SPECIAL MESSAGE TO READERS

This book is published under the auspices of

THE ULVERSCROFT FOUNDATION

(registered charity No. 264873 UK)

Established in 1972 to provide funds for research, diagnosis and treatment of eye diseases. Examples of contributions made are: —

A Children's Assessment Unit at Moorfield's Hospital, London.

•

Twin operating theatres at the Western Ophthalmic Hospital, London.

•

A Chair of Ophthalmology at the Royal Australian College of Ophthalmologists.

•

The Ulverscroft Children's Eye Unit at the Great Ormond Street Hospital For Sick Children, London.

You can help further the work of the Foundation by making a donation or leaving a legacy. Every contribution, no matter how small, is received with gratitude. Please write for details to:

THE ULVERSCROFT FOUNDATION,
The Green, Bradgate Road, Anstey,
Leicester LE7 7FU, England.
Telephone: (0116) 236 4325

In Australia write to:
THE ULVERSCROFT FOUNDATION,
c/o The Royal Australian College of Ophthalmologists,
27, Commonwealth Street, Sydney,
N.S.W. 2010.

THE CARPENTER'S WIFE

1865: Mary Moore must leave her cottage after her husband, John, a shepherd, dies from pneumonia. Pregnant and with two young children to care for, Mary moves back to her mother's in Yarnscombe. She makes friends with the wife of the village carpenter, Jane Dark, who is pregnant with her eleventh child. Mary's son is born healthy, but Jane's child is stillborn and she dies heartbroken. Desperate for a new wife to care for his ten surviving children, Jane's husband, Reuben, passionately proposes marriage to Mary. But should she take on such a daunting challenge? Can she ever love another man?

*Books by Peggy Loosemore Jones
Published by The House of Ulverscroft:*

MOON OVER MEXICO
DARE TO DREAM
LOVE DANGEROUSLY
REMEMBERED WITH LOVE
THE LUNDY SUMMER
A STRANGER RIDING
A HAUNTING AFFAIR
THE LOVE SEASON
WHITHER THOU GOEST
A TOUCH OF MAGIC
A SUMMER FOLLY

PEGGY LOOSEMORE JONES

THE CARPENTER'S WIFE

Complete and Unabridged

ULVERSCROFT
Leicester

First Large Print Edition
published 2001

All rights reserved

British Library CIP Data

Jones, Peggy Loosemore
 The carpenter's wife—Large print ed.—
 Ulverscroft large print series: family saga
 1. Domestic fiction
 2. Large type books
 I. Title
 823.9'14 [F]

ISBN 0–7089–4373–X

Published by
F. A. Thorpe (Publishing)
Anstey, Leicestershire

Set by Words & Graphics Ltd.
Anstey, Leicestershire
Printed and bound in Great Britain by
T. J. International Ltd., Padstow, Cornwall

This book is printed on acid-free paper

1

John was now very late and Mary could not settle to anything. She knew that his chest was bad. He had come home the previous day wet through, the harshness of his breathing telling her that he was heading for another attack of bronchitis. Yet he would go out that morning in the streaming wet, saying he had to take fodder to the sheep in the top pasture and bring them down if the weather worsened.

'You think more of them sheep than you do of me!' she had yelled after him and felt sorry now. It wasn't his fault. It was the weather. She hated November. It was the same every year, cold and bleak, and every year John's chest seemed to get worse. He wouldn't be able to lead the singing in the village chapel on Sunday, that was for sure.

The rain had turned to sleet now and it felt appreciably colder. She poked at the glowing embers in the grate to raise a flame and added a couple of logs. The piece of bacon cooking with vegetables in the pot hanging over the fire was ready to eat and the kettle was steaming. Irritably, she moved it to one side. Why didn't he come? He was never this late.

Little George tried to haul himself up by her skirts and began to whinge. 'Don't pull at me, Georgie!' she snapped at him. 'You'll get yourself scalded, one of these days.'

'He's hungry, Ma,' Eliza said and looked up at her mother with beseeching eyes. 'Can't us have tea?'

'Not till Dada comes. Be a good maid and see if you can put the cloth on the table. He won't be long, now.'

The children were picking up her anxiety, Mary knew so she tried to smile at Eliza as she struggled to spread the cloth on the well scrubbed wooden table. She was four years old, with John's clear blue eyes and fair hair, curling like his over her forehead. Something about the likeness caught at Mary's heart, making her snatch up Georgie and hold him close, ashamed of her earlier sharpness. What would she do if anything happened to John?

Needing to be occupied, she carried George to the dresser. Like the pendulum clock on the wall, it had come from her grandmother's house and was her pride and joy, its drawers full of the cutlery she and John had been given at their wedding, and its shelves stacked with her pewter dishes and painted cloam plates. Each one told a story and George chuckled as he pointed. 'Gee-gees!'

Mary gave him a hug. 'That's a clever boy!' She found the knives and forks and spoons she needed, put George down and handed them to him. 'Take these to Lizzie!'

She watched him fondly as he staggered towards his sister. He was twenty months old and a late walker, chubby but determined, hampered as he was in his baby skirts. He half stumbled and she was moving to catch him when there came a sudden scampering and barking at the door. Her heart leapt at once. The dog was back so John could not be far behind!

As soon as she lifted the latch Toby burst in, dripping wet and excited. 'Out!' she commanded and pointed to the back kitchen. 'Bad dog! Out!'

But he ignored her and returned to the lane, then made little dashes to and fro, whining as if begging her to follow him. Mary's heart plummeted then. She pulled her old shawl from the hook on the door, covered her head with it and turned to the children. 'Bide inside!' she told them. 'I'm going out to meet Dada.'

She stepped from the warmth of the cottage into the driving sleet and shuddered. It was bitter cold and already dark. The light from the oil lamp she had placed in the window glinted on the sleet but cast only a feeble glow along the dripping hedges.

The dog was running on ahead so she strained her eyes and called, 'John?' She waited, then thinking she caught a distant cry, called again, 'Be that you, John?'

Toby barked in answer and when she hurried towards him, her long skirts clinging between her legs, she could see her husband coming, stumbling and shambling along like an old man. She ran to him in fear. 'Oh, Lord, John! What's the matter?'

He clung to her for support, coughing and retching. When he could breathe, he croaked, 'I'm fearful bad, Mary.'

She put her arm round him and half dragged, half carried him to the cottage. The children were watching from the doorway, their faces beginning to pucker into tears.

'Get in out of the wet'! she stormed at them, making them both howl. 'I told ee!' she raged at her husband. 'I told ee not to go out today!'

'Ay,' he whispered. 'Just — a drink, Mary — '

'You need more'n a drink! You need your bed and the doctor!' He was shivering violently and began coughing again when the warmth of the fire reached him. She pulled his sodden cap from his head and the dripping sacking from his shoulders and helped him to his old wicker chair. When he collapsed into it the dog crept in unnoticed and sank on its belly beside him.

Mary saw her husband's misery, and tenderness flooded through her as she knelt to unlace his boots. 'I must get ee out of these wet things,' she said, 'and into a warm bed. Lizzie, fetch the hot water bottle for Dada! 'Tis on the shelf in the back kitchen.'

The child went running and came back staggering under the weight of a flat bottomed, stone hot water bottle

'Now his night shirt from under the pillow on our bed,' Mary instructed, sending Eliza clattering up the wooden staircase to her parents' room.

George was watching round-eyed, with one thumb stuck in his mouth as Mary removed his father's steaming jacket, his flannel shirt and woollen vest and began towelling him dry as if he were a baby. When he could get hold of one of his hands, George clung on to it as if he would never let it go.

Eliza brought the night shirt and Mary held it in front of the fire to warm, then slipped it over John's head and began easing it down over his shoulders. 'Let go of Dada's hand, Georgie!' she scolded but the child only clung tighter until Eliza gently coaxed him away.

Once the rest of John's muddy clothes had been removed and he was warm and dry and enveloped in his night shirt, Mary asked him, 'Can ee eat anything?'

He shook his head, looking so frail she was afraid. She wiped his forehead which was shining now with sweat instead of rain and felt it burning.

'Just a drink,' he whispered. 'Feed the children!'

She straightened up to make the pot of tea and, as she did so, felt the baby in her womb give a sudden, urgent kick as if to remind her of its presence. You, too! she thought. I know all about you! and willed herself to forget this further claim on her strength.

She made the tea and filled John's tin mug, stirred in extra sugar and held the mug to his lips because his hands were trembling so.

'Feed the children!' he croaked again.

'When you'm in bed. They can wait.'

As soon as he had drunk all he could, she filled the hot water bottle and carried it up to the iron bedstead she shared with him, pushed the bottle deep into their old feather mattress and covered it with the darned blankets her mother had given her and the patchwork quilt she had made herself.

The children trailed after them when she

helped John up the stairs. Then they stood solemnly watching as their father sank into his bed with a sigh.

'Sleep now!' she told him and he nodded. 'Kiss Dada goodnight!' she urged the children.

They approached him warily instead of jumping on him the way they usually did and were subdued when they went downstairs again. They ate their meal in silence, mopped up the last of the gravy with chunks of bread and went to their cots without protest as soon as they had finished.

They know! Mary thought, just as she knew herself that night when she slipped into bed beside John, heard his breath rasping in his chest and felt his body burning against hers. She could not sleep but lay rigid and fearful beside him.

By the morning he was delirious, raving that the sheep were coming in the window and that the stream was rising. She knew he needed a doctor but the one who had attended him before was miles away in High Bickington and she had no means of getting there even if she could have left John and the children. She knew it would be no use appealing to the farmer who was an intolerant man and would not spare one of his workers to take a message. But her mother lived in Yarnscombe, a mile and a half uphill from Westcott farm. She could send her a note if she could catch one of the Potter children from the cottage next door when they passed on their way to the church school in the village. Her mother would surely find somebody to call the doctor?

She dressed hastily, woke Eliza and set her to watch from the kitchen window, then scribbled a note to her mother. The sleet had turned back to rain but the damp struck chill in the cottage as the fire had burned down in the night. So she fetched wood and coal from the shed and coaxed it into burning brightly again, then went to the pump for water. Some she heated to sponge John's face and hands and then made tea and porridge for them all.

But John only wanted to drink and stared at her wildly, rambling incoherently about ewes and the stream rising. He tried several times to get out of bed and she had trouble restraining him.

Then Eliza shouted that the Potters were coming by in the lane so she had to leave John and run downstairs. Ten year old Minnie was sensible and would remember what she was told.

The Potter children squeezed thankfully into the cottage doorway, their boots thick with mud and their heavy jackets steaming.

The shawl over Minnie's head was already soaked and her long hair hung in streaks over her face. But she listened carefully to Mary's instructions. 'Charlie could run back and tell Ma 'bout Mr Moore being poorly,' she suggested.

'I'd be late for schule,' Charlie objected, 'and teacher'd give me the cane.'

'No, 'er wouldn't 'cos I'll tell 'er why.'

'A ha'penny if you'll do it, Charlie,' Mary said, 'and a penny for you, Minnie, if you'll tell my mother 'tis urgent.'

She fetched her purse and paid the children, then watched as Charlie squelched back towards his own cottage and Minnie shepherded her four other brothers and sisters on their way to school. Their mother was a rough and ready woman, feared by some for her sharp tongue but Mary knew that she was good hearted and would help her if she could.

Relieved, she went back into the cottage to find Eliza staring wide-eyed up the stairs. John was on the top step, clinging to the wooden handrail and swaying, pale and ghostlike in his white night shirt.

'Dada be going to fall,' Eliza whispered and before Mary could move he had buckled at the knees and begun tumbling down, rolling from step to step until he landed at her feet.

'Oh, John!' she moaned as she knelt to cradle him. 'What have ee done now?'

Upstairs, George started screaming and Eliza began to cry. Mary did not know where to turn between the three of them. Then, to her relief, John raised himself up a little and stared uncomprehendingly at her. 'Why be us sitting on the floor, Mary?' he asked.

It was as if the shock had jolted him back into something like normality. ''Cos you fell downstairs, you maze man!' she said and, near to tears herself, she hugged him and kissed his cheek. 'Can ee get up?'

He frowned. 'Why be the children crying?'

'They want their breakfasts. Try to get up, John!'

He made the attempt but even with her help he could not stand, so he shuffled to the foot of the stairs and heaved himself on to the bottom step where he sat with his head in his hands, mumbling that he should be setting off for work.

He was still there and Mary was wondering how she could get him back into his bed when Poll Potter opened the cottage door and let herself in.

'Oh, my!' she said as she took in the scene. 'You'm in a pretty fine pickle!' She pulled off the piece of sacking she had flung round her shoulders, shook some of the wet out of it and hung it on the door hook. Then she advanced on John. 'Come on, now, John Moore!' she said. 'You can't bide there in everybody's way. That poor cheel upstairs needs fetching. As for you Lizzie,' she scolded Eliza, 'you be a good maid and stop that noise! There be nort the matter with you!'

She was a large woman with strong arms, muscular like a man's. She pulled John to his feet and turned to Mary. 'Take one side an' I'll take t'other. Us'll get'n up. I've sent Charlie down to the farm to tell Maister your man's sick.'

'The yaws,' John was mumbling as the women heaved him up the stairs. 'Stream's rising.'

'He's been on about nothing else all night,' Mary said. 'He was wet through when he came home. 'Tis his chest again and he's terrible bad.'

'Never was strong,' Poll said. 'Didn't 'is father die young?'

Mary shuddered. 'That was consumption. John's bain't that. 'Tis just his bronchitis. He gets it every year.'

They reached the bedroom and sat John on the bed under the slope of the ceiling, then lifted his legs and covered him. He closed his eyes, looking pale and exhausted, the fever momentarily burned out of him.

Poll Potter shook her head. 'He be fit for nothing, poor man.'

'The doctor'll give'n his usual. He's been like this before, only not so bad.'

'Best let'n sleep, then. You fetch that poor cheel or 'e'll make 'isself sick yelling! I'll put the kettle back to boil. You look all in yerself.'

'I couldn't sleep,' Mary admitted, 'he was burning so.'

She was reluctant to leave John but he seemed quiet enough so she went to lift George from his cot. He was dripping wet so by the time she had cleaned him up and carried him downstairs, Poll Potter had made a fresh pot of tea and given Eliza a bowl of porridge. She ladled out a big helping and pushed it across the table to Mary. 'Eat, girl! You must keep up your strength to help your man. Give Georgie to me! I'll see to'n.'

She sat George on her knee and began feeding him with a spoon. Mary could hardly force the porridge down her own throat but she ate because she knew that Poll was right. She had to stay strong for all their sakes.

'Thanks, Poll,' she said when her neighbour had to go. 'You've been very kind.'

'No more'n you'd do for me. I'll send Minnie up when 'er's home from schule. Tell 'er if there's anything you want and what the doctor said. Have ee enough to pay'n?'

Mary flushed. 'I've a bit put by.'

'You'll need that for when the baby comes.'

'I'll manage.'

But what if John's off work for a long time and we lose his thirteen shillings a week? Mary thought. It was bad enough last year when he was sick and Maister was threatening to hire another shepherd. It would break John's heart if he did that.

'Is your Billy still helping with the sheep?' she asked. Billy was Poll's eldest, twelve years old now and working.

'Depends where Maister sends'n.'

'Well, will ee ask'n to look at the sheep in the top pasture? John's been on about the stream rising and he was wet through when he came home — boots an' all. He could've been in the water.'

'I'll ask Billy but I don't s'pose them sheep have come to much harm!'

Poll went and there was nothing Mary could do then but wait for the doctor. Between cooking and cleaning and keeping the children quiet she periodically checked on John who was in an uneasy sleep, rolling his head from side to side. He was sweating and yet his hands felt cold.

He's been like this before, she tried to reassure herself, knowing all the time that this was different.

It was late in the afternoon before Toby barked a warning and she heard the sound of horse's hooves in the lane. She flung open the cottage door, expecting to see the doctor but it was her sister Anne's husband who was hitching his horse to the gate post. He was wet through, his hair plastered to his head and he looked grim when he came in.

'That lazy old bugger, Jonas, wouldn't turn out in this weather,' he told Mary. 'Your mother was so worried I rode up to High Bickington soon's I could but all Jonas's done is send a bottle of the physic he gave John last time he was sick. Much good it didn't then! How be'n, Mary?'

'Bad, Bert — terrible bad.'

Bert bounded up the stairs to look at his brother-in-law. The children would have followed him until Mary held them back. They loved their uncle Bert, an easy going giant of a man who tossed them around in boisterous play, so different from their quieter father.

When he came down again Bert was looking troubled. 'I've never seen'n this bad, Mary. 'Tis worse than bronchitis, I reckon — more like pneumonia. That Jonas wants whipping.' He fished in the deep pocket of his jacket and pulled out a brown bottle. 'Here! I s'pose 'tis worth a try. Jonas said to give'n some straight away and he'll come in the morning. I'm sorry, Mary.'

'Tain't your fault, Bert. 'Tis the weather. John would go out to the sheep even though his chest was bad. I told'n to stay at home.'

'Well, us all knows how John feels about them sheep. Can't understand it meself. If 'twas hosses, now!' Bert was a saddler and horses were his bread and butter. He patted her shoulder. 'Try not to fret, Mary! He's pulled through before. How be you, anyhow? Can't be long now to your time.'

''Tis not till March.'

'Well, take care! You know where to come if you need help.' George was tugging at his breeches so Bert scooped him up with a chuckle. 'I swear you'm getting more like your granfer Pugsley every day, Georgie! Same pug nose and boxer's jowl! 'Tis a good job you take after your ma, Lizzie.' He ran a hand through the little girl's curls and bent to give her a kiss. 'You be a good maid and help her while your dad's poorly.' He turned to Mary. 'I'll come by tomorrow and see how things be. Send word if — ' he hesitated, ' — if John should worsen.' Then he set George down and made for the door.

Mary watched him go, a cold feeling at her heart. What did he mean, if John should worsen? What was he trying to say?

The medicine bottle felt heavy in her hand. Without much hope she found a spoon and dragged herself upstairs where she stared at John who had not opened his eyes all day to look at her. In despair, she dropped the bottle and spoon on to the bed and flung herself down beside him, putting her arms around him and holding him close.

'No!' she cried. 'You'm not to die, John Moore! I won't let ee! You'm too young and you've gived me three children. What should I do without ee?'

He stirred in her arms and she remembered their early, tremulous attempts at making love and her immense surprise at the fierce uprush of passion that had swept through her when she first came to climax. She could not bear to think that they might never make love like that again. In panic, she shook him, trying to make him open his eyes and look at her with his usual tenderness. But when his eyelids fluttered back his blank stare held no recognition and she sank her face on to his chest and wept.

Someone touched her shoulder and she sat up to see Eliza there. 'Minnie's come,' she whispered. 'Don't ee cry, Ma!'

Mary brushed a hand across her eyes. 'I bain't crying, Lizzie. I'll come down and speak to Minnie.'

'Her's brought an apple pudding for our tea. Dada likes apple pudding.'

'P'raps he'll eat a little, then.'

But Mary knew that John was past eating and she went downstairs with a heavy heart to thank Minnie and to send a message to Poll Potter that she feared John had pneumonia. Afterwards, she attempted to force some of the brown, syrupy medicine into his mouth but it only ran down his chin, so she left the bottle on the washstand and went down to give the children their tea.

They were in the middle of it when the dog barked and ran to the door, wagging its tail expectantly. Somebody knocked and when Mary opened the door she found young Billy Potter there.

'Maister be coming!' he warned her. 'Ma said to run and let ee know. There be two yaws on their backs in the stream — drownded. Maister knows an 'e's mad's a bull — said John Moore should've brought 'em down lower.'

'How could he?' Mary cried. 'He was too bad. He must've tried last night and that's why he's so sick!'

'Well, watch out! Maister's comin' up the lane and I don't want'n to catch I 'ere!'

Billy ran off and Mary saw him scramble through a gap in the hedge into the field beyond so that he would not be discovered in the lane.

She went back into the cottage, shut the door and leaned against it, her heart racing. Josiah Blackmore was an impatient man, hard on his men and intolerant of mistakes. Even though John was lying close to death, he would blame him and want restitution. When one of his horses went lame he blamed his head horseman and docked the cost of treatment from the man's wages.

I will not let him blame John! Mary resolved. He shall not even see him! John's only ill because he put the sheep before his own health. I shall tell Josiah Blackmore so.

She was waiting for him when he came but her courage almost failed her when he stooped under the low lintel of the door and met her face to face. He was a big man, heavy shouldered and bearded with dark eyes that seemed to pierce through her. He took off his cap and shook the wet out of it, then stood, huge in his heavy jacket and breeches, his gaitered legs aggressively apart as he glowered down at her.

'Where be John Moore?' he demanded. 'I want words with he!'

'Sick in bed and can't see nobody.'

'He'll see me!'

'No!' He would have moved to the stairs

but she blocked his way. 'You can't go up! He's too sick. You'd best tell me what you want.'

'I want what I can't have — two good yaws that be dead and swollen because of his neglect! Out of my way, woman!'

He would have pushed her aside but Mary stood her ground. 'Don't you touch me!' she blazed at him. 'John din't neglect your yaws! He went out to 'em when he was ill and came home wringing wet and half froze. Now he's got pneumonia and could die 'cos of your yaws. D'you think they'm more important to me than my man and my children?'

Josiah Blackmore's face turned dark red as he glared at her. 'Us'll see what's more important to you, my girl — John Moore's job and this cottage or the pair of you turned out into the fields with your brats! Tell your man that when he's fit enough to listen!'

He swung round, aimed a kick at the dog which was growling at him and stomped out of the cottage, slamming the door behind him. Mary hurried to bolt it fast and the children, who had been hiding under the table, ran to her, wailing.

'Hush!' she whispered as she gathered them to her. 'You'll wake Dada. 'Tis all right. Maister's gone now.'

But he would be back, she knew, and

hardly dared imagine what might happen to them if he made good his threat and gave John the sack. He had argued before that John was not strong enough to be a shepherd and this latest sign of weakness might give him the excuse he wanted.

Then I must be strong for us all! Mary vowed as she cradled her children. They, at least, were sturdy and healthy, as she was herself. Whatever happened, they would manage.

She was thinking that when there came an unexpected sound from upstairs. The children raised their heads to listen, then looked at their mother in wonder.

John was singing. His usually strong baritone voice sounded thin and reedy but the words of the old Wesleyan hymn floated down to them clearly. 'Gentle Jesus, meek and mild, look upon a little child. Pity my simplicity. Suffer me to come to Thee.'

With an exclamation, Mary pushed the children from her and ran for the stairs just as John started on the second verse. 'Fain I would to Thee be brought. Dearest God, forbid it not . . . ' His voice faltered and when she rushed into the bedroom she saw that he was sitting up, staring straight ahead of him with a fixed smile on his face.

She knew a moment of terror. 'John — ?'

He did not hear her. His breath rattled in his throat and his head slumped to his chest. She knew, even as she caught him in her arms, that he was dead.

When the doctor arrived the next morning, all he could do then was sign a death certificate for John Moore, aged twenty-seven years, who had died of pneumonia on November twenty-ninth, eighteen sixty-five.

2

It was a cold December day for the funeral and the little wooden chapel at Yarnscombe was crammed as everybody knew John Moore, who had led the singing there so regularly. His own family arrived in a hired carriage from nearby Atherington — John's widowed mother and his uncles who were blacksmiths, his two brothers with their wives and his only sister with her husband. The Moores were a proud family and had insisted on paying for the funeral as they did not want Mary to appeal to the parish. John's brothers and Mary's two brothers-in-law carried his coffin and they all sat together during the service, a dark, sombre group.

Mary's mother and sisters wept quietly into their handkerchiefs but Mary herself was dry-eyed throughout the ceremony. She had felt numb ever since John collapsed into her arms and her throat only contracted when the congregation sang 'Gentle Jesus, meek and mild,' his favourite hymn. She clutched George on her lap and snuggled Eliza close beside her, hardly aware of what went on. The shiny elm coffin and the air of solemnity in the chapel seemed nothing to do with her or John because she kept remembering his delight the day he had taken her there for its inaugural service. He and his fellow Bible Christians had met in a cottage until they had collected over a hundred pounds to erect their wooden tabernacle in a corner of a field on Ward farm. They had put it on six wheels so that the landowner could never claim it when the farmer's lease ran out.

That was only four years ago, just after Eliza was born. Now John would never sing there again and she was a widow at twenty-five, with two children and another on the way. What was she going to without him?

After the service, when they all moved to St Andrews' churchyard for the burial she still could not cry, even when she stood on the wet grass and watched John's coffin being lowered into his grave. People approached her afterwards to offer their sympathy and to wonder what she was going to do but she could find no words to answer them. The only person who did not ask her that was Josiah Blackmore. She had not expected to see him in the chapel as he was a church goer but he had sat at the back and joined in the singing in a loud, confident voice. He had no need to ask because he knew that the first thing she would have to do was move out of the tied cottage he would require for the shepherd he was hiring to replace John. She saw that certainty in his eyes when he gruffly offered his respects.

Her mother had insisted that all the family should go back to her cottage for something to eat when it was all over. Mary and Poll Potter had baked meat and potato pasties and apple pies, thinking that everybody would go down to Westcott. Instead, they had to pack it all in a basket which Mary took with her when Bert came down with the pony and trap to take her and the children to the chapel.

Mary was sorry that Poll would not go with them for she did not know what she would have done without her. It was Poll who had looked after the children when she ran in the rain all the way to the village to tell her mother that John was dead and Poll who helped her lay him out the next morning. They had washed him together, straightening his young limbs and brushing his hair until it shone.

'A real beauty, your man was,' Poll said and Mary had cried a little then.

Poll had cared for the children again when Mary went with Bert into the village to make arrangements for the funeral and when Reuben Dark, the carpenter and undertaker came to measure up for the coffin. A tall, austere looking man, more respected than liked in the village, he had been unexpectedly gentle with her, saying he was in no hurry for his money and that Mary could pay him when she was able. So many people had been kind, she did not know how she could ever thank them.

Now, in her mother's cottage kitchen, she helped make tea for the womenfolk, poured cider for the men and passed around the provisions.

'But what be ee going to do, Mary?' her mother asked for the third time. 'You won't be able to stay at Westcott.'

'I know that. I'll have to find work — go back to the gloving, p'raps.' She had worked in the factory at Torrington before her marriage, lodging with her Aunt Maude and only coming home on Sundays.

'How can ee, with two children and big for another? You'd best come to me till you've had the baby.'

'There'd be no room for all of us with you, Mother!'

'Us'll make room! Us managed when you was all small. There's only Becky with me now that Anne and Sarah be wed. How long's Joe Blackmore giving ee at Westcott? Has'n said?'

'Not yet. No more'n a couple of weeks, I reckon.' Mary thought of her own cosy kitchen which was full of the things she and John had scrimped to buy. She would have to sell most of them if she moved in with her mother.

As if she had read her thoughts, her sister Anne said, 'If you'm getting rid of your dresser, Mary, will ee give me first chance?'

Mary shook her head. 'Not the dresser, Anne. I'm keeping that.' And John's wicker chair, she thought and my clock and the rag rugs I made.

'You won't be able to bring too much of your clutter,' her mother put in. 'You'll have to get rid of John's dog, for a start. I can't be doing with'n here, chasing the cat!'

Eliza pulled at Mary's hand when she heard that. 'Ma?' Her lips began to tremble.

John's brother, William spoke up then. 'Toby's a good dog. I'll give ee five shillings for'n, Mary.' He scooped up Eliza and bounced her in his arms. 'Then you can come and see'n sometimes, little maid.'

'I don't want your money, Will,' Mary said. 'Just so long as Toby gets a good home. John would've wanted you to have'n, I'm sure.'

'Then I'll pick'n up before us goes back home. When you have to leave Westcott, you just let us know and I'll bring the hoss and wagon to shift your things up to your mother's.'

It seemed that everything was being decided for her and Mary had no strength of will to object. But later on, when she and the children were alone again in their own cottage, she wondered if she was doing the right thing and said as much to Poll Potter who called to see how she was faring.

'I'll be sorry to see ee go, for one,' Poll said. 'But I s'pose 'tis for the best as you'll 'ave to move out of 'ere. You won't 'ave much trouble gettin' rid of your bits and pieces, that's for sure. You've got some lovely crocks,' and she stared admiringly at Mary's dresser.

Impulsively, Mary selected one of her precious plates and handed it to her. 'Here! Take this one to remember me by! And for all your kindness, Poll.'

Poll stared speechlessly at the plate. When she looked up at last, Mary saw that she had tears in her eyes. ''Tis beautiful,' she said. 'I've never 'ad such a present. Thankee, Mary.' She patted her on the shoulder. 'You bore up well today, maid. Stay strong and you'll be all right.'

When she had gone, Mary turned to the children who had been quiet and subdued all day. 'Time to take your best clothes off now,' she said, 'and go to bed.'

Eliza's blue eyes were questioning. 'Where be Dada, Ma? Did they put'n in that big box?'

Mary winced. 'I told ee. Dada's gone to Jesus.'

'Why?'

'To look after his sheep.'

'Who's to look after us, then?'

'I'll look after you and Georgie. And when us gets to Gran's, she'll look after all of us.'

Eliza nodded. 'When I'm big, I'll look after ee, Ma.'

Mary held her tight. 'You'm a good maid,' she whispered and, for the first time that day, she felt a sob rising in her throat and tears running down her cheeks.

Early the next morning, Josiah Blackmore knocked at the cottage door and before Mary had time to open it, he had stepped into the kitchen.

She had a bowl of water on the table and was washing Georgie's face and hands clean of his breakfast porridge. His mouth quivered when he saw Josiah and Eliza ran to hide in her mother's skirts. The farmer towered over them and Mary held her breath because she knew why he had come.

She felt his searching gaze travel over her and flushed as it lingered on the swelling under her apron. Defensively, she crossed her arms to cover it and waited for him to speak.

'I've a new shepherd coming at the week's end,' he said abruptly. 'A married man, so he'll need this cottage. 'Twasn't the time to tell ee yesterday, so I waited.'

He seemed to be expecting her to comment but when she said nothing, he scowled.

'I bain't a hard man,' he continued. 'I figured you'd want to have words with your folks and decide what to do. I can give ee five days to move out.'

Still Mary did not speak and she caught a flash of irritation in his eyes. 'About them yaws,' he said. 'I know 'tis no use expecting you to pay up, so I'll take John Moore's dog instead. That's giving ee the best of the bargain.'

Mary drew herself up then, the better to confront him. 'The dog's not here,' she said calmly. 'John's brother took'n yesterday.'

Josiah's bushy eyebrows met in a frown. 'Took'n? Took'n where?'

'To where he'll 'ave a good home and not be kicked by the likes of you!'

'You had no right!'

'I had every right! John bought that dog as a puppy and trained'n well. The pair of 'em looked after your sheep, Maister, better'n you look after your men! If John hadn't gone out in all that weather, he'd be alive today! So don't talk to me about rights! You and your sheep took my man and I don't owe you a farthing!'

He seemed taken aback by her outburst and she saw his expression change to grudging admiration. 'So! John Moore's missus has got more fire in her little finger than he had in his belly! Where be going when you leave here then, Mary? There could be a place for ee back at the farm if you want.'

Mary stiffened. She had helped out in the farm dairy when she was first married, humping the heavy pans and churning the butter, grateful for the ninepence a day she earned and the occasional jug of skimmed milk when she was expecting Eliza. But she had been glad to escape the farmer's roving eye and his occasional familiar slap on her bottom.

'And end up in the fam'ly way, like the rest of your maids?' she said tartly.

He sneered. 'You'm in that already, so what's the odds, Mary?'

She felt her cheeks flame. 'The odds, Maister, be that I'm a respectable woman and aim to stay that way! Now — if you've had your say, I'll ask ee to leave. The cottage is mine till the end of the week.'

'I could put ee out tomorrow, if I chose!'

'And have your name dragged through the mud more'n 'tis already? You wouldn't dare put me out, Josiah Blackmore! 'Cos if you did, I'd go to the agent. You may be cock o' the walk round here, but you'm only a tenant farmer on the estate.'

'Ay! And I've lost two yaws and still have to find a hundred and twenty quid come Lady Day for me half year's rent! Think Bill Morgan'd listen to the likes of you?'

'I'd make'n listen! If he didn', I'd write to his Lordship, I swear I would. I'm on me own now, Maister, and ready to fight for me and mine.'

He grimaced mockingly. 'Then I'd best get out of your road, Mary, before you do me some mischief! Just remember — you'm out of this cottage come Sat'day!'

'I'll be glad to go — glad to be where I can breathe a cleaner air!'

After he had gone, she shut the door and bolted it fast. Then she sank into John's old chair and put her head in her hands. Her heart was pounding and the blood was beating in her temples. She could not remember when she had been so angry.

George came whimpering to climb into her lap so she picked him up and held him close. She saw that Eliza was eyeing her as if she were a stranger. 'Ma?' she whispered. 'Be ee cross, Ma?'

'Not with you, Lizzie.'

'With the nasty man?'

With everything, Mary thought. She was

angry with the way her life had been so cruelly shattered, with the new weight of responsibility laid upon her and the knowledge that she was on her own to face it all. Worst of all, she realised in despair, she was angry with John who had died so needlessly.

'Ay!' she cried. 'I'm cross, Lizzie. But don't mind that nasty man! Us'll be all right, whatever happens.'

Things began to be better after that for somehow, in the confrontation with Josiah Blackmore, Mary had renewed her spirit. She still grieved for John and took George into bed with her at night to make up for his loss but she was so busy packing everything she wanted to take to her mother's she sometimes forgot him for minutes or even hours at a time. Poll Potter passed the word around that she had things to sell so there was a constant stream of women knocking on her door, looking for a bargain.

John's brother, Will, called to know when she had to leave the cottage and promised to bring the horse and wagon early on Saturday morning. 'I had that old bugger, Blackmore after me yesterday,' he told her, 'wanting John's dog to make up for the yaws he lost.'

'You didn't let'n have Toby?'

'Not I!' Will grinned. 'The Moores bain't beholding to he. Neither be you, Mary, so don't let'n bully ee!'

The Moores were well respected in the area and Mary had often wished that John had become a tailor like his late father or had taken on a smallholding like his brothers instead of working in the fields in all weathers. But that was all he wanted, the freedom of the hills and the moors and the company of Toby and the sheep. There had been a solitary, dreamy side to John and Mary had often thought that he was happiest on his own or making music, singing in the chapel or playing tunes on the penny whistle he always carried in his pocket. She was keeping that for George in case he turned after his father.

She watched the children playing with Will who was pretending to take halfpennies out of their ears and making them chuckle. What would they be like, she wondered, when they were grown? Eliza had her father's colouring and his gentleness but George's hair and eyes were darker, more like her own and he was already showing a stubborn streak. As for the one as yet unborn, she could not begin to imagine what he or she might be like.

So she sighed and poured Will a mug of cider to cheer him on his way. 'I'll be ready Sat'day morning sharp,' she said, ''cos I don't want Maister coming here to put us out. You be sure to keep Toby safe, Will! I wouldn't put it past Josiah Blackmore to try to pinch'n one dark night.'

Will laughed. 'Toby wouldn't go with he! Bite'n, more like! Don't ee worry, Mary! You'll soon be shot of Josiah Blackmore!'

But late on Friday night, when the children were in bed and Mary was finishing the last of her packing, she thought she heard footsteps outside in the lane. The cottage door was bolted so she hastily doused the lamp and listened, regretting the loss of Toby who would have warned her and given her some protection.

There came a rattling of the latch and she heard the sound of heavy breathing. Then a familiar voice said, 'Be ee in there, Mary Moore?'

She held her breath as a shadow loomed against the window. Even though she knew she could not be visible in the darkness, she crouched low beside the kitchen wall.

The shadow moved and Josiah Blackmore banged his fists against the door. 'Open up, Mary! I reckon you owe me summat for them yaws so I'll take the only other thing you've got to offer. Come on! Open the door and I'll show ee what a proper man can do with a ripe young woman like you be!'

His voice was slurred, telling her that he

had been drinking.

'Aw, come on, Mary!' he pleaded. 'Open up! You must be missin' it! 'Twill be a farewell present, from me to you. You'll like it, I can promise ee that.'

He rattled the latch again and banged several times, then started kicking at the door and cursing. Suddenly fearful that he might try to break in the back way which was not so secure, she bent low and scuttled to the back kitchen where she dragged the heavy mangle across the door, not caring now if he heard her or not.

Upstairs, George began to scream and she dug her nails into her hands in frustration, uncertain whether to go to him and reveal she was awake or to stay where she was. Then it sounded as if Josiah Blackmore aimed a final, angry kick at the door because it was followed by silence.

She waited but nothing else happened so she crept back into the kitchen and listened. Had he really gone?

George had awakened Eliza now so she hurried upstairs to quieten them and carried George to the bedroom window that overlooked the lane. There was a watery moon, hazy between the clouds and in its faint light she could just make out Josiah Blackmore weaving his drunken way down towards the farm. She knew of his reputation but had not supposed that he would have tried to take advantage of her so soon after John's death. Was this what it was going to be like now that she was a woman on her own?

For the first time she was thankful that she was leaving the next day. She had not wanted to give up the cottage where she and John had been so happy, or the little patch of garden he had planted with vegetables to feed his family. Now she could hardly wait to escape from it all.

When Will arrived the following morning she was ready with her boxes packed, the children fed and dressed and so eager to get away he looked at her in astonishment.

'You be an early bird and no mistake!' he said as he began loading her pieces of furniture on to the wagon. 'I thought you'd be shedding a few tears today, Mary.'

'I can do that later,' she said. 'I just want to put some distance between me and Maister. I never want to see his face again.'

Will paused in what he was doing. 'Did he come bothering ee, then?'

'Last night. He would've come in, and you know what for. But the door was bolted fast and the lamp was out so he must've thought I was abed.'

'The dirty old devil!' Will's face was grim.

'Wants teaching a lesson, he do!'

'No, Will!' Mary put a hand on his arm, remembering that he and his brother were quick with their fists. 'I don't want trouble. I just want to get out of his road.'

'Then you shall, m'dear.' Will said. He lifted Eliza aboard, helped Mary and George on to the seat beside him and clicked his tongue to get the old horse moving. As the wagon rumbled up the lane towards the village, Mary looked back at the cottage with its thatched roof and whitewashed cob walls and felt that the best part of her life was already over.

3

There was a cold wind blowing which struck chill when they reached Yarnscombe for the village was high up and exposed, perched on a ridge five hundred feet above sea level. It was not much more than one winding street with a tiny, central square, its skyline dominated by the ancient church of St Andrew. Because it was Saturday, the children were not in school so the wagon was soon surrounded by a curious crowd of whooping youngsters, running alongside it as it rumbled into the village. A few women came to their doors to see what all the excitement was about and called a welcome to Mary when they recognised her. They all knew she was coming home to stay and she felt a lump in her throat as she smiled down at the friendly faces she remembered so well.

'I can see Gran!' Eliza shouted, jumping up and down in excitement when they were within sight of her grandmother's stone and slate cottage, one in a row opposite the church.

Mary's mother had appeared at her door when she heard the wagon arriving. She was soon followed by Mary's three sisters, Sarah, Anne and Becky, and Anne's two boys, Bertie and Tom who grinned and made rude faces at Eliza.

Mary's children were kissed and cuddled and then they all crowded into the kitchen, thankful for the warmth of the open fire. Mary's paternal grandmother had stayed prudently inside for she was well into her eighties now, the undisputed head of the family. At the sight of so many women, William stood looking bashful until Mary pushed him into a sagging armchair. The kettle was steaming and her mother was soon making tea in her big brown pot. Then she produced a pan of freshly made scones from the cloam oven in the wall by the fire, fetched butter and honey and urged William to eat up as he had to drive all the way back to Atherington.

Mary's grandmother, white haired and straight as a poker, perched herself on a high-backed chair in the middle of the room from which she could survey all that went on. Looking almost regal in her black gaberdeen skirt and black silk blouse with its ruffle of white lace at the neck, she stared hard at William.

He put down the scone he was eating in embarrassment and turned to Mary. 'Where do ee want all your bits and pieces putting then, Mary?' he asked. 'I'd best get it all unloaded before them young devils outside gets their hands on it.'

'Me and Bertie can do that, Uncle Will,' Tom offered and he and his brother escaped gleefully outside. They soon began bringing in boxes and sacks which they dumped in the corner by the stairs. William had to help them carry in the dresser and when Mary's mother saw it she cried, 'There be no room for that! Why did ee bring it, Mary?'

''Cos 'twas old Granny Chugg's and left to me.'

'You should've let me buy it when I offered,' Anne said.

'But I need it for me crocks!'

William made a suggestion then. 'Put'n in the chimbley corner! There'd be room if us moved the harmonium.'

'And where be that going?' Mary's mother demanded.

'Under the window. The aspidistra can go in the corner.'

''Tis too dark there! Aspidistras need light!'

'Nonsense!' Mary's grandmother spoke with authority. 'Aspidistras'll flourish anywhere.'

Nobody dared argue so everything was

moved around so that Mary's dresser could be installed where William had suggested. Then the wooden box containing all their clothes was carried up to the biggest bedroom Mary would be sharing with her mother. There was just enough space for George's cot alongside their double bed. Eliza's little truckle was jammed next to Becky's in the other much smaller room, so tightly she had to climb over it to get inside. Mary wondered what would happen when her baby was born and sighed as she remembered the joy she and John had felt when they first moved into their little bedroom in the farm cottage.

But there could be no looking back. She and the children had a roof over their heads and for that she was thankful. She had some money saved and had added to that by selling the things she could not bring with her. They could manage for a time but she did not want to be financially dependent on her mother who took in dressmaking to make ends meet, or on young Becky who was working as nursemaid to the vicar's children. She would have to look around for a little light work she could do before she had the baby.

When she went downstairs again, her grandmother Pugsley fixed her with a penetrating stare. 'Now then, Mary,' she began, ''tis time to think of your future. You'm young yet and healthy so you could get married again. But there bain't many men'll want to get saddled with another man's children. So you'd best go as housekeeper when a chance comes your way. I've spoken to the vicar's wife and she'll put in a good word for ee when the time comes. 'Tis too early for that yet, so you can come to me for a few hours every morning doing the cleaning. The flibbertigibbet I had working for me has took herself off so I could do with some help. I can pay ee three shillings a week.'

She waited, expecting a reply. Mary hesitated. Becoming a housekeeper was not what she had in mind. She had other plans for after the baby was born and she knew that her grandmother would not be easy to work for. She looked at her mother, who nodded. 'I can mind Lizzie and little Georgie for ee,' she said. 'Tis very good of your gran, Mary.'

Still Mary hesitated. Three shillings a week did not seem much but at least it was something. 'I'll do it, then,' she said reluctantly. 'When do ee want me to start?'

'Monday morning, eight o'clock sharp till one. That should give ee plenty of time to do the washing.' She stood up to go. 'Well, I've said what I came to say so I'll leave ee now to get settled in.' She bent, meaning to kiss Eliza but the child shied away. Hastily, Mary lifted George and presented his cheek instead which the old lady brushed with puckered lips. When she made for the door, William leapt to open it for her and, as soon as she was safely out of earshot, they all laughed.

'Rather you than me, Mary!' Sarah said. 'Her's a right old besom! Can't keep a maid for more'n five minutes! No wonder Granfer Pugsley upped and died!'

'At least he left her well provided for!' Mary's mother said with a touch of envy.

Will chuckled. 'And us all knows how he did it! I could tell ee plenty of tales about Jack Pugsley.'

Mary knew that her grandfather had been a horse dealer, a plausible rogue who was half gypsy with a reputation his widow had been trying to live down ever since.

'That be all past and gone,' her mother said disapprovingly, 'and there's no need to speak ill of the dead! I reckon Mary ought to keep on the right side of her gran.'

'At three bob a week?' William mocked. 'Mary could do better'n that! I'll keep an eye open for something going our way, once the baby's born.'

'Tis kind of ee, Will,' Mary said. 'But we'm best off here. Thanks for taking the time to bring us. Be there anything left on the wagon?'

'Just foodstuff — a side of bacon, a jar of pickled eggs, a sack of potatatoes and that apple pie your neighbour passed in just before us left.'

'Poll Potter.' Mary smiled. 'She's been good to me, Will. You all have. I'll never forget that.'

'Just remember,' Will said, 'you'm John's widow and if you ever want for anything, you'll know where to come. But I'd best be off. There's plenty of work waiting for me back home.' He patted her clumsily on the shoulder. 'Send word when you've had the baby!' He lifted Eliza for a kiss and she clung round his neck. 'You be a good maid for your ma, Lizzie! Then you shall come and see Toby one day.' He took George in the crook of his other arm and kissed him, too. 'As for you, Georgie boy, us'll make a farmer of ee yet!'

Watching him with the children, Mary felt a rush of sorrow that they had no father now to cradle and tease them, just as she had no man to lie beside her at night to comfort her. She took them outside to wave William on his way once he had unloaded her foodstuffs and they watched together as the wagon slowly rumbled farther up the hill to take the road to Atherington. It was as if their last link with

John had been broken and she had to grip her lips tightly to prevent them from trembling. That night, when she lay in the unfamiliar double bed on the lumpy flock mattress with her mother's snoring keeping her awake, she could hold back her tears no longer but sobbed silently into her pillow.

She did not accompany her mother and Becky to church the next morning. She had grown away from the Anglican service after being introduced to the chapel by John and had soon discovered that she preferred the Baptists' simpler approach and more rousing hymns. Now he was not with her to walk to the chapel, so that Sunday morning she made the excuse that she needed to unpack her belongings and find places for everything, promising to have the dinner on the table for when her mother and sister came home again.

She wanted to be alone with the children as they showed signs of being unsettled after the move. George kept whingeing, clinging to her skirts and Eliza had climbed out of her bed in the middle of the night and come looking for her. So she found the bag of wooden blocks John had made for George and sat him down to build with them on one of her familiar rag rugs. Then she and Eliza carefully unpacked her plates and dishes and arranged them in the same order they had always been on her dresser. Eliza found her rag doll in one of the sacks and begged her mother's old shawl to make a bed for it in John's wicker chair.

Mary could leave the children happily playing then while she went out to the back to draw water from the pump for peeling the potatoes and scrubbing the parsnips she would roast with the piece of pork in the side oven. Then they could have Poll Potter's apple pie and clotted cream for afters.

By the time the others came home from church she had removed her mother's red plush cloth from the table and covered it with a plain white one. The cutlery was in place and the meal was smelling appetisingly. Becky rushed straight to the fire to warm her fingers and Mary's mother looked pinched when she appeared, even though she was wearing her heavy skirt and jacket and her fur trimmed bonnet.

'Twas bitter cold in church this morning,' she grumbled. 'They'd lit the stove but that only kept the vicar warm. 'Tis nice to come home to a hot meal, Mary, and not have to think about cooking.'

'I might be a bit of use to ee then and not just a nuisance!'

'You'm never a nuisance, m'dear and nor be the little lambs. Just look at Georgie there, building a castle! And what be you doing, Lizzie — putting your baby to sleep?'

When Eliza took her grandmother's hand to show her the bed she had made, Mary suddenly felt that they were a family again and her heart was full when she went to the oven to check on the meat and potatoes. They were going to be all right, so she would keep her future plans to herself for a while.

During the meal, her mother said, 'Tell ee who was in church this morning, Mary — Mr Dark, the carpenter and his wife. I had a word with'n afterwards, and thanked'n for the way he managed John's funeral. A fine figure of a man he looked, all in his blacks and tall hat when he walked in front of the coffin. But Mrs Dark's looking proper poorly — nearly as big as you are, Mary, expecting her eleventh child, poor soul. Can't be all that young, neither.'

Mary remembered the carpenter's wife, a tall, slender woman when she was not expecting, with dark hair plaited in coils over her head. She had a certain refinement about her which people in the village put down to pride, blaming her mother who had been a lady's maid and had brought her daughter up with ideas above her station. Everybody was surprised when she married Reuben Dark, a self-made man reputed to rule his wife and his large family with a rod of iron.

'Do they still live in that big house at the top of the hill,' Mary asked, 'next to Granny Pugsley's?'

'Ay. Not likely to shift, neither, now that Reuben Dark's built a bigger workshop in the yard. He's doing well — gets all the work in the village and the farms about — even some in Barum they tell me. And he's the best wheelwright round here. The two biggest lads have learnt the trade and moved on. Now he's training the next one. All boys they be, 'cept for two. Pretty well one every year, the poor soul's had.'

'I remember one girl, a few years younger than me.'

'Em'ly!' Mary's mother sniffed. 'A wild one that, and no better than she should be. Took off about twelve months ago, nobody knows where.'

'She was very pretty.'

'Pretty is as pretty does! Just about broke her mother's heart, Em'ly did.'

Mary was silent, remembering the vivacious girl she used to know. All the lads were around her when she was only eleven or twelve and she was daring even then, so it was unlikely Emily would have lasted long in Reuben Dark's strict household. As for his wife, Mary could not imagine how she could have submitted to being made pregnant for the eleventh time when she must be at least forty. Perhaps she would see her when she was at her grandmother's house. It would be interesting to talk to somebody who was also in the family way.

But it did not seem there would be much opportunity for a neighbourly chat the next morning. Mary arrived a little late because George had screamed when she tried to leave him and Eliza's eyes had filled with tears. It had taken all of Mary's and her mother's powers of persuasion and promises of sweeties to pacify them.

Her grandmother was not disposed to listen to excuses. 'That boiler should've been lit long before this,' she scolded, 'if the sheets are to be on the line by ten o'clock. You'll have to do better than this, Mary!'

Old Mrs Pugsley's house was stone built and solid with a porch at the front, a parlour as well as a kitchen, a back kitchen and a built on wash house which contained a copper boiler, an innovation in the village. This was set up on bricks and Mary hastened to fill it with buckets of water from the pump. She raked the cold ashes from under it and set sticks and paper to rekindle a shovelful of hot coals she fetched from the kitchen range. When the fire was was well ablaze she topped it up with fresh coal and sorted out the washing. The whites could be put to boil but her grandmother's woollen stockings and underclothes and her more delicate petticoats and blouses would have to be washed by hand. So she filled the big iron kettle and set it on the range for more hot water while she took a knife to shred the slab of yellow soap her grandmother had given her.

It took a while for the copper to begin bubbling but at last she could fling in the soap and push down the sheets, the pillow cases, bolster cases, towels and tablecloths with the dolly stick. The wash house filled with steam and her face was flushed as she bent over the tub, rubbing and wringing her grandmother's clothes, needing to scrub her long black skirt on the wash board, it had collected so much dirt. She had to fetch more water for rinsing and the whites needed a freshening from the blue bag before she could put everything through the heavy mangle. By the time she went out into her grandmother's garden to hang it all on the line, Mary was exhausted.

It was a bright, December morning with a cold breeze which cooled her hot face and blew her hair loose from its pins. She pushed it away from her eyes wearily before flinging the first of the sheets over the washing line.

As she did so, she caught sight of a movement in the garden next door. Two hands were reaching up to peg a towel to a long line which stretched between tall posts and was already partly filled with children's clothes.

Curious, Mary moved towards the dividing hedge and peered over. A woman was bending to take another garment from the clothes basket at her feet and, as she straightened up, she put one hand on the small of her back as if in pain. The telltale bulge under her long white apron told Mary who she was.

'Morning,' Mary said. ''Tis Mrs Dark, I think.'

The woman turned, startled. Then she smiled. 'Mary Pugsley! I heard you were coming.' She looked much older than Mary remembered but her smile was still sweet.

''Tis Mary Moore now. I'm back at me mother's since — but I 'spect you've heard.'

'Yes.' Jane Dark's eyes clouded. 'I was very sorry, Mary. 'Tis a sad thing to lose a husband so young, and you, like me, in the family way. When's your baby due?'

'End of March.'

'Mine's not till June and I won't be sorry. I'm finding it a lot harder this time.'

She looked tired and drawn and was obviously in trouble as she bent and stretched to lift and hang up the washing.

'You could do with some help with that,' Mary said.

Jane smiled ruefully. 'The girl who usually comes sent to say she's sick.'

'Can't one of the children give you a hand?'

'They're all at school except for Joey, who's working with his father and Freddy, who's asleep in his cot. Sally wanted to stay home today but I wouldn't let her.'

And Emily's gone! Mary thought. 'Then I'll come over when I've finished,' she said.

'You will not, Mary Moore! You're nearer your time than I am!'

Mary nearly said that she was also several years younger but bit that back when she saw Jane Dark guess what she was thinking. In any case, her grandmother called at that moment from the wash house.

'Mary! Don't bide there gossiping! That's not what I pay ee for!'

Mary grimaced and turned away from the hedge. She heard Jane Dark laugh softly. 'Take no notice!' she murmured. 'Come and have tea with me tomorrow, Mary — three o'clock before the children get home. Bring your little ones and they can play with Freddy.'

Mary smiled and nodded her thanks before

she bent to lift another sheet to fling over the line. It would be good to have somebody to talk to, somebody who would understand and sympathise. Jane Dark might be nearer her mother's age than her own but she sensed that they might have a lot in common, if only because they were both expecting another child.

4

As her days in Yarnscombe lengthened into weeks, Mary's life slipped into a new pattern, broken only by Christmas. This was the hardest time. John's brother, William, came over from Atherington with an armful of holly and a fat goose and the children hung up their stockings as usual. But when they discovered them stuffed with sweets and nuts and oranges on Christmas morning and bounced into bed with their mother and their grandmother, Mary could only think of previous years when she and John had shared their excitement.

She was glad when the festivities were over and she could get back to the strict routine of work in her grandmother's house — washing on Mondays, ironing on Tuesdays on the kitchen table with two flat irons she heated in turn on the range, blacking the stove on Wednesdays and scrubbing the kitchen floor, cleaning the bedrooms on Thursdays and the parlour on Fridays with special attention given to polishing the furniture with beeswax, all the odd jobs like cleaning the windows on Saturdays. This was the only day she looked forward to as it was when she was paid her hard earned three shillings. She kept a shilling of it to put into her tin box with the money she was saving for the baby and gave the rest to her mother to help towards their keep.

Jane Dark's first invitation to tea was followed by more, usually once a week. Mary enjoyed the change and felt that Jane was glad of her company. The children were shy at first but soon looked forward to going to the big house where there was a cupboard full of the Dark children's abandoned toys. Little Fred Dark was about the same age as George but it was always George who took the lead in their games and Eliza who acted as peacemaker if there was ever any trouble. Usually they played happily together, leaving their mothers free to talk as they sipped their tea and commiserated with one another over increasing tiredness and swollen ankles.

It was to Jane that Mary confided her plans for the future, telling her how she had worked in the glove factory in Torrington before her marriage to John and wanted to get back to it. She had started at thirteen as a humble end-tier, snipping and tying the thread ends left by the machinists, but had gradually progressed to working on the machines herself.

''Tis all cloth gloves they make at

Vaughan's,' she said, 'ladies' gloves mostly out of taffeta and silk and milanese, lace sometimes. We'd part machine them on the treadles and the rest was hand-finished by home-workers. The best bit was the pointing — the decoration on the backs of the gloves. I was good at that. Towards the end of my time I could machine three rows of stitches inside an eighth of an inch, none of them touching. 'Course, I know I can't go back to Vaughan's full-time but I could work at home, doing the finishing. What do ee think, Jane?'

Her friend smiled encouragement, 'I'm sure you'll do it and do it well. I wish I had your courage.'

'But you don't need it. You've got a husband.'

'Yes.' Jane turned away with a sigh. 'I've a husband and ten children but I rarely see some of them now that the older boys are working away from home. As for Emily — ' she paused. ' — I miss Emily every day that passes. Sally tries to take her place and Reuben's taken her out of school to be with me. I wish he hadn't done that. She's a bright girl and Miss Baker's best pupil when the Inspectors come. She's passed her Standard four tests already, even though she's not quite ten.'

Mary put a hand on her arm. 'Ma told me

Em'ly'd run off. Don't ee ever hear from her?'

'Not a word. And it was all over nothing — a stupid row. She was always headstrong.'

'I remember her,' Mary said. 'She was very pretty.'

'Too pretty for her own good! I worry about her Mary. If she would just let me know she's all right . . . '

Mary could tell that Jane's eldest daughter was her favourite and that her sudden departure had hurt her deeply. She wondered about the reason for it, whether it had something to do with Reuben Dark, that silent, domineering man she had so far seen only once in the big house. He had burst into the parlour where she and Jane were drinking tea. Muttering an apology, he had made for a desk in the corner of the room and begun rummaging in it, grumbling under his breath when he could not immediately find what he wanted. His presence put a stop to the women's chatter and the children's play. It was not until he was striding out of the room with a paper in his hand that he glanced down at Mary. For a moment his eyes met hers, startling her with intensity of his gaze. Then he nodded, as if in approval, and moved on.

'He works too hard,' Jane said, as if that

explained everything. She smiled gently at Mary and changed the subject. 'Are you enjoying the book I gave you to read?'

She was a great reader, particularly fond of poetry and had persuaded Mary to take home one of her precious, leather bound volumes and tell her what she thought of it.

Mary hesitated. 'Some of it's lovely,' she said, 'but I didn't understand a lot of it. I'm not as clever as you.'

'You're just as clever, Mary! You must borrow another of my books. The more poetry I read, the more life becomes clearer to me. Poets get to the heart of things, don't you think?'

'P'raps,' Mary said doubtfully. 'But most of them won't know what ordinary folks lives are like. They wouldn't know what it means to be having a baby, for a start.'

Jane laughed. 'You're so wise, Mary! They're mostly men so they wouldn't know at all what it's like! They wouldn't understand about these long weeks of waiting. They're the most peaceful times for me because I feel I'm still in charge of my body. 'Tis only later . . .'

'When you'm birthing?' Mary grimaced. 'Tisn't you that's in charge then, is it? 'Tis the baby, pushing and shoving to get out!'

'Oh, that! I wasn't meaning that. I meant — afterwards.'

'When there's all that feeding and squalling? It don't finish then, neither. Goes on for years!'

Jane sighed and Mary had a feeling that she might have missed the point her friend was trying to make. 'Afterwards' — that was a word that could have meant anything.

'Well, 'twon't be for much longer now,' she said, trying to sound optimistic, 'first me, then you!'

'You'll let me know when it happens, won't you?'

''Twill be all round the village before I've even given suck, if I know Yarnscombe!'

The last few weeks of her pregnancy dragged. Towards the end of it she had to cut down on her work at her grandmother's and often turned to Jane's books for comfort, finding herself abstracted, in a kind of dream, as if the period of waiting would go on for ever. In a way, she did not want it to end, for while it lasted she felt as if she still had a part of John with her.

When her baby eventually decided to enter the world he was born in her mother's bed a few minutes after midnight on March 20th, 1866. A red faced, bawling boy, he came in such a rush that Ma Shaddick, who acted as the village midwife, only just arrived in time.

George's cot had been moved downstairs

for the event but Eliza came stumbling in from her bed to know what all the noise was about. She was promptly shooed away by the midwife and set up such a wailing she woke George, too. So Becky had to bring them both into the big bedroom to meet their new baby brother who was just being cleaned up in a bowl on the wash stand.

They stood beside the bed in silent amazement, watching as Ma Shaddick handed him to their mother who put him to her breast for the first time.

'What's'n going to be called, Ma?' Eliza asked at last.

Mary looked down at her son, feeling the urgent tug of his mouth as he nuzzled into her. His head was covered with wispy black hair and he had a little pug nose. His eyes were tightly shut and his tiny fists pummelled her breast as he sucked. 'John!' she decided. 'He's going to be called John, after your dada and he'll grow up to be a big, strong man.'

There was much coming and going in her mother's house that day as family and friends called with gifts for the new arrival. Granny Pugsley was one of the last to arrive, bringing a knitted shawl she had made herself. Mary's mother was kept busy in the kitchen brewing tea for the visitors while Mary and baby John held court upstairs in the big bed. When at last it seemed that everybody had been and had mostly gone again, there came another knock on the cottage door. Becky answered it and was surprised to find Jane Dark there.

'I won't come in,' Jane said. 'I heard the news and just want to ask after Mary. And to leave this for her.'

Mary's mother came bustling to the door as soon as she realised who was there. 'Of course you must come in!' she cried. 'Mary'll be glad to see ee. Her's doing fine and so's the baby. Becky — show Mrs Dark upstairs while I make a fresh pot of tea.'

'No, no!' Jane said. 'Mary must be very tired. As long as I know she's all right.' She handed over a small package. 'Will you give her this, Mrs Pugsley?'

Mary's mother accepted the package grudgingly. 'If that's what you want, Mrs Dark. You must suit yerself, of course but you'm welcome enough to come in.'

'I know. But I'm sure Mary's had enough visitors for one day. Tell her I'll see her another time.' She smiled, turned away, then began walking slowly and painfully back up the hill.

'Well!' Mary's mother said after she had shut the cottage door. 'So my cottage bain't good enough for Jane Dark! Dunno why she should give herself such airs. Who's Reuben

Dark, when all's said and done?'

'Keeps herself to herself,' Granny Pugsley said. 'Always has done. I've lived next door to her for years and never had more'n the time of the day. Seems her's took a fancy to Mary, though.'

'Keeps lending her books. Trying to turn her into a scholar, or summat.' Mary's mother looked at the package in her hand. ''Tis a small thing to be giving a baby,' she said and turned to Becky. 'You take it up! 'Tis hardly worth my while climbing the stairs!'

Mary was almost asleep when Becky looked in on her and the baby was dozing contentedly in the crook of her arm. Becky touched her sister's hand. 'You've had another visitor,' she whispered.

Mary opened her eyes and struggled to sit up. 'I thought everybody'd been.'

''Twas that Mrs Dark, the carpenter's wife.'

'Jane? Why didn't you bring her up?'

'Her wouldn't come. Said you'd be too tired.' Becky grinned. 'Mother thinks her's stuck up.'

''Tis just shyness. You have to get to know her.'

Becky produced Jane's present. 'Her's left this for little Johnny. Shall I open it?'

'Please.'

Inside the brown paper wrapping there was

a little leather box and when Becky opened it she found a baby's silver spoon and a gold sovereign. There was also a card on which Jane had written, 'For Mary and her new baby, with kindest regards from Jane Dark.'

'Caw!' Becky said when she held up the spoon. 'Solid silver! And a whole sovereign! You could buy a lot for Johnny with that!'

I could, Mary thought, but I shall not! For she knew, with certainty, that Jane had intended the money to help tide her over the period when she was working her way back into the gloving that would make her independent. As soon as I'm up and about, she thought, I shall take Johnny to see her and thank her. And if I can ever do anything for Jane in return, she has only to ask.

But other things had to be seen to first. It soon became obvious that different sleeping arrangements would have to be made to accomodate the baby. Mary's mother grumbled about being woken up in the night when Johnny had to be fed, especially as George, whose cot had been moved back into the bedroom, usually woke up, too. The vicar's wife made things easier for everybody by offering Becky a bed at the vicarage where she was working as nursemaid. George was then able to move into the little bedroom with Eliza and, although Mary and her mother still had to share the double bed, the baby could sleep in the cot which George had grown out of, anyway.

None of this was really satisfactory and Mary longed for the day when she could find a place of her own. She wanted to get on with her plans and discuss them with Jane. It irked her to be lying in bed but it was several days before Ma Shaddick would allow her downstairs. Even then, Mrs Pugsley insisted that she should be 'churched' before going visiting. Mary was in the habit of going to Sunday evening services at the little wooden chapel but her mother considered it inferior for such an important event. So, on the second Sunday after little John was born, Mary carried him to the ancient church of St Andrew to be cleansed and blessed by the vicar.

Then John's brothers brought their wives and their mother over from Atherington for a visit and Poll Potter walked up from Westcott to see the new baby. There was so much going on, it was a while before Mary was able to find the time to visit Jane Dark and when she did, she was shocked to see the change in her.

She was carrying her baby very low and looked weighed down with it. Her face was drawn and her ankles and legs so badly swollen she had difficulty in walking. But she greeted Mary cheerfully enough and was charmed with little Johnny, holding him in her arms and talking softly to him. She only handed him back when he began to whimper and then to yell.

Mary laughed as she took him and loosened her bodice. 'He's hungry,' she said when he clamped his mouth upon her nipple. 'Always lets me know it, too! Greediest baby I've had, this one!'

Jane sighed as she watched her. 'I hope mine will be so healthy and that I'll have plenty of milk this time. Little Freddy was pining until I found him a wet nurse.'

'Well, you won't have far to look now!' Mary said. 'I've enough for two if you should have trouble.'

Jane leaned forward eagerly. 'D'you mean that, Mary? I'd sooner hand my baby over to you than to anybody else. That last girl — ' She pursed her lips. 'I couldn't bear to see her with Freddy, she flaunted herself so. I sent her away and Reuben was angry because I had to put Freddy on cow's milk and water. He thrived somehow.'

'He's lively enough now!'

'But not as strong as your Georgie.' Jane put a hand on her swollen stomach. 'I hope for a girl this time. So promise me you'll be here for my baby, if — ' She broke off and Mary saw a tear trickle down her cheek.

'Of course I'll promise!' she said. 'But t'won't be the end of the world if you can't feed your baby! Lady Anne put all hers out to a wet nurse so's her could get her figure back! Nobody thought the worst of her for that!'

Jane smiled sadly. 'I wonder if she realised what she was missing, poor woman?'

'Poor woman! Living in that big house with all them servants, decked out in jewels and fancy dresses and off to Lunnon whenever her takes the fancy? There's nothing poor about Lady Anne!'

'Poor children, then,' Jane murmured.

Mary shook her head. 'You don't miss what you've never had. Johnny here won't miss his father because he'll never know'n. That breaks my heart sometimes. But he'll grow up, same's Lizzie and Georgie will, 'cos that's how life be, I reckon. I'll do my best for 'em, just as you'll do your best for yourn. Us can't do more'n that, Jane.'

What Mary had in mind, though, was to do the best, not only for her children but also for herself as she had no wish to continue working for her grandmother. She knew that Bert regularly drove into Torrington with completed orders for the saddles and other gear he had made and that he spent some time there, picking up new orders from the farmers or buying a fresh stock of leather from Chapple's yard. So, on the last Thursday in April, she begged a lift into the town for herself and Johnny, making the excuse that she had to buy things for him.

Her brother in law deposited them in the square which was always busy on market days. But Mary soon left the crowds and hurried towards New Street, feeling a quiver of excitement when she reached the glove works she had first entered twelve years before. It was a tall, handsome building and when she went inside she passed the counting house on the ground floor and glanced in at the cutters' room where the men worked. A long room, it was lined with tables on which stood the hand shaped punching machines for the final shaping of the material. Bales of stuff were stacked on the shelves — silk, lace, taffeta, all kinds of fabrics in dozens of different colours.

She had to climb the stairs to the machine room and could hear the familiar whirr of the treadles as she made her way up, wondering if Meg Connibear was still in charge and if she would remember her. It all looked much the same when she opened the door and saw the April sun streaming in through the fanlights in the roof on to the bent heads of the women, busy at their work. One or two looked up and recognised her, murmuring a greeting as she moved carefully between them with Johnny in her arms.

Meg Connibear was at the far end of the room and when she turned, Mary saw her eyes light up with recognition. 'Why, if 'tisn't Mary Pugsley,' she said. 'I never thought to see you here again!'

'I'm Mary Moore now and back looking for work. I've been widowed this past six months.'

'With a new baby as well!' Meg clucked her tongue sympathetically and peered at Johnny. 'A fine boy by the looks of him. Well, if you'm looking for work, Mary, you've come to the right place. We're fair run off our feet with all the orders that's coming in. Twentyfour thousand pairs of gloves us have sent off this week!'

''Tis home working I'm wanting,' Mary said. 'I'm back living with Mother in Yarnscombe. Do ee collect and deliver from there?'

'Carter goes round on Fridays. He collects from Alverdiscott so I'll ask'n to branch off to Yarnscombe. Tell me where you live and I'll see you get a parcel next week. Payment's the following Friday if the work's satisfactory. But you was always good at it, Mary, so I've no worry on that score.'

Mary smiled her thanks and left the factory feeling jubilant. She bought some cheap material in the market to make a new gown for Johnny but did not tell Bert where else she had been or why. She only wanted to confide in Jane and made up her mind to go and see her friend the next day.

Their way back into Yarnscombe took them past the carpenter's house and, as they approached it, Mary was startled to see Sally, Jane's young daughter, come running out in tears. She was followed by her father who shouted something to her.

'Stop a minute, Bert!' Mary said and leaned out of the trap. 'What's the matter, Sal?' she called.

''Tis Mother!' the girl sobbed. 'Her's been took for the baby!'

'But 'tisn't due yet!'

'I know. I'm to fetch Ma Shaddick.'

'Us can do that! Get back in and look after your ma!'

'But I don't know what to do! Her's screaming something terrible!'

The girl was almost hysterical. Mary pushed Johnny into Bert's arms and leapt from the trap. 'Take Sally to Ma Shaddick's, Bert, and leave Johnny with Mother! I'll see if I can help.'

She ran to the house and banged on the door. Reuben Dark opened it, looking wild eyed. 'What be you doing here, Mary Moore?'

'Come to help Jane if I can. I've just seen Sal — '

He moved to let her in. 'Jane's upstairs — '

A scream from above them led Mary to Jane's room where she found her friend rolling in agony on a blood stained bed. She struggled to sit up when she saw Mary.

'The baby — ' she cried. 'I'm losing the baby — '

Mary knelt down beside her and held her hand. 'No! Hold on, Jane! Ma Shaddick's coming.'

'Too late!' Jane tossed her head from side to side and gripped at Mary's hand. 'The pain — '

'Hang on to me — tight's you like!' She winced as Jane's fingers clamped in a vice like grip. 'Try to ride the pain, Jane and don't push! Not yet!'

'But I'm tearing apart!'

Reuben Dark appeared in the doorway. His hair was standing on end as if he had been dragging his fingers through it. 'How be her?'

'Bad. But bearing it.'

He groaned and turned away.

A door banged below and a moment later

Mrs Shaddick bustled into the bedroom with Sally. 'Hot water!' she demanded. 'Plenty of it! And everybody out of 'ere 'cept Mary!'

Sally ran to fetch the water and for the next two hours Mary and the midwife did their best to help Jane through her torment. When she gave a final, despairing cry, there slithered into Mrs Shaddick's waiting hands the lifeless body of a tiny baby girl, six weeks premature. The horrified midwife would have spirited her away until Mary intervened.

'No!' she cried. 'Let me wash her for her mother to hold. You see to Jane, Mrs Shaddick! Her's lost a terrible lot of blood.'

'But who's to tell the father?' the midwife asked fearfully.

'I will. Just see to Mrs Dark!'

Jane had collapsed in exhaustion and when the midwife whispered to her that her baby was dead, tears ran silently down her cheeks. ''Twas a girl,' Mrs Shaddick said. 'Mary's cleaning 'er up for you to see.'

But Jane turned her face into her pillow and would not look even when Mary brought the baby to her, washed clean and wrapped in a napkin.

'But her's beautiful,' Mary said. 'Hold her for a minute, Jane!'

'No. Take her away! I don't want to see her!'

Rebuffed, Mary drew back. She had never seen her friend in such a state, she was usually so calm and gentle.

'Mr Dark should fetch the doctor,' she said to the midwife. 'And he'll have to be told.'

She laid the dead baby gently on a bedside chair and left the midwife ministering to Jane while she went downstairs to look for Reuben Dark. She found Sally sitting miserably in the kitchen with the younger children and the girl burst into tears when she was given the news.

'You must be brave for your mother, now,' Mary told her, 'and the first thing you can do to help is fetch fresh linen for her bed, so her's clean and tidy when your father goes up. Where's he gone, Sally?'

'To the workshop. Said he couldn't bear it no longer in the house.'

The sound of hammering met Mary even before she reached the wooden building Reuben Dark had built for his carpentry. The outer door was open and she stood watching him for a moment as he stood at his work bench in his shirt sleeves and carpenter's apron, hammering away at a window frame.

Then he seemed to sense her presence because he looked up. 'Be it over, then?' he asked.

'Ay' Mary moved into the workshop. 'And I'm sorry, Mr Dark.'

He frowned. ''Tis dead, then?'

Mary nodded. ''Twas a girl — perfect but born too soon.'

'And Jane?'

'Poorly, her's lost so much blood. You'd best fetch the doctor, Mr Dark.'

Reuben put down his hammer and untied his apron. 'I'll go to her, then. Thankee, Mary Moore, for your help.'

I'd have done a lot more if I could, Mary thought as she watched him striding away towards the house. I'd have fed that poor mite for Jane if she'd wanted me to.

She cupped her hands under her breasts, feeling them heavy and painful and remembered that it was several hours since she had last fed Johnny. She could imagine his lusty yelling and her mother's frantic efforts to pacify him and knew that it was time to return to her own responsibilities.

First she wanted to say goodbye to Jane. She returned to the house and went upstairs to the big bedroom but when she looked in and saw Reuben Dark supporting his wife in his arms she knew that for the moment she was not needed and would only be an intruder. So she beckoned to the midwife and left a message that she would call again the next day. Then she hurried back to her mother's cottage where she took a red faced, bawling Johnny into her arms and bared her breast for him. But even as she rejoiced in the urgent pulling of his mouth at her nipple she was weeping for her good friend's grief and disappointment.

5

The next afternoon, once her morning stint at her grandmother's was over, Mary left Johnny at home and called at the carpenter's house. A tearful Sally opened the door to her and told her that her mother was much worse. She could not be persuaded to eat even though Sally had prepared a thin gruel for her and an egg beaten up in milk. So her father had ridden to High Bickington to fetch the doctor who had prescribed rest and quiet and no visitors.

'She's grieving terrible,' Sally said, 'and won't even talk to Father. I'm at me wit's end 'cos Freddy cries for her now the young uns are at school and the boys out working.'

Mary felt sorry for the girl who was not much more than a child herself. 'Where's your dad now?' she asked her.

'In his workshop, making a coffin for the baby.' Sally's eyes flooded over at the thought and she sobbed aloud.

'I'll go and see'n,' Mary said. 'I know your mother's supposed to rest but she might talk to me if he says I can try.' She patted Sally's arm. 'Get inside and brew up a pot of tea.

'Twill make ee feel better, Sal.'

She left the porch and crossed the yard to the workshop. There was no sound of hammering and when she looked inside she saw the carpenter standing at his bench, brooding over the tiny coffin he had just finished making. He looked hunched and dejected with his large, capable hands splayed out on the bench in front of him.

'Mr Dark?' Mary spoke softly and he jerked his head towards her. 'Sally tells me Jane's very bad.'

'Ay. You can't see her!' he said roughly.

'I know. Leastways, I know that's what the doctor said. But p'raps 'twould help if I did. Jane and me often talked.'

'Her's not talking now. Her won't even talk to me so her won't talk to you, Mary Moore! Leave her be!'

Rebuffed but undaunted, Mary moved towards the work bench and looked at the little coffin. It was beautifully made, its joints dovetailed as carefully as if it had been an expensive piece of furniture. Reuben had lined it with a soft, white material, embossed with a pattern of roses.

'This is lovely,' she said, 'as lovely as the poor mite that's to rest in it. Have ee named her yet?'

He shook his head. 'I can't get no sense out

of Jane. She was hankering after another girl but this be the end of that, I reckon. There'll be no more now.'

His lips were gripped tight as if he was angry. Mary ran her hand along the lining of the coffin, wondering how to approach him. ''Tis so soft,' she said, 'like a little cradle. You should take it in for Jane to see.'

'No!' He spat out the word. 'Her wants no part of it. I've spoke the vicar and he'll say a prayer over the little maid before I bury her. So there's nothing more to be done. You'd best go now, Mary Moore. This be no place for you, never having lost a baby.'

Mary felt her cheeks burn. 'I've lost a husband,' she reminded him sharply, 'and one loss be much the same as another to a woman with feelings.'

'Ay.' Reuben Dark's expression changed and his voice softened. 'I spoke out of turn. Later, p'raps, you can talk to Jane, when her's picked up a bit.'

'I'll call again tomorrow, then.' Mary moved towards the door but turned back. 'Why don't ee call the baby Jane? That might please your wife when her's more herself.'

She called every afternoon after that but it was a week before Sally was able to tell her that her mother was a little better and might see her. She was still in bed and likely to be there for some time.

Mary went up to the now familiar bedroom, where she found Jane propped up on pillows, looking pale and thin in her voluminous nightgown. Her greying hair hung loose about her face, making her look older but she managed a wan smile when she saw Mary. 'You've been before?' she asked.

'Every day.' Mary drew up a chair beside the bed and saw that Jane had an open book near to her hand. 'Poetry?'

'It's a great comfort.'

There was an awkward silence while both women avoided the subject which hung like a cloud between them. Then Jane asked abruptly, 'How are the children?'

'They'm all right. Lizzie started school after Easter now her's turned five. Georgie misses her but he'll soon have Johnny to play with, he's growing so fast. Greedy as ever!'

She saw Jane wince and could have bitten her tongue. She had left Johnny with her mother so as not to remind her friend of her own loss. Reproaching herself, she took hold of her hand. 'But I'd have made'n wait his turn, and nursed your poor little maid for ee, Jane, if only her'd been spared. But 'twasn't to be and that was a sadness to us all. Only the Lord knows why He took her, just as only He knows why he took my John. 'Tis a great mystery. But some'ow us have to go on, 'cos of them that's left. That's all us can do, Jane.'

A tear trickled down Jane's cheek as Mary squeezed her hand. 'You're stronger than I am,' she said. 'I left everything for Reuben to do, even the naming. He called her Jane. In my heart, I was calling her Emily so it's as if I've lost my daughter for a second time.'

'No! Your Emily'll come back! I feel it in me bones. And you've still got Sally — her's a good maid. And you've got your boys and your man! You'll soon be up and about, once you get your strength back.'

Jane shook her head. 'I can never be a proper wife to Reuben again. The doctor's told me that. 'Tis going to be hard for him, being the man he is. At least you haven't that to think of, Mary.'

Shocked, Mary stared at her friend, understanding, in a moment of insight, Reuben Dark's anger in the workshop and Jane's earlier use of the word 'afterwards.' Was that what she had feared, then — her husband's persistent advances that would have made her pregnant again? After eleven children, who could blame her?

'Well,' she said awkwardly, 'that's between you and Mr Dark. You'll be a good wife to'n in other ways, I reckon.'

'I'll try,' Jane said. 'But I'm not as brave as

you are. So you must come and see me when you can, Mary, and cheer me up. Bring the children! Freddy misses your Georgie.' She tried to smile. 'But you haven't told me yet how you got on at the glove factory. Are they going to give you work?'

Mary beamed. 'I'll be getting my first parcel of gloves tomorrow. I haven't told Mother yet, nor Granny Pugsley — haven't told nobody, 'cept you.'

'They won't mind, will they?'

'Bad job if they do! I aim to be my own mistress, Jane, beholding to nobody!'

Her grandmother's reaction was much as Mary expected. 'What be I going to do?' she demanded when she learned that Mary would not be working for her after the weekend.

'Same's you always did — find some other maid to work for next to nothing!' Mary retorted, hardening her heart.

Even her mother sounded doubtful. 'How be ee going to settle to glove making with the children about?' she asked. 'I can't be minding 'em all the time.'

'There's only George and Johnny now that Lizzie's at school. And there's times when they'm asleep. I'll work at night, if I have to, under the lamp.'

'And ruin your eyes?' Her mother shook

her head. ' 'Twill be too much for ee, Mary.'

The first parcels of gloves were delivered by the carter that Friday afternoon. Mary opened them eagerly. There were six pairs of gloves in each pack, one set of grey milanese with matching threads for stitching and pearl buttons for the cuffs and one set of cream taffeta with matching threads and lace for frilling. There were also two packets of different sized needles and each pair of gloves was ticketed with the worker's name so that it could be traced back in case the finishing was not done well.

'I shall work on the table,' Mary said, 'with my back to the light,' and she began straight away.

She was slow at first, as she knew she would be, painstaking and determined that each stitch should be perfect. Johnny was asleep after his feed and George had wandered into the back garden with his grandmother so she made good headway until Eliza came home from school and wanted to help. She was set to counting the buttons and by teatime Mary had finished one glove. She knew then that she could do it and her confidence rose.

The next morning she went to her grandmother's for her last Saturday's work and the old lady was not in a good humour when she handed Mary her three shillings.

'You won't be seeing so much of your friend, Mrs Dark, now that you'm working at the gloving!' she said spitefully. 'They'm saying her's gone into a decline since losing that baby. Never got over it, did her?'

Mary said nothing, knowing that her grandmother was only probing. But she worried about Jane who showed no signs of improvement. Reuben Dark had already taken on a woman to see to the running of the house and the care of the younger children, as if he did not expect his wife to get better. So despite her new commitment, Mary determined to call on her friend whenever she could.

She finished her first parcels of gloves in time for collection the following Friday, but instead of opening the new ones, she put them aside and took George and Johnny to the carpenter's house that afternoon. This welcome break became a weekly arrangement and during her visits to Jane, Mary tried to interest her in life outside the big house, telling her all the village gossip. But she remained frail and languid, lying on the sofa downstairs when she was not in her bed, reading her books or sometimes doing a little embroidery. Mary felt concerned for her family as Jane seemed to be drawing away from them. Reuben Dark occasionally looked in on her when Mary was there and he seemed morose and sounded impatient. Once he embarrassed her by bursting in when she was feeding Johnny and his eyes had held a despairing, hungry look as she hastened to cover herself.

Every week Jane said, 'If only Emily would come. If I could just see her once more.'

That made Mary fear that her friend was resigning herself to dying, so she asked around in the village, especially among Emily's old school friends, if anybody knew where she might have gone. Some thought she had begged a lift in a traveller's cart towards Exeter, others that she could have run off with the fair folk from Barum because she had disappeared in September when the fair was in town. It was obvious that nobody really knew.

'Wherever that maid went,' Mary's mother said, 'you can be sure her's come to a bad end. You don't want to bother no more about her, Mary.'

So Mary stopped asking but she did not stop worrying, especially as Betsy Harding, the woman Reuben had engaged as housekeeper, whispered to her that the doctor was talking of pernicious anaemia, brought on by Jane's losing so much blood when she gave birth prematurely.

Even when the warmer days came, she could not be persuaded to ride out with Reuben or sit in the garden, but stayed inside, growing paler and weaker. Mary sometimes took the younger Dark children out into the lanes with her three, picking primroses and violets for their mother and dog roses when spring turned to summer. Then it was blackberries and crab apples for the pies and jellies Jane would once have made but now had no interest in. Mary made them instead and took baskets of preserves to the carpenter's house for his family.

Around Christmas time, Jane seemed to rally a little, especially when the older boys brought in holly and mistletoe to hang from the beams in the kitchen. Mary began to hope for her and was able to join in the festivities more happily herself than in the previous year when she had so recently lost John. But January came in cold and bleak and she watched, with despair, as Jane slipped back into her former apathy.

One Friday afternoon in February she called on her as usual, leaving George and Johnny with her mother as Jane had been so tired the week before. Now she was much worse, back in her bed and unable to speak or even to smile at her.

Betsy Harding shook her head. 'The doctor's been,' she whispered, 'and said her's failing fast — can't take in so much as a sip of water, poor soul.'

'But us can't let her go like that!' Mary cried. 'I'll sit with her and see if she rallies.'

She drew up a chair close to Jane's bed and saw that her favourite poetry book was on the table beside her. Picking it up, she opened it at random.

'Jane,' she murmured. 'Can ee hear me, Jane? Shall I read to ee for a bit?' There was no response but she cleared her throat and began. She read slowly, carefully, so that she would not make a mistake and when she finished one poem she began another, sometimes stumbling over a difficult word and often not fully understanding what she read. Every now and then she glanced at Jane to see if there was a change in her and thought once that her friend might be smiling.

She was still reading when Reuben Dark came into the room and stood looking down at them both. Mary's voice tailed away in embarrassment and she closed the book.

''Tis no good, Mary Moore,' he said gruffly. 'Her's going. Doctor reckons her won't last the night.'

'Then I'll stay beside her and wait!'

'No! 'Tisn't your place to do that. 'Tis mine. You've plenty other calls on ee, anyhow. So I'll bid ee good-day and I'll send word when 'tis all over.'

Mary had tears in her eyes and her lips were trembling when she stood up to go. She could not hold back a sob. 'Jane's been a good friend to me,' she choked.

Reuben Dark nodded. 'And a good wife to me, when all's said and done. 'Twas kind of ee to call, Mary Moore.' To her surprise, he clasped her hand in his. 'Jane thought a lot of ee, I know. But even the best of things come to an end.' His eyes met hers and she saw the suffering in them.

'I'm very sorry, Mr Dark,' she whispered, 'for you and the children.'

'Ay. Seems the Lord's hit the pair of us bitter hard, Mary, but 'tisn't for us to ask why.'

He released her hand and she knew it was time for her to go. She looked at Jane who was lying pale and still, just as John had in their old double bed. Impulsively, she bent and kissed her gently on the forehead.

Sally brought the news the next morning that her mother had died in the night. The girl was so choked up with grief she could hardly utter the words. 'Funeral's to be on Tuesday in the church,' she said. 'Father's making the coffin,' and then burst into such a torrent of weeping, Mary held her close.

The old church was full for the funeral service. Reuben Dark was well respected in the village and even those people who had thought Jane held herself aloof could not fault her as a wife and mother. Her four eldest sons carried her coffin and the vicar spoke well of her devotion to her family and the church. It was only afterwards, when they all went out to the graveyard for the burial that Mary caught sight of a young woman, wearing a black shawl over her head, standing watching from the shadow of the yew trees.

She knew at once that this was Emily and waited for one of the Darks to recognise her. But they were all clustered around Jane's grave and too absorbed in their sorrow to notice. When it was all over and people began to move, Mary saw the girl about to slip away so she hurried after her.

'Emily?' she asked and the girl started. 'You've come too late, I reckon.'

Close to, she saw that Emily's face was streaked with tears and her condemnation turned to pity. She took the girl's arm and led her farther away from the mourners. 'Your mother was asking for ee,' she said. 'Every day she asked. So you'll not go now without speaking to your father?'

'I came for her, not for him and I'd have come before if I'd known she was so sick. Seems 'twas another baby finished her. I told'n that would happen years ago. He killed my mother so I've nothing to say to'n.' She looked at Mary closely. 'But what be you doing here, Mary Pugsley? I heard you was married.'

'Married and widowed, Emily. Your mother's been a good friend to me this last year and more, so I think I knew her as well as most. She wanted that baby — wanted another girl to take your place. You can't blame your father for that! He could do with you now, in that big house. Can't you find it in your heart to go to'n and grieve alongside your brothers and Sally? 'Twould be what your mother wanted.'

Emily stared blankly at her, then shook her head. 'Things were said once that can't be took back. He won't forget and nor will I. I've said goodbye to Mother which is why I came. So now I'll go.'

'Wait! At least tell me where you'm living, in case you should be needed.'

'Needed? Who by? I haven't been so far away they couldn't have found me if they'd wanted. I'm best on me own. I've learned how to look after meself. You'll be learning that now, Mary, I reckon.'

She began walking quickly away and Mary watched her go. The wilful girl she remembered had grown into a strong minded, handsome young woman, but Mary was glad that there was still enough heart in her to weep for her mother.

The funeral party was leaving the graveyard and when she began following them she saw that Sally was waiting for her to catch them up. 'Father said to ask if you'd like to come back to the house,' she said. 'There's food prepared for family and friends.' She looked questioningly at Mary. 'Who were you to talking to just then? 'Twas too far away for me to see.'

'Just somebody I used to know.' Mary hesitated. 'I won't come to the house, Sal. 'Twill be mostly your father's friends and close family. I'd best get back to the children before they drive Mother mad! Thank your dad for the offer and tell'n I'll remember you all in my prayers.'

And Jane, she thought, and the little baby with the same name. It was comforting to think that they would now be together in Heaven.

She hurried back to her mother's cottage, wanting only the presence of her children. It was as if death had closed another chapter in her life for there would be no more visits to the carpenter's house and cosy chats in Jane's little sitting room. She squeezed her eyes tightly, knowing that she was going to miss her friend badly.

Yet her funeral had not, it seemed, completely turned the page for that Sunday morning somebody knocked at the cottage door. Mary opened it and was astonished to see Reuben Dark there, holding a book in his hand.

'I'm on my way to church,' he said awkwardly, 'and I've brought ee this. 'Tis the book you was reading to Jane. I don't hold much to poetry meself but I thought you might like it to remember her by.'

He handed over the book and when Mary looked up to stammer her thanks she caught the same hungry look in his eyes she had avoided once before. Then Eliza and George came clamouring, pulling at her skirts.

'I see you'm busy,' he said and turned to go. 'Jane would've wanted ee to have summat, I reckon.' He doffed his cap and strode away, leaving Mary standing nonplussed, with Jane's favourite poetry book in her hands.

6

Mary did not fully appreciate how much Jane's friendship had meant to her until she was so cruelly deprived of it. She missed her weekly visits to the carpenter's house and Friday afternoons now seemed empty. Whereas before she had put aside her new parcels of gloves, she now opened them with relief and started work at once. The more intricate it was the better she was pleased for she was quicker at it now and had earned praise from the factory, even being asked if she could take on more.

She had refused the offer because it was already difficult enough to find time for the work between sharing the household chores and the care of the children with her mother. Then, a few months later, something happened to make her change her mind.

The elderly couple in the cottage next door suddenly announced that they were going to move into Barum to live with their son. As theirs was the first property to become vacant since Mary had returned to Yarnscombe, the chance of taking it seemed too good to miss. The rent, like her mother's, would be two pounds fifteen shillings a year, due in half yearly payments at Michaelmass and Lady Day. She had not touched the sovereign Jane had given her when Johnny was born so she already had enough saved to put down the first half year's rent and calculated that she could cover the second if she completed three parcels of gloves a week instead of two. She could work without distraction if her mother would look after the boys for a few hours a day now that Eliza was at school. Johnny had been weaned on to gruel and gravy mash so that would make things easier for them both.

The more she thought about it, the more Mary yearned to move next door. They would all have more room and, best of all, she would be independent.

Her mother shook her head in disapproval when she was told of the idea. 'I turned this place upside down to fit ee all in,' she grumbled, 'and now you'm ready to be off and leave me without so much as a thankee. You'll never make enough at the gloving to pay the rent and feed the children proper! And what'll ee do about furniture?'

'I could get twice as much work done if I was on my own,' Mary argued, 'and I've got the few bits and pieces I brought from Westcott — '

'Oh, ay! And your mother next door to take

the children! You've got it all worked out nicely, I see! Well, 'tain't good enough, Mary! You've gived no thought to me at all!'

Mary was dismayed. '"Twasn't meant like that, Ma! I've been grateful to ee, you know I have. But I've got to make my own way sometime!'

'Well, you needn't expect me to be at your beck and call whenever you think fit!'

Mary was so worried she had upset her mother that she went to see her eldest sister who only laughed. 'Don't fret yourself!' Anne said. 'You know Ma! She'll calm down. If her don't, I'll have the children when I can. Take the chance of a place of your own, Mary! Most of the stuff in that cottage'll have to be sold so you could pick up some of it dirt cheap.'

Encouraged, Mary made discreet enquiries about renting the cottage and the possible sale of its contents. She said no more to her mother but felt her inquisitive eyes on her whenever she was working at her gloves.

At last Mrs Pugsley could contain herself no longer. 'What be ee doing about next door, then?' she demanded. 'Be ee going or staying?'

'That's up to you, Ma,' Mary said calmly. 'I'll stay if you want me to. But if I go, Anne's offered to help out with the children.'

Mrs Pugsley bridled at once. 'There be no need for that! I've got nothing against the little dears. I'd miss 'em if they wasn't around.'

'Then would ee look after the boys for a few hours a day if I move next door?'

Mrs Pugsley sighed. 'I see you'm bent on it, Mary, so I won't stand in your way. I daresay there's a few things I could let ee have if you get the cottage. There'll be more after it, mind!'

Most of the village properties belonged to the estate as did all the surrounding farms. Mary hoped the agent would deal kindly with her now that she was widowed and she found him friendly when she went to see him because he remembered John. There followed an anxious wait until at last she heard that her application had been accepted. At once she sent word to the glove factory that she would be able to take on extra work in a few weeks time.

Everybody in the family rallied round, as they had done before, giving her spare curtains and rugs or pots and pans and she spent a few shillings of her savings on an extra bed and two oil lamps from the sale. Will came over from Atherington with the wagon, bringing a high backed settle and two chairs, while both her sisters helped to scrub through the empty cottage so that everything would be spick and span.

It was a cold day in October when they were at last ready to move in. The children were reluctant to leave their grandmother at first but cheered up when they realised that they could go in and out between the two cottages whenever they wanted. Mary had no doubts. Once everything was in place and a cheerful fire was burning in the grate, she looked around at her new kitchen and gave a sigh of satisfaction. This was all hers. It was almost two years since John had died and now it was wholly up to her to make a new life for them all.

So many people had been kind, bringing presents to her door, she was not surprised when there was another knock as she was preparing their first supper. But she was astonished when she opened the door and found Reuben Dark waiting just outside. In the glow of her hanging lamp she saw that he was carrying a small sack over his shoulder.

'I heard you was moving, Mary,' he said, 'and might be short of a few things. So I've took the liberty of bringing ee this.' He unslung the sack and held it out to her. 'Tis just off-cuts of wood for a bit of kindling. This cottage'll need warming, I reckon, after being empty so many weeks.'

Mary accepted the sack with reluctance. 'Tis very kind of ee, Mr Dark,' she managed at last and when he showed no signs of moving, wondered if he was expecting to be asked in. She did not want to encourage him but felt obliged to enquire, 'How be the children?'

'Missing their mother terrible, the young 'uns in particular. Freddy keeps asking after your George, you used to call so regular. So if you'm ever up our way, Mary, with the children, 'twould be a kindness if you'd call in sometimes, or p'raps take Freddy out with you, the way you did before Jane died.'

Caution made Mary hesitate. 'I won't have too much time, Mr Dark,' she said. 'I'm taking on more of the gloving, now I've a place of my own.'

'Ah!' He frowned. 'I see. That must be hard for ee, Mary. I hope I bain't intruding. I just thought I'd bring ee the wood and tell ee about Freddy. Goodnight then, missus.'

He went and she was left with the same feeling of bewilderment as when he had given her Jane's book. What did he really want? She was sure there was more to his request than just the hope of a playmate for Freddy. She remembered the hungry expression she had sometimes seen in his eyes when he looked at her and recoiled, just as she had done when

Josiah Blackmore had hammered on her door at Westcott. One thing she did not want was another man! She was free from all that and, anyway, nobody could take the place of John in her heart.

All the same, she was not prepared for the loneliness she often felt when she began to sit, hour after hour, in the quiet of her new home, stitching away at the piles of gloves that arrived with monotonous regularity every Friday. The housework she had shared with her mother was now her sole responsibility. She had to rise early each day to draw water and light the fire, then wake the children and prepare breakfast before seeing Eliza on her way to school and leaving George and Johnny next door. Only after that could she settle down to several hours at the gloving.

Sometimes she could hear the children playing and longed to be with them but knew she could not stop work until it was their dinner time. Her mother insisted on cooking for them all which gave her a break in the middle of the day but then it was back to the stitching until Eliza came home from school. It was a relief to collect the boys and have them all with her for supper but even after they were in their beds she often felt compelled to finish off any gloves she had abandoned partly done.

Now that she was starting on her new parcels on Fridays she tried to keep Saturdays free, spending the mornings washing and baking and the afternoons for the children. One crisp Saturday in late December she dressed them in their warmest clothes, wound them tightly in woolly scarves and bundled Johnny into the old wicker baby carriage her sister Anne had handed on to her. They were going for a walk in the lanes, she told them, to see if they could find some holly for Christmas and perhaps a sprig of mistletoe.

'Can Tommy come?' Eliza asked eagerly. Tommy was the youngest of the Dark children at school with her and fast becoming her best friend.

'And Freddy?' George chimed in. 'Can us bring Freddy?' He was nearly four years old now and never stopped talking.

'Perhaps,' Mary said. She had avoided the carpenter's house since he had called with his gift of wood but thought now that it was a pity to exclude his children, too.

As soon as they reached the top of the hill, Eliza ran on ahead, with George trailing after her and they were into the porch and knocking on the door of the big house before Mary could stop them.

Sally came out and beamed when she saw

who was there. 'Where be you off to, then?' she asked.

'Picking holly with Ma,' Eliza said. 'Can Tommy come?'

'And Freddy!' George piped up.

Mary had joined them now. 'I thought — as us be going, anyway — ' she began but stopped and felt herself blushing when Reuben Dark suddenly appeared behind his daughter. She had not expected to see him on a Saturday, especially not in his riding jacket and breeches.

When she caught his eye, he looked embarrassed. 'I be just off to Alverdiscott,' he said, 'to measure up old Tom Gifford. Died in his bed last night. But you'm welcome to come in, Mary.'

'I haven't come to stay,' Mary said. 'I've come to take the children out, like you asked.'

'Oh! That's kind of ee. Freddy'll be glad to see George, I know. A fine boy he's getting to be, too!' He patted George on the top of his woolly cap. 'P'raps you'd care to stop off for a cup of tea on the way back?'

Mary shook her head. ''Twill be getting dark by then, the days be so short.'

'Ay! Well, I'd best be off before old Tom's missus thinks I bain't coming. Good-day to ee, then, missus.'

He strode past them out of the house and

she saw him begin making his way to where he stabled his horse. He was a fine figure of a man, upright and confident in his riding clothes and something stirred in her as she watched him go. It was an unexpected feeling and she turned impatiently away, meeting Sally's curious eyes on her.

'I'll get the boys dressed,' the girl said. 'Can I come with ee, Miz Moore? I know all the best places for holly.'

She became a child again as she raced on ahead with the little ones when they were in the deep lanes and shut in by the high beech hedges. Then she ran back for Johnny in his baby carriage so that he could catch up with them and helped Mary gather armfuls of holly. Later on, when they were all getting tired, she said, 'I'm glad us came with ee, Miz Moore. 'Twas nice when you used to call to see Mother. I wish you could still come sometimes, 'cos the young uns don't like Missus Harding. She slaps 'em when they'm naughty and Mother never did that. Father takes his belt to the lads if they'm really bad but he mostly only has to tell 'em once.' She laughed. 'Father's bark's worse than his bite, I reckon.'

Sally was growing prettier, Mary thought, more like her sister, Emily. Her cheeks were rosy from the cold and her eyes were bright and she had pinned her long brown hair in coils around her head, in imitation of her mother's.

'How old are you now, Sally?' she asked her.

'I'll be twelve next birthday. I'd like to be out working but Father says I'm best staying home to help with the children. He wanted Em'ly to do that, but she wouldn't.'

'D'you miss her, Sal?'

'Not now. I used to, 'cos us shared a bed and I'd wake up cold in the night and cry. I don't do that any more.' She sighed. 'I don't want to go away for good, not like Em'ly. I'd just like to see some place different and earn a few shillings, the way you do with your gloving. You must be clever to be able to do that.'

Mary laughed. 'You don't have to be clever, Sal — just willing to take pains. Is there anything you'd specially like to do?'

'Only what Mother said once.'

'So what was that?'

''Twas after Miz Baker at school told her I was good at my lessons and with the little ones and said I could p'raps go as a pupil teacher when I was old enough. She kept giving me books to read and making me practise arithmetic and spelling and Mother started teaching me how to talk better. But the other children only laughed at me and I didn't think I'd be good enough. Then Mother was taken poorly and I had to leave school so nothing came of it.'

'You could still try, Sally!'

'No. Father needs somebody with'n, more'n just the lads and Missus Harding. That's why 'twould be nice if you could call sometimes, Miz Moore.'

The girl's eyes were guileless but Mary wondered what she was thinking and why it seemed as if events were propelling her towards Reuben Dark. No! she thought again. This is not what I want! It is too early for me and much too early for him, with poor Jane hardly cold in her grave.

So she did not call for the Dark children again. Christmas was almost upon them and Eliza was making paper chains at school and bringing them home to hang in the cottage. Will brought another goose from Atherington so Mary made puddings and invited her mother and Becky to share their Christmas dinner in their new home. That evening Anne and Lou came with their husbands and children to taste her cake and drink a punch of ale and cider. It was all very different from the miserable Christmas Mary had spent aching for John, missing the warmth of his body next to hers and his tenderness in bed.

She had tried to put all that behind her and to some extent had succeeded by immersing herself in her work and her children. But when she saw her sisters laughing with their men and watched them going home, arm in arm together, she felt a surge of the old pain. She was young and spirited and had known passion. The fires were still there, just waiting to be rekindled. But not yet. It was too soon, even if she could risk being hurt like that again.

Then Christmas was over and the old year ended. It was eighteen sixty-eight and she was the head of her household, dependent upon her gloving to keep herself and her children housed and fed. Sometimes, as she sat alone stitching, it was as if this was all she had ever done. Then her mind would go back to the cottage at Westcott and the things that had happened there, like the day John had brought home a squealing piglet, the runt of a litter Josiah Blackmore had given him in rare moment of generosity. They had kept it in the old sty and fattened it up on a mash of potato peelings and barley until the day the pig butcher came to slaughter it. Eliza had run screaming into the lane and Poll Potter had taken her in. Then there had been all the trouble of blanching the carcass in the big cauldron, cutting it up on the kitchen table and salting and hanging the joints. It had lasted them all winter even though they had given a lot of it away, but Mary never wanted to rear a pig again.

She smiled as she stitched and remembered Poll Potter. One day, when she had time, she would walk down to Westcott to see her for Poll had been as good a friend, in her own way, as Jane. But it was Jane she missed. When the children were in bed, she often turned to the poetry book Reuben Dark had given her, trying to understand what it was in the poems that Jane had found so necessary to her.

Some passages had been underlined and Mary read these over and over, thinking that they must have had some special meaning for Jane. Two lines in one poem she found particularly puzzling. 'Thus, to prevent my love from being cruel, My heart's the sacrifice as 'tis the fuel.' What could they mean? Even reading the whole poem did not help. It seemed to be about love. But what sort of love? Had Jane felt the poem reflected her own life, that she had sacrificed her heart to Reuben? Surely not to prevent him being cruel?

Mary could make no sense of it so she put the book away, telling herself it was just clever poetry with no particular reference to Jane at all. But the words occasionally returned to trouble her and to reinforce her determination to keep out of Reuben Dark's way.

In February, Granny Pugsley took to her bed with influenza and the whole family was soon kept running to and fro, taking it in turns to look after her. Mary made a pot of chicken broth which she carried up to the house and persuaded the old lady to sample. 'Twill warm ee nicely, Gran,' she said, 'and there's plenty for tomorrow if Annie hots it up for ee.' Annie was the girl who had taken her place to do the housework.

'The maid's a fule!' Granny Pugsley groused. 'You never should've left me, Mary. I'd have seed ee all right if you'd stayed — a lot better off than you be with the gloving!' She sneezed and looked pathetic. 'But I'm just an old woman and a bother to ee all. I'd be better off out of it.'

'Oh, come on, Gran!' Mary said. 'You bain't going yet — not for a long whiles. Have another spoonful of broth before it goes cold.'

When she left her grandmother's house, she glanced across at the one next to it and saw that somebody was at the window. Whoever it was waved and beckoned and a minute or two later, Sally ran out from the front door, calling.

Mary waited as the girl came up to her.

'Nothing wrong, is there, Sal?' she asked.

'No!' Sally seemed excited. 'I just wanted to tell ee Miz Baker came to see Father last night. Seems there's more children at school this term and she could do with some help. She wants me to go back for a few weeks to work for my Standard five and help with the little uns. I'd be a monitor and get a shilling a week! If I like it and do well, I could p'raps be a pupil teacher later on if the vicar thinks I'm good enough. Miz Baker said he's promised to give me extra lessons in Scripture and Grammar! What do ee think, Miz Moore?'

'I think you should go back and see how you do, Sal! What does your father say?'

Sally's face fell. 'He hasn't said much — not yes or no, but I can tell he don't want me to go back. Teacher needs an answer this week, so I was wondering — ' She hesitated. 'Could you talk to Father, Miz Moore? He might listen to you.'

'I can't think why he should!'

''Cos you and Mother were good friends and you know what her wanted for me.'

'Only because you told me, Sal!'

'Oh, please, Miz Moore!' In her agitation, Sally took hold of Mary's arm. 'There's nobody else I can ask. Father's in his workshop today with Joey, making new window frames for the vicarage — '

'Then they won't want me stopping 'em, if they'm busy!'

'But 'twould only take a minute!'

Mary found herself being reluctantly urged along towards the carpenter's workshop. When she and Sally went into the shed, Reuben and his son, a strapping sixteen year old, handsome like his father, looked up in astonishment.

The carpenter frowned, rubbed his hands clean on his apron and stepped towards them. 'Sally? What be doing, bringing a visitor out here?'

Mary cleared her throat in embarrassment. 'I bain't exactly visiting, Mr Dark. I just happened to meet Sally outside.'

'Oh, ay?'

He waited until Mary stumbled on. 'She's been telling me her good news — how her's been asked to go back to school to be a monitor and p'raps a pupil teacher if she does well.'

Reuben shook his head dismissively. 'Sally left school once,' he said. 'No point in going back.'

'But if her's clever and good with the little uns — ?'

'There's little uns still at home for Sally to look after.'

'Not for much longer. Your Freddy and my

George'll soon be at school and your other boys are getting big enough to look after themselves. Don't you think Sally should have her chance, Mr Dark?'

Reuben glowered at her. 'Sally's chance'll come when her finds a man to marry her. And the better her is at managing a house and children, the better that chance'll be!'

Mary felt her anger rising. 'So 'tis only your lads that'll get a proper training, then? You'm teaching them your trade so's they can make their own way in the world. So why not your daughter? 'Tis harder for women. There bain't much to choose from round here 'cept farmwork or going into service. Teaching's a respectable job, Mr Dark, and I know your wife wanted it for Sally.'

'So's her could end up an old maid like that old stick, Miz Baker?'

'No! So's her could better herself and hold her head up! If her's got the brains for it, you should at least let her try!'

When Mary's eyes met Reuben's there sparked between them a challenge and counter challenge. For a moment neither of them spoke or looked away and Mary sensed in the stillness of Joey and Sally a feeling of shock.

Then Reuben shrugged his shoulders. 'Seems I'll have to consider the opinion of a working woman, then,' he said ironically, 'gloving being one step up from housework!' He turned to his daughter. 'So you may as well go back to school till the summer, Sal. Then us'll talk again.'

Mary's colour was high when she faced him. 'Gloving may be only one step up from housework, Mr Dark, but 'tis keeping me and my children fed!' Furious with him, she turned to go. 'You won't regret giving Sal a chance. 'Tis better to do that than risk losing another daughter!'

She stalked out of the workshop, leaving the same shocked silence behind her. Then Sally caught her up, babbling her thanks. Mary brushed them aside and hurried down the hill to the sanctuary of her cottage and her independence. Once inside the door, she leaned back against it and stood breathing hard, her hands clenched. So this was the man Jane had put up with for all those years! One thing at least was clear. She was not going to fall into the same trap herself!

7

Towards the end of February, just before Eliza's seventh birthday, snow fell heavily for two days. All the lanes to the village were blocked so nobody could get through with the milk and the carter from Torrington was unable to deliver Mary's usual parcels of gloves. The village children were overjoyed because the school had to be closed as none of the pupils from the farms could reach it. There was sledging on the big field behind the church instead and Sally Dark came slithering down the hill to Mary's cottage in great excitement.

Her brothers had their sledges out and her father had made a special small one for Freddy. So could George and Eliza come to share it with him? She had started back at school and was working hard but it was lovely to have time off and she was sure she could look after George and Eliza if Mary could not come with them.

Mary smiled at her eagerness. 'I've no work just now,' she told Sally, 'so I'll leave Johnny with Mother and come, too. 'Tis a long time since I was sledging.'

It was very cold but the sun was out after the downfall and the village looked its best, sparkling under white roofs. In their thick clothes and boots and wrapped around with shawls, Mary and Sally, Eliza and George trudged up through the snow to the field behind the church, hearing the shouts and laughter of children even before they reached it.

Sally's three young brothers were taking it in turns to pull Freddy on his little sledge, but they were glad enough to pass that job over to their sister and return to their own bigger ones when she arrived. Even the two older Dark boys were there as they had been given an hour off work by their father to enjoy the snow while it lasted.

Joey winked at Mary. 'Want a ride, missus? I could take ee from the top of the field right to the bottom.'

She smiled and shook her head. 'If I ride, I'll go with Sally. Take Lizzie, if you'm careful.'

But Eliza hung back, too shy to go with him and waited her turn to be pulled by Sally. Then Charlie and Tom offered to take Freddy and George on to their sledges while Philip pulled Eliza on the little one. Mary stood laughing as she watched them all.

Somebody spoke quietly in her ear. 'Not

sledging, Mary? You'm spritely enough to try.'

It was Reuben Dark who had walked up behind her.

'P'raps I will, then,' she dared him, 'if you go first!'

He grinned and shouted to Joey. 'Hey, Joe! Give us a turn, will ee? 'Tis time I showed you young uns a thing or two!'

Joey came sliding down on the sledge and passed it over to his father. 'Going to give Miz Moore a ride, be ee, Dad?' he asked cheekily.

'Not till I've seed he's safe!' Mary retorted and watched as Reuben dragged the sledge to the top of the field and launched himself off.

He came whizzing down and stopped within a foot of her, then sat there laughing, triumphant. 'What did ee think of that then, Mary?'

Her heart missed a beat as she stared down at him. She had never seen him like this, so light hearted. His cap had slipped rakishly over one bright eye and he looked almost boyish in his red woollen muffler. Had he forgotten Jane already, then?

'Be ee ready to chance yerself with me?' he demanded. 'I'll hold on to ee tight so's you won't slip.'

She felt her colour rise. 'I don't think I'll risk it.'

'Oh, come on, Miz Moore!' Joey urged and Eliza and Sally clapped their hands in expectation. 'Come on, Ma!' Eliza cried. 'I've never seed ee on a sledge.'

She took hold of one of her mother's arms and Sally took the other. Together, they began pulling her through the snow up the steep slope of the field while Reuben Dark followed with the sledge. Once at the top he held out a hand to Mary and told her to sit in front.

'Tuck your skirts up, Mary,' he said, 'and trust me!'

He squeezed himself in behind her and she felt the strong grip of his thighs against her hips and the warmth of his body as he wrapped his arms round her. Then they were off and all the children stopped to watch and cheer as Mary and Reuben careered a zigzag path down the field. The cold whipped at her cheeks which were flaming already because of his nearness and her heart began racing alarmingly. When they finally jerked to a stop, she tumbled backwards into his arms and felt the roughness of his beard against her cheek as he whispered in her ear, 'Something for ee to remember, Mary.'

He swung himself off the sledge and helped her to her feet. For a moment she leaned unsteadily against him. Her breath was coming fast and she dared not look him in the face for fear of what she might read in his eyes. Then Sally and Eliza came running and the dangerous moment passed.

She made great play of brushing the snow from her skirts as the girls laughed up at her.

'Did ee like that, Ma?' Eliza asked. 'Was ee scared?'

'Course her wad'n scared!' Reuben Dark answered for Mary. 'Your mother knows her needn't be scared with me. Shall us do it again, Mary?'

'No!' Mary's voice was sharp. ''Tis time for us to go before the little uns catch cold. The sun's going in and us could have more snow. Fetch Georgie, Sal and tell'n to say goodbye to Freddy!'

'Oh, can't us stay,' Eliza begged, 'just for bit longer?'

'No! Your Gran'll be wondering what's happened to us. Be a good maid and help Sally with George!'

Reuben moved closer to her as the girls scampered off. 'This be the first time for twelve months I've felt my heart lighten, Mary,' he said and his voice was low and warm.

She tried to answer him carelessly. 'Must be all the fresh air and exercise, Mr Dark!'

''Tis more'n that. 'Tis your company, Mary and remembering what 'tis like to hold a woman close — '

'Don't! You shouldn't say such things!'

'Why not, if they'm true? I've watched ee, Mary. Even when Jane was alive, I watched ee — '

'Then you should be ashamed! Have ee forgotten her already?'

He shook his head. 'I'll never forget Jane. 'Twas a great grief to me when I lost her. But a man can't be sad for ever and there comes a moment when life stirs again. P'raps 'tis different for women. I bain't wise enough to know. But you must know, Mary, having lost your man.'

Oh, I know! Mary thought. I know it isn't all that different! She dared not say so for she was full of confusion and only anxious to get away from this man who was making her feel things she thought she had forgotten. To her relief she saw Sally and Eliza coming down the hill, dragging a reluctant George between them.

'The children are coming,' she said, 'so I have to go. You must put these thoughts out of your mind, Mr Dark. They bain't fair to me and mine or to your own family, neither.'

'Must I wait, then? Do ee think 'tis too soon?'

'I don't think of it at all and neither should you! So I'll beg of ee not to speak of it again.'

George came running as soon as he saw his mother and flung himself against her legs. She scooped him up and held him close, feeling his cheeks cold against her flushed ones and telling herself that the children were all she needed. But she could not forget the strength of Reuben's thighs against her body and the warmth of his breath when he had whispered in her ear, 'Something to remember!' He had give her that for sure and she was fearful for her own weakness if he persisted in pursuing her.

She tried to put him out of her mind but it was all round the village the next day that she and Reuben Dark had gone sledging down the church field together.

Mrs Pugsley was affronted. 'I'm surprised at ee, Mary,' she said, 'making such a show of yerself! As for Reuben Dark, what could ee be thinking of with 'is poor wife dead no more'n twelve months!'

''Twas the children,' Mary tried to explain. 'They dared us. There was no harm in it.'

'That's as maybe! It's made a lot of talk and I don't like our good name being bandied about. Us've always been respectable.'

'Save for Granfer Pugsley!' Mary could not resist reminding her mother. 'He wad'n too particular!'

'That was men's affairs, Mary! 'Tis different for women. Now you'm on your own, you should be specially careful!'

Mary was too busy during the following week to be anything other than careful. A sudden thaw melted the snow, allowing the carter to get through the sodden lanes with a double amount of work for her from the glove factory. She was kept stitching all day, every day and even in the evenings when the children were in bed, in an effort to catch up.

Late on the Thursday night, when she was about to pack her work away and get to bed herself, she was startled by a soft tap at the cottage door. She had already bolted it fast and could not think who could be calling at that hour, unless her mother was in some sort of trouble.

She went to the door but did not open it. 'Who be there?' she asked.

A man's voice answered. 'Don't be scared, Mary. I seed your lamp was still lit. I must talk to ee.'

'Mr Dark?'

'Ay. Open up! I won't do ee no harm but there be things I must say. For Jane's sake, Mary.'

'Jane's?' She did not believe him. 'What's Jane got to do with you and me?'

'I'll tell ee if you'll let me in. You won't

regret it, I promise.'

Mary hesitated, then unbolted the door and opened it a crack. 'Say what you have to say and go!'

'It can't be said outside where others might hear! 'Tis private.'

'Then I don't want to hear it!'

He had his hand round the door now. 'I bain't the sort of man to force me way in, Mary, so I won't. But for all our sakes, I beg of ee — open the door proper and listen to what I've come to say!'

Reluctantly, she pulled the door wider, stepped away from it and let him in. When he closed it behind him she took up a defensive position between the kitchen table and her dresser.

He motioned to John's old wicker armchair. 'Won't ee sit down?'

'I prefer to stand. So don't take too long about it!'

'Mary!' He softened his voice and smiled at her. 'I wouldn't hurt a hair of your head, you must know that. I haven't been able to stop thinking about ee since us took our ride on the sledge. No — don't stop me from saying that! I know you think 'tis too soon for me to be speaking me mind, but there 'tis! I can't help being the man I am. Jane knew that, so when her was so sick and knew her wouldn't live, she said to me, 'Turn to Mary when I'm gone!' '

'No!' Mary cried. 'I don't believe you!'

''Tis gospel truth. I didn't think much to it then, being too grieved for her, but I've thought of it since, specially since our ride in the snow. And I know Jane was right. You an' me, Mary, we have need of each other. 'Tisn't seemly to make that public yet but I wanted to speak for ee before another man did.'

'Another man? What sort of woman do ee think I be?'

'A young and comely woman, Mary, with plenty of spirit. The sort of woman any man would want.'

'With three children?'

'I've got ten already, so what be another three to me? You'd be a good mother to mine and I'd take care of yourn. Two of 'em be boys so I could put 'em in the way of a good trade, like I'm doing for me own. What sort of prospects would 'em have otherwise?'

'John's folk would find 'em something!'

'Farm labouring? I can do better for 'em than that. I'm asking ee to marry me, Mary. Not yet, 'cos I reckon I should wait another six months or so, but as soon after that as be decent.' He moved towards her. 'Tain't just for my convenience, neither, but because I long to have ee near me and in my bed!'

'Mr Dark! How dare you be so bold with me!'

' 'Cos I've been bursting all week to say these things and can't keep 'em in no longer! I spoke from the heart, Mary, and now 'tis done. You can give me your answer when you think fit and if you'm agreeable, I'll court ee respectable till the end of the year. Then I'll ask the vicar to marry us and you and yourn can give up this cottage and move in with me.'

Mary felt overwhelmed. 'But I like my cottage! 'Tis home to me now! And what about my gloving?'

'You won't need that when we'm married!'

'S'pose I don't want to give it up? I'm making my own life here and I like being independent.'

'Independent?' He laughed. 'I can't believe you'm not as lonely as I am, Mary, and aching for a man. Your blood runs hot like mine and us could make a fine fire between us! Think of that, m'dear, when you'm cold in yer bed tonight!'

'I'm sure I won't think of that! I'm a respectable woman and you've said things to me you shouldn't! So I'll ask ee to go. I don't want to hear no more, Mr Dark!'

'Then I'll wait for your answer. And when you give it, I hope you'll be ready to call me

Reuben. 'Twill sound sweet, Mary, coming from your lips.'

'Just go! You shouldn't have come here so late. S'pose my mother'd heard ee, or the neighbours on t'other side?'

'Their lamps be all out. That's why I knocked, seeing yourn were still lit. But I won't shame ee by coming late again. I can wait, now I've had me say. Just don't keep me waiting too long, Mary. Goodnight to ee.'

He went and she bolted the door with relief, hardly able to believe what she had just heard. When she was in her bed she could not sleep but went over and over in her mind the things Reuben had said. Had Jane really suggested that he should turn to her? That might just be true as she had been willing enough to hand over her baby. But her husband?

Mary recalled the words Jane had underlined in her book of poetry — 'My heart's the sacrifice, as 'tis the fuel,' and how she had more than once wished she could be as strong as her friend. Perhaps she had thought that Reuben and herself were better matched, strength for strength. Hadn't he just suggested that they burned with the same fire?

She remembered the feel of his arms round her on the sledge and clenched her hands in shame as a flicker of desire caught her unaware. Reuben was years older than herself and more experienced. John had been a gentle, shy lover and they had learned the ways of love together through youthful, innocent fumblings. How could she bear to give herself to another man who might be rougher with her? Suppose she had more children, one every year like Jane? And what about her own three? How would they fare in Reuben's strict household?

She tossed and turned on her bed and could not come up with an answer. He would not give her long to decide, she knew, and there was nobody she could confide in. She did not want to speak to her mother or her sisters as she was sure they would only see the advantages of a marriage to Reuben Dark and think it best for her. There was more to it than that as she already knew to her shame. If Jane had been alive she would have asked her, but if her friend had lived, there would have been no question then to answer.

Just before dawn, when she was drifting into sleep, Mary decided what she must do. She had been meaning to call on Poll Potter for some time so she would walk down to Westcott and have a talk with her. Poll was sensible and straightforward and not involved in any way. Mary was sure she would give her an honest opinion.

After the snow and the wet, March came in like a lamb, so that Saturday afternoon, Mary dressed the children, put Johnny into his baby carriage and set off in sunshine with them to walk the mile and a half to the cottages at Westcott.

It seemed strange to pass by the one they had lived in for so long and to see children they did not know, hanging round the gate. Eliza recognised the cottage but George had been too young when they left to remember it at all and Johnny had not even been born. But Poll Potter was the same as always. She welcomed them enthusiastically and was soon brewing up tea for them all. Then Minnie, Poll's eldest, took the little ones out to hunt for primroses in the hedges, leaving their mothers to talk.

At first it was only farm and village gossip. When Mary eventually began hesitantly to tell Poll about Reuben Dark's proposal and her doubts about accepting it, her friend listened attentively. Then she said, 'He's a well respected carpenter, Mary, and a decent enough man from what I've 'eard. You and yourn would be well looked after. But do ee like'n well enough to take'n to your bed?'

Mary flushed. 'I don't really know that much about'n, only from what his wife told me and from meeting up with'n sometimes.'

'Never mind how much you know! How much do ee feel?' Poll grinned. 'I can see by your face you feel summat! If you couldn't abide'n, you wouldn't be asking me what to do! You'd 'ave said no straightaway.'

'But I have to think of the children, Poll, and what would be best for them. I've got my own place now and can manage to make a home for 'em with the gloving. But who's to know what might happen later on?'

'When they'm grown up and left ee and the gloving's ruined your eyes? Think of yerself, Mary and do what's best for ee!'

'That's just the trouble! I don't know what's best! Be ee saying I should marry'n, Poll?'

'No! I'm saying, think of yerself! If he wants to wait for a few more months since his wife died, then let'n court ee so's you'll get to know'n better. You can always cry off if he don't come up to scratch. If he do, you can invite me to the wedding!'

Mary laughed. 'I knew I'd do well to talk to ee, Poll.' Impulsively, she reached across and kissed her old neighbour's cheek. 'You was always a good friend to me, especially when things were bad.'

Poll made a face. 'They bain't too good now. Maister reckons the farm don't pay so he's laying off more of his men. Seems prices be down at the markets. He sent my Billy packing in the summer but he's been took on as stable lad at Barrows, over to Alverdiscott.'

'Your man's still kept on?'

'Till now. Can't think where us'd go, if Jake lost his job. 'Tain't for what ee earns, neither. Every Lady Day, wages seem to be worse.'

So Reuben Dark might have been right, Mary thought, when he said he could offer my boys better prospects than in farming. That was something in his favour but she knew she could never marry him just for what he could provide for her and her family. There had to be feeling as well. So she would take Poll's advice and tell him he could officially court her, provided she had the final say about marriage.

When she was back home in her cottage at Yarnscombe and the children were in bed, she wrote him a formal letter, laying down her conditions, then wondered how best to deliver it.

She knew he would be in church the next morning and that her sister, Becky, who always spent her day off from the vicarage at her mother's, would be attending the service with Mrs Pugsley. Mary had fallen into the habit of cooking the Sunday dinner for them all as recompense for her mother's feeding them during the week, so when Becky arrived, she took her aside and slipped her the letter.

'Tis just some business I have with Mr Dark,' she told her. 'No need to make a show of giving it to'n. Let'n have it when the service is over and everybody's outside. No need to tell Mother, neither.'

Becky's eyes widened. 'Can't think what sort of business you could have with the carpenter, Mary.'

'Tis a little job I need doing,' Mary said. 'He knows all about it. The letter's to say I'm agreeable.'

Which is true enough in a way, Mary thought. But she had only offered Reuben a provisional agreement and after Becky and her mother left for the church she imagined him reading her letter and wondered what he would make of it. Knowing the man he was, she was sure he was quite capable of throwing it back in her face if he did not approve of it.

8

Mary did not hear from Reuben for two days — two long days during which she agonised over whether she had done the right thing. Then, on the Tuesday, Eliza came home from school bursting with importance because Sally had entrusted her with a letter for her mother.

'I put it in me pinny pocket for safety,' she told Mary, ''cos Sal said 'twas important.'

Mary wondered if Sally had guessed what the letter was about and her heart began to thump as she broke the seal and unfolded the single page.

The letter was written in a bold, strong hand. Like her own, it was formal and to the point. 'Dear Mary,' she read, 'I thank you for your reply to my proposal and feel honoured that you will allow me to pay court to you with marriage in mind. If you are not otherwise engaged on Sunday, perhaps you and your children would like to come to tea with us. Yours respectfully, Reuben Dark.'

There was no mention of the stipulation she had made that she should have the final say about marrying him. But that, Mary thought, was typical of the man.

Eliza was watching as she crumpled the letter between her fingers. 'Was it important, Ma?' she asked eagerly.

Mary shook her head. 'No! 'Tis just inviting us to tea with the Darks on Sunday.'

Eliza's eyes lit up at once. 'Can us go? Shall I tell Sally us can?'

'No. It has to be done proper. I'll write a note you can give to Sally tomorrow.'

'Saying us'll come?'

Mary nodded and Eliza clapped her hands.

But although she and George were delighted that they were going to the carpenter's house again, Mary found the prospect of having tea with his family alarming. When they arrived on Sunday she was invited to sit, with Johnny on her lap, at the bottom end of the long oak table Reuben had made to accomodate his large brood. He sat to the right of her. His eight sons, for even the two eldest, who were working away, always tried to come home on Sundays, filled up the sides of the table, with Sally at its head. Eliza and George were tucked in between Freddy and Tom.

Mary was relieved that Betsy Harding, the housekeeper, had the day off for she found it embarrassing enough having to meet the curious eyes of the older lads and ignore the nudges and winks of the younger ones. Even Reuben seemed ill at ease. But Sally was unperturbed. She poured the tea, doled out large helpings of apple pie and cream and ordered her brothers to pass the cakes or the scones as if she had always done so. Going back to school and having extra responsibility seemed to have brought out in her some of her mother's poise.

Mary thought that Jane would have been proud of her and said as much to Reuben when his sons had scattered to their own pursuits after tea and Sally was entertaining the little ones.

'Sal does well enough.' Reuben said. He had lit his pipe and looked relaxed in his old wing chair in front of the blazing log fire. 'But 'tis good to see you sitting opposite me, Mary, and to think that one day you'll be taking Sal's place at the head of my table.'

Mary stiffened. 'I wouldn't want to push Sal out! There's a long way to go before that and a lot to think about.'

He stretched his legs and closed his eyes contentedly. ''Tis enough for me that you'm here now and that us've made a start. Once the evenings get lighter I'll be able to call on ee and us can walk out together if your mother'll have the children. Then there's times I take the wagon into Barum to stock up for the trade and you could come too. That'll make the months pass quicker till us can be joined together proper as man and wife.'

'I did tell ee I might cry off,' Mary warned him.

He smiled. 'I bain't feared of that. 'Tis only natural you should act modest and hold back at first. But I can be bold for both of us, Mary, 'cos I know 'tis meant us should be together. Why else would the good Lord have put ee in my way if He didn't want us to comfort one another, after He took my Jane and your man?'

Mary gazed at him in stupefaction. ''Tain't for us to say what the Lord has in mind, Mr Dark! 'Tis for us to take what He sends and be thankful!'

'True enough! When I was in church this morning I thanked Him for sending me Jane and now for sending me you.'

'Mr Dark!' Mary sprang from her chair. 'What be ee saying? You'm talking as if I have no say in the matter and that Jane didn't, neither! I have feelings, like Jane, and a mind of me own. 'Tain't right you should use the Lord in such a way, specially after the things you said to me in my cottage t'other night! 'Twadn' what the Lord wanted then, 'twas what you wanted! And if us do come together, 'twill be 'cos I want it, too!' She reached for her shawl which she had flung over the back of her chair and wrapped it round her shoulders. 'I think 'tis time I took the children home, before it gets dark.'

Reuben stood up, too, and clasped her hands in his. ''Tis your spirit that draws me to you, Mary,' he said, 'and your fire that warms me. I thank the Lord for that, too. But if you feel I spoke out of turn, I beg your pardon. I'll be going into Barum this Thursday on business. Would ee like to join me in the wagon?'

She withdrew her hands and shook her head. 'I'll be busy finishing off me gloving for Friday.'

'Ah!' He frowned. 'Then bring the children to tea again next Sunday.'

Mary hesitated. 'So long's you understand, Mr Dark, that I haven't made up me mind yet about marriage. I have to get to know ee better, first.'

He nodded. 'That's what these few months be about, Mary. I'll court ee proper, like a gentleman should. There's no need to be feared of me.'

It was not that she was afraid of him, Mary knew. She was more afraid of herself. She turned away in case he noticed any sign of weakening in her eyes. 'I must fetch the children,' she muttered, 'and get back home,'

'Then I'll walk ee down the hill.'

'No need for that! 'Tain't dark yet.'

But he insisted and even steadied Johnny's baby carriage over the cobbles as they walked down the village street together. It was very quiet as everybody was indoors. Nobody noticed them until George and Eliza ran on ahead and Mary's mother came to her door when she heard them arrive. She stared at Reuben who doffed his cap awkwardly before saying an abrupt goodnight and striding back the way he had come.

Mrs Pugsley followed Mary and the children into their cottage. 'What be Reuben Dark doing, walking ee home like this?' she asked suspiciously.

'He meant it kindly. We've been up to tea, so's the children could play together.'

'I see! First the sledging, now this. 'Twill make more talk, Mary!'

'Not unless you start it! 'Tis my business, Mother, so leave it be!'

It was not long, however, before tongues began wagging that Reuben Dark was courting Mary Moore. Although they were discreet, only meeting at the carpenter's house or for the occasional trip into town, the village was too small for their relationship to go unnoticed. After Reuben made Johnny a little wooden cart for his second birthday, Mary's mother began reluctantly to think of him as a possible new son-in-law, even as a good catch, despite his being so much older than her daughter. Later on, as the Spring evenings lengthened and either Mrs Pugsley or one of Mary's sister was called on to look after the children while Reuben took Mary out walking, the whole village realised what was going on. Some people thought the carpenter was in too much of a hurry to look for another wife but most were tolerant, saying it would be a good thing if two bereaved families could come together.

Only old Granny Pugsley voiced her disapproval. She had never liked Reuben Dark, she said. He was a hard, overbearing man and she was sure Mary would rue the day if she married him.

As for Mary, she began to feel that she was being swept along towards a marriage from which she thought she had procured an escape if she wanted one. She was no longer sure if she did. Reuben was kind and did not force his attentions on her. He bought her little presents when they went into Barum and flattered her mother by asking her to join them sometimes for Sunday tea.

Mary felt confident that his family would accept her. Sally seemed delighted that her father had found someone she liked to take her mother's place and Mary's own three soon found their favourites among the Dark boys. So there seemed to be nothing standing in the way of her final acceptance of Reuben except her own hesitancy and she could not put into words what it was that made her draw back.

He rarely touched her but sometimes when he offered her his arm if they were out walking, or held her close for a moment when he helped her into his wagon, she sensed a tension in him of passion tightly controlled. A responsive tremor ran through her then and she knew that what she was most afraid of was her abandonment to this man who already had the power to stir her physically. She thought of Jane, who had sought refuge in poetry and tried to tell herself that she was different. She was an independent woman who could make her own living. She had no real need of Reuben Dark.

But the more she saw of him, the more she realised that he would be difficult to refuse. Spring turned into summer and she began to panic that the end of the year would come before she had come to a decision. Then John's brothers came over from Atherington because rumours had reached them that Reuben Dark was courting Mary and they wanted to know if they were true. She expected their disapproval but instead they told her that she could not do better than the carpenter who was an honest, well respected craftsman, certain to provide a good home for her and the children.

'But if he don't,' William assured her, 'just let us know, Mary, and us'll come and sort'n out!'

Mrs Pugsley gave a dismissive sniff after he and his brother had gone. 'Well, of course the Moores'll be glad if you marry again, Mary! They won't feel responsible for ee then! Not that they've done much to help ee, as 'tis!'

Mary felt too despondent to argue. Everybody, it seemed, except old Granny Pugsley, would be glad if she married Reuben Dark.

The school closed early in the summer so that the children from the farms and the older village lads could help with the hay making. Eliza was at home all day and Mary could tell that having her to look after as well as the boys was becoming too much for her mother. So she began working on her gloving early in the mornings and late in the evenings, leaving the afternoons free for the children. When it was fine she took them out and Sally came with them sometimes, bringing Freddy and Tom. They packed their tea in a basket to take to one of the nearby fields where the children could run about and play. One warm Saturday at the end of August, Reuben decided it was time he took some time off, too, so they crammed all the young children into the wagon and set off for Torrington where he promised them a picnic by the river. They could paddle their feet as he knew of a safe place with a shingle beach under the bank and a stretch of grass to play on when they tired of the water.

They drove through the town and down the steep hill to the river valley, then on past the old Town Mills to his chosen place. Here he parked the wagon and left the horse to graze. It was a bright, sunny day but cooler under the trees and the Torridge ran clear and sparkling over its stony bed. Reuben had brought a rug which he spread on the grass for Mary and Johnny. He was toddling now and needed more watching so it was Sally who helped Eliza and George to unlace their boots and pull off their stockings. They soon scrambled down the bank after Freddy and Tom, squealing as their feet met the water.

'I should've brought a net,' Reuben said. 'There's tiddlers in there — bigger fish, too. I used to come here a lot when I was a lad. Brought up in Torrington, I was.'

'I didn't know that,' Mary said. 'When I

worked at the glove factory I lodged in Mill Street with my Aunty Maude. She's dead now but I've got cousins about still.'

'Daresay I have,' Reuben said, 'but I don't see 'em now. Us went our separate ways when I set meself up in Yarnscombe.'

'Be they carpenters too, then?'

He shrugged. 'They had their chance. Father and Uncle Will were brothers and worked together, Father the carpenter and Uncle Will the wheelwright. So all us lads got taught the trade but I was the only one who made much fist of it. When Father died I could see they'd all be leaning on me, so I got out soon's I could. Never looked back since.'

He removed his jacket, rolled up his shirt sleeves and lay back on the rug beside Mary, closing his eyes against the sunlight which dazzled between the trees. She stared down at him, at the strong lines of his features and the fierce jut of his jaw and tried to see in his face the young man who had walked out of a family partnership when it ceased to be profitable to him. Reuben's dark hair and moustache were streaked with silver now and his forehead was lined. A hard man! That was what Granny Pugsley had said.

Yet his mouth looked soft now that he was relaxed and she wondered what it would feel like if he kissed her. His shirt was open at the neck and, like his forearms, his throat was tanned from working so often outside. A fine line of dark hairs sprouted from the base of it and she imagined it continuing down his chest and lower still.

Just at that moment he opened his eyes and looked up at her. 'What be ee staring at, Mary?'

She blushed. 'Nothing special.'

He caught hold of her shoulders and pulled her down to him. 'Be ee sure? There was something in your eyes then — something that made me think — '

'No!' She struggled to sit up. 'There was nothing. I noticed your hair's going grey, that's all.'

He frowned. 'You think I'm too old for ee, is that it?'

'No. I don't think that.'

'What, then?'

How could she tell him what she had just been thinking? Confused, she looked away and saw that Johnny had moved from the rug and was staggering at speed over the grass towards the edge of the bank. She leapt up to rescue him, grateful for the distraction.

'Here!' she said and dumped him down beside Reuben. 'Keep tight hold of this little monkey while I fetch the basket! I'd best give'n something to eat.'

She could hear the other children laughing excitedly and glanced down to see what they were doing. George and Freddy were still paddling in the shallows, holding on to Sally's hand but Eliza had moved in deeper and was watching Tommy who was splashing about after something.

'Don't let 'em go in too far, Sal!' Mary called.

She went to the wagon and collected the basket. When she came back she saw that Reuben was lying down, playing with Johnny, holding him in the air and making him chuckle by pretending to throw him away. There was a catch in her throat as she watched them, for John had played with George and Eliza in much the same way. It was a while since she had thought of him so vividly and she felt a surge of resentment against this other man who was seeking to take his place.

Then Reuben realised she was there and smiled up at her. 'I shan't be able to do this for much longer Mary. The boy's getting too heavy!'

She said nothing but sat down beside him and began unwrapping the napkin containing the pasties she had made. She broke one in half and gave a piece to Johnny. 'Here! Sit yourself still and eat this!'

Reuben rolled over and regarded her. 'Summat troubling ee, Mary?'

'No. What should there be? Do ee want a pasty?'

'Ay.' He sat up and accepted one. 'But 'tis more'n a pasty I want from ee, Mary. You know that.'

''Tis how much more you want that bothers me!'

His brow furrowed. 'I want no more than a man expects of a wife.'

'Like you expected of Jane and took as your right? Like you expected and took from your father and your Uncle Will but didn't give back when 'twas needed?

His eyes darkened. 'That was business! What a man does in business be different from what he does with his wife!'

'Seems to me there should be giving as well as taking in all things, Mr Dark, specially in marriage.'

He looked perplexed. 'I'd be good to ee, Mary, like I was good to Jane. Haven't I been good to ee these last few months?'

She sighed. 'You've treated me fair, there be no gainsaying that. But 'tis easy to be fair when you'm courting. 'Tis after you'm wed that the trouble starts. Now — will ee give a call to the children to come for their tea?'

He did not immediately rise to his feet but stared intently at her. 'I swear to ee, Mary, I'll never ask more of ee that you'm willing to give. Never!'

She smiled and shook her head. 'I'll p'raps remind ee of that one day.'

His eyes gleamed. 'One day? Do that mean — ?'

'Nort just yet! So call the children!'

He strolled to the river bank and looked down, then shouted back to her. 'They bain't there! They must've gone farther downstream, round the bend!'

'They can't have!' Mary picked up Johnny and ran to join Reuben. 'Sally'd never let 'em wander!'

Reuben's face was grim. ' "Twill be Tommy, mark my words! He'll 'ave spotted a fish and gone after'n. Bide here, Mary! I'll fetch 'em back.'

He began striding along the bank towards the bend in the river but before he reached it, Mary heard a child scream. She could not tell from that distance who it was but it sounded like Eliza. Anxiously, she began hurrying along after Reuben, hampered by her long skirts and Johnny's weight.

Reuben was running now and she saw him reach the bend and jump from the bank. There was a splashing and a clamour of children's voices, one high pitched and clear she recognised as Sally's. Johnny started to yell, alarmed by the noise and his mother's heavy breathing as she struggled on, fearful of what she might find.

She reached the bend and looked down. There was a sheer drop from the bank with no shingle and the river was running fast. The water was deeper here and Reuben was up to his knees as he waded in. She could see George and Freddy near the bank with Sally but there was no sign of Eliza. Tommy was shouting and pointing and when Reuben reached him he dived head first into the middle of the river, then came up holding a bedraggled white bundle.

'Lizzie!' Mary screamed.

Reuben wiped the wet hair from his eyes and waded towards her. 'The maid's all right,' he called. 'Only went under once.'

'Give her to me!'

'No. 'Tis too high to reach. Get back with Johnny! I'll walk t'others round to where they can climb up easier.'

'Oh, Lizzie!' Mary moaned as she hurried back towards their picnic place with the yelling Johnny. 'Lizzie! I could've lost ee!'

She was waiting with her shawl to wrap Eliza in when Reuben clambered up the bank with her. The child was coughing and retching and was sick when he gently put her down. 'Let her bring it all up!' he advised. 'Her's all right, Mary.'

Mary held her daughter as she vomited and then began to cry. 'Oh, Ma!' she sobbed.

'Now you'm all right, Lizzie.' Mary wrapped her round with the shawl. 'Don't cry! You'm all right.'

'I want to go home!'

'Presently. I must get ee dry first.' Mary stared at Reuben who was dripping wet. 'How did it happen?'

Reuben cuffed Tommy across the head and pushed him forward. The boy shuffled his feet and mumbled, 'Us saw a trout and I went after'n. I nearly catched'n, only Lizzie slipped and fell in. I tried to pull her out, Miz Moore — '

Reuben cuffed him again. 'That'll do! I'll deal with ee proper when us gets home. As for you — ' He rounded on Sally. ' — why didn't ee stay where I showed ee? What was ee thinking about, letting 'em go downstream?'

The girl flinched. 'I tried to stop 'em but they would go after Tommy — '

'You should've had more sense! You'm the eldest and the most to blame.'

'No!' Mary protested. ' 'Twas as much our

fault as theirs. Us should've kept a better eye on 'em and not left it all to Sally.' Her voice softened. 'But you'll catch your death, Reuben, if you don't get out of them wet things!'

He laughed. 'On a day like this? I'll get rid of me boots, take off me shirt and dry off in the sun. See to Lizzie! I'll give the rest of 'em their tea 'cos they'm starving, no doubt.'

So Mary took Eliza to the wagon where she removed the girl's outer garments and rubbed her dry as best as she could with her shawl. Then she slipped off her own underskirt and draped it round Eliza, pinning it with the brooch John had once won for her at Barum fair.

'There!' she said. 'Now you'm a proper lady. Come back to the others and get your stockings and boots on. Then us'll have some tea.'

'Ma,' Eliza asked anxiously, 'was I nearly drownded?'

'No! Mr Dark wouldn't let ee drown.'

'I'd best say thankee to'n, then.'

'Yes. I must, too, so shall us do it together?'

When they rejoined the others, the boys were ready to laugh at Eliza's strange garb until Reuben silenced them. He had stripped off his shirt, revealing that his chest, unlike his arms, was pale. The line of dark hairs which began at his throat stretched to the belt of his breeches and Mary closed her eyes briefly as an unexpected sensation pierced her.

Abruptly, she pushed Eliza towards Reuben. 'Say what you have to, Lizzie!'

'Thankee, Mr Dark,' the girl said shyly, 'for saving me from the river.'

He had been sitting with the children but now he stood up and moved towards Eliza. 'You'm like one of me own now, Lizzie,' he said. 'So of course I saved ee!'

'I must thank ee, too,' Mary said, 'from the bottom of my heart, Reuben. Lizzie means a lot to me.'

'I know,' he smiled at her. 'But you've thanked me twice now, Mary. You've twice called me Reuben and that be all the thanks I need.'

She remembered how he had once said that his name would sound sweet from her lips. She had not realised she had used it. So what did that mean? When she met his eyes and saw the warmth in them, she knew at once what it meant. She could no longer hold back from this man who had saved her child and could be hard or gentle as the mood took him. He would not be easy to live with, that was certain, but she was finding it impossible to ignore the strong physical attraction that drew her to him.

So she smiled back at him. 'P'raps I'll find even better ways to thank ee later on then,' she said. 'When the time comes!'

9

As soon as Reuben realised he had won Mary over, he began making plans. Jane had been dead for over eighteen months and he saw no reason to wait any longer. So, without telling Mary, he approached the vicar of St Andrews and arranged for the banns of their marriage to be called on the first three Sundays in October.

'You said the end of the year!' she protested.

'Twill be near enough the end by the time us be wed! And there's plenty for us to do before that, Mary!'

First there was the sleeping accomodation for Mary's children to think about. Eliza could move in with Sally but Reuben's six sons still at home were already sleeping three to a room. Reuben had shared the master bedroom with Jane for twenty years and did not consider moving out until Mary told him it held too many sad memories for her. She had watched her friend miscarry and die in that room and said she would be happier somewhere smaller. So he set to work during September and towards the end of that month took Mary upstairs and proudly showed off his handiwork.

He had stripped the master bedroom of its original furnishings and moved all his sons into it, the three youngest sharing the big double bed. George and Johnny could have the small bedroom next to the one he had chosen for himself and Mary. This overlooked the garden and he had completely redecorated it, bought a new brass bedstead and feather mattress in Barum and made a wash-stand, a cupboard for her clothes and a bedside table in his workshop.

'Anything else you want, you can have,' he told her. 'I'll leave the fripperies for ee to choose next time us goes into town. But 'tis all new in this room, so us can make a fresh start with nothing to remind us of past sorrows. What do ee say, m'dear?'

For a moment she was lost for words, touched that he had tried so hard to please her. ''Tis lovely, Reuben,' she said at last. 'Can I choose some pretty stuff for curtains?'

'Choose whatever you like if it'll make ee happy.'

He was looking so boyishly pleased, she reached up impulsively and kissed him on the cheek. 'I'm happy now.'

At once he caught her to him and held her close, kissing her on the mouth with such passion she was startled. 'I could make ee happier still,' he said roughly, 'this very minute and in this very room — '

'No!' She pulled away from him. 'Not yet! Us've waited till now and can wait a few weeks longer — '

'The need be powerful strong in me, Mary — '

'Then strengthen your will to deny it! 'Twill be all the sweeter if us wait.'

He gave a sigh that was almost a groan. 'I've held back from ee all these months to give ee the time you wanted, though I've been sorely tempted.'

'I know. And I thank ee for holding back. 'Twill not be for much longer.' She looked at him anxiously. 'Will ee be gentle with me, Reuben, on our wedding night?'

He folded her to him and rocked her in his arms. 'Gentle as a lamb or fierce as a lion, however you want me, my lover. After the wedding, I'll carry ee off to Barum and us'll spend the night in the Golden Lion, out of the way of prying eyes. 'Twill be our honeymoon.'

Her heart missed a beat as she gazed at him. 'But what about the children? I thought they'd be moving in here with me soon's us were wed.'

'Us'll move 'em in the day before with all

your bits and pieces. Sally'll keep an eye on 'em. You can stay that night at your mother's and I'll meet ee at the church on our wedding morning.'

It seemed he had everything arranged. She felt her liberty slipping away from her and some of her old uncertainty returned. But it was too late for doubts now. The banns were being called for the first time that Sunday and she had promised to go to church with him for the service.

She moved to the bedroom door. 'I'd best go down and fetch the children,' she said. 'I've work waiting for me back home before the carter calls.'

He frowned. 'But you've told 'em at the factory you'm finishing?'

'Next week, I said. I'm doing one more load.'

'And you've given notice that you'm leaving the cottage?'

She nodded.

'Then there be nothing standing in our way. I'll call for ee on Sunday morning and walk ee to the church, Mary. 'Twill be good to hear the vicar speak our names together. Bring Lizzie with ee! Her's old enough now to understand what such things mean.'

There would be more people than Eliza who would understand that, Mary knew and her heart quailed at the thought of meeting the inquisitive eyes of the congregation. But she steeled herself that Sunday morning to dress in her best and walk openly with Reuben and Eliza up the hill to the church. Sally and the older Dark boys were already in their family pew and, as they moved up to make room for their father and his companions, a hushed whisper ran through the assembly.

Once the service was over and they were outside in the churchyard, Mary and Reuben had to face the many well-meaning or frankly curious people who came up to offer them congratulations. This delayed them so they were among the last of the stragglers as they walked down the path. Mary was looking out for the children who had run on ahead when she suddenly noticed a figure standing just outside the gate in the shadow of the trees. Immediately, her mind flashed back to Jane's funeral and she halted, pulling at Reuben's arm.

'Stop a minute!' she whispered. 'Let the folks go by.'

He glanced at her, puzzled. 'Summat up?'

'Could be, or p'raps not.' She pretended to be reading one of the gravestones as the rest of the church folk passed them. Then she straightened her shoulders, linked arms with

Reuben and said, 'Seems there's somebody else waiting for a word. So best face it.'

Emily confronted them at the gate and Mary saw the scorn in her eyes when she looked them up and down. 'Well, Mary Moore,' she said, 'you'm a bigger fool that I took ee for to tie yourself to the man at your side!'

'What be you doing here?' Reuben demanded harshly. 'I thought I'd seed the last of ee three years ago.'

'And so you did! I wouldn't be here now only I heard the banns was to be called and couldn't believe it till I'd heard 'em for meself! So you've found another woman to be at your beck and call and bear your children till her heart breaks or her bleeds to death!'

'That's foul talk!' Reuben's face had whitened. 'Don't speak of your mother like that! You'm not fit!'

'Not fit? What'll ee do, then? Take your strap to me like you did before? I got out then and I'd have taken Mother with me, only her wouldn't come. Couldn't leave ee, her said.' Emily gave a bitter laugh. 'You'd best watch out, Mary Moore, before he gets a hold on you, too!'

Reuben raised a fist and Mary gasped, afraid he was going to strike the girl. But he lowered his arm and said, in an ominous voice, 'Get out of here, Em'ly, before I do ee some mischief!'

'Oh, you wouldn't do that,' Emily taunted, 'not with your woman by your side! I wish ee well of him, Mary Moore! Fine friend to me mother you've turned out to be, setting your cap at him, soon's her died.'

Mary flinched but was too shocked to retaliate. Reuben caught hold of her arm in a firm grip and said, 'Come Mary! Us'll listen to no more of this!'

He pushed Emily out of the way and began marching Mary down the path from the churchyard. The girl laughed again, a mocking sound which made Mary pull away from him. 'Walk on!' she told Reuben. 'There's something I have to say to Em'ly while I have the chance.'

'No! Leave her be! Mary! Come back here!'

He called after her but she was already hurrying towards the girl who seemed astonished that she should return. 'So!' she said. 'Found your tongue at last, have ee, Mary Moore?'

'If I have 'tis only to warn ee to watch yourn! I don't know much about your mother's life but I do know that her thought a lot of your father and he of her. P'raps they wasn't best suited some ways and p'raps he can be hard. But I've found good in him, too, Em'ly, that you must've missed and more's the pity. I'm marrying him with my eyes open and I aim to be a good wife to'n. If you ever lose the bitterness that's eating your heart and want to come back to your father's house, you won't find me standing in your way. Well — I've said what I wanted to say so the rest is up to you.'

She watched as Emily struggled to find an answer. At last she said, 'He's no father to me now. I won't come crawling back while he's about. You'll find out soon enough what sort of man he is, specially if you'm only marrying him for what you can get! If you make that sort of bed for yourself, Mary Moore, you won't be comfortable lying in it!' She turned to go, then hesitated. 'How be Sally and the boys?'

'All well. Sally misses ee.'

'Then tell her — ' Emily began but shook her head. 'No — don't tell her you've seen me! I get to hear what's going on and she knows I'll come and fetch her if she ever wants to get away.'

'Can't you just let her know where you'm living, so's her could get in touch?'

''Tis better this way.' Emily glanced down the hill to where Reuben was waiting. 'Better hurry back to your bridegroom, Mary Moore!

He looks to be getting restless!'

Reuben was not so much restless as furious. 'Why did ee go against me?' he demanded when Mary rejoined him. 'I told ee to leave her be!'

'Em'ly's your daughter, Reuben, and soon to be my stepdaughter! I can't abide ill feeling in fam'lies!'

'What did ee say to her?'

'It made no difference what I said 'cos her wouldn't budge! Whatever happened between you and Em'ly must've been terrible to leave such bitterness.' She saw that Reuben's mouth was set in a thin, tight line. 'Did you really take your strap to her?'

'If I did 'twas only because her goaded me — always off with the village lads, egging 'em on and laughing in their faces. Then one night her never come home — been over to Barton's farm with one of the horsemen. Jane couldn't tame her and I feared her'd come to no good.'

'So you took your strap to her?'

He looked shamefaced. 'I swear I never touched her before, Mary. I just couldn't bear the shame her was bringing to my poor Jane.'

'But Em'ly loved her mother! I know that from things her's said.'

'You spoke to her before, then. When?'

'At Jane's funeral. Em'ly was there but

never came forward so I was the only one to see her tears.'

Reuben said nothing and for a while they walked on in silence. Mary wondered what he was thinking until he asked, 'I s'pose Em'ly spoke of me too then, Mary.'

'Maybe her did.'

'Bad things?'

'Not so much bad.' Mary did not know how to put it. 'But her thought — well, her thought you wore her mother out with too many babies too quick.'

'And killed her with the last one? Was that what her said?' Reuben caught at Mary's arm and made her stop. She saw that his face was contorted with grief. 'Do ee think I haven't blamed meself ever since for my selfishness? But Jane wanted that baby, Mary, and after it died 'twas as much a sorrow to her as to me that I couldn't come near her again as a husband should. I have strong feelings — strong, passionate feelings. That don't make me a bad man, do it?'

'Not so long's such feelings can be mastered. You blamed Em'ly for being wanton. P'raps her's more like you than you know. She's quieter now, just as you've been, Reuben, these past few months of waiting.'

He seized on her remark with relief. 'Then I've proved to ee that I can hold back when need be. So you don't have to be feared of me, Mary.'

She met his eyes levelly. 'I've only been feared of ending up like Jane.'

She saw him wince. Then he took her hand and said, 'That'll never happen. I'll cherish ee as a precious gift from the good Lord. You'll never regret marrying me. I'll make dang sure of that!'

But the meeting with Emily made Mary wonder if she might be making a mistake. If Reuben could be so hard on his own children, how might he treat hers? The force of his personality had swept her towards marriage and now it was too late to draw back. The banns were already being read.

She spent the next three weeks trying not to think of her wedding, unlike her mother and her sisters who busied themselves making new skirts and blouses and insisted on Bert's taking them into Barum so that they could buy ribbons and feathers for their hats. Mrs Pugsley bought a length of blue velvet and fashioned a jacket and skirt for Mary to wear with her best blouse as she was too intent on finishing off her gloving to make anything for herself. Then the children had to be spruced up, George and Johnny with little sailor suits and Eliza with a new flounced dress and pinafore.

'You'll wear yourself out with all this sewing, Mother!' Mary protested. 'There's no need for such a fuss.'

But Mrs Pugsley said she was not going to give people room for talk that she had failed to do her best for her daughter's wedding. She even wanted to have all the guests back to her cottage after the ceremony until Reuben pointed out that there would be more room in his house. But she still insisted on preparing most of the food, convinced that Betsy Harding, Reuben's housekeeper, would not do justice to the occasion.

Only old Granny Pugsley remained unmoved. She was not going to doll herself up to see Mary married to Reuben Dark whom she could not abide she said. She was not even sure if she would show up at the church.

In the event, both families were there in force, apart from Emily. Reuben's eldest son, Walter, acted as his best man and Mary's brother-in-law, Bert, gave her away. Poll Potter walked up from Westacott and John's eldest brother, William, drove over from Atherington. Mary had not been sure if she should invite any of the Moores until Will remarked that wild horses would not keep him away from seeing that she was properly wed and would be well cared for.

Mary herself floated through the ceremony in a daze, only waking up to the significance of what she was doing when Reuben slipped his ring on her finger. It was solid gold, a thicker, heavier ring than the one John had given her and that she had put away in her box that morning. Reuben's felt unfamiliar and seemed to weigh on her all through the rest of the day.

He was eager to be off to Barum once the guests had been fed but Mary felt a lump in her throat when Johnny clung round her neck as soon as he realised he was going to be left behind. He had cried in his strange bed the night before and she hated having to leave him again.

'He'll be all right,' Reuben said brusquely. 'Sally'll see to'n.'

'Where be going, Ma?' Eliza asked anxiously. 'Be ee coming back?'

'Of course! I'll be home again tomorrow. Be a good maid and help Sally look after Johnny and George.'

When Reuben brought the pony and trap to the front of the house, the three children came out to wave them off, looking so small beside Sally that Mary felt close to tears. It was only the second time she had left them overnight and she watched and waved until Reuben turned the pony on to the Barum road and she could no longer see them.

He smiled at her and put a hand on her knee. 'Not nervous, Mary?'

'No.' But instantly she was and all her studied calm deserted her.

''Twas a good day,' he said with satisfaction, 'and 'twill be a better night. I've taken the finest room at the Golden Lion and ordered us a fish supper. Fresh in today at Barum Quay the landlord promised. 'Twill be a change for ee from farm food. Us'll drink a glass of wine with it and do it in style. How 'bout that, Mary?'

She nodded and smiled back but could not help remembering the first meal of boiled bacon she had prepared for John in their cottage on her other wedding night eight years before. They had moved in straight away and could not afford more than a jug of farm cider to give them courage for the night ahead. Not that they had needed it. She closed her eyes as a flood of sweet sorrow swept over her. Be gentle with me, Reuben! she prayed inwardly. Be gentle!

It was beginning to get dark by the time they reached Barum and drove towards the Square. The Golden Lion was on the corner of it and there was a resting place for the pony next to the Golden Tap where all the servants stayed. Reuben arranged for the animal to be fed and watered and rubbed down and then he escorted Mary into the inn. The landlord himself welcomed them, beaming at Mary and winking at Reuben who was well known to him as he often spent time there when he was in the town on business. They were assured that their meal would be ready as soon as they wanted it and a lad was called to show them upstairs to their room.

It was on the first floor and Mary gasped at its splendour. Its ceiling was elaborately decorated with plasterwork and its walls covered in a dark red flocked paper. Its wooden floor had been polished until it shone and the four poster bed had a canopy of red brocade curtains. There was a blue and white china jug and basin on the washstand and two chamber pots of the same design under the bed. A huge oak wardrobe stood in one corner and an oak dressing table with a stand-up mirror in another.

'Didn't I tell you this was the best room?' Reuben boasted.

She moved to the bed and felt the mattress. 'Feather,' she said and blushed.

He came up behind her and wrapped her in his arms. 'Soft for us to tumble in,' he whispered in her ear. 'But take off your shawl, Mary, and come down to supper. Mustn't waste too much time thinking about it when us've come all this way!'

'I don't know I'm all that hungry,' she said and blushed a deeper pink.

He hugged her tight. 'Then I've appetite enough for two! 'Tain't often you get a taste of fish. You'll enjoy it.'

To her surprise, she did. It was a large fillet of whiting caught from over the bar at Bideford, served with scalloped potatoes and washed down with a good white wine. Reuben kept refilling her glass so that by the time she climbed the stairs again she was warm inside and light-headed. He unlaced her boots for her and when she modestly turned her back to undress, he turned her round again and undid her buttons and bows and loosened her skirt so that it fell to the floor. He took the pins from her hair, letting it tumble to her shoulders and in between undressing her he was pulling off his own clothes until they stood gazing at one another's nakedness.

Mary had always covered herself before getting into bed with John and she had never seen him completely naked until the day she and Poll Potter had washed his dead body. Yet she felt no shame as she looked wonderingly at Reuben and began learning the muscular shape of him and the way he was so finely balanced on his strong legs. She even reached out a hand and began tracing the line of hairs that began at his throat, down and down until Reuben caught her to him with an exclamation and carried her to the bed.

He was tender at first, his hands so delicately searching she lay unresisting. Then he became more urgent and passionate until he had roused her to cry out for him. Twice he took her before they fell into a deep sleep. In the morning, when they woke, she was eager for him again and was so heavy-eyed with love when they went down to breakfast, that he smiled at her.

'You'm a woman again, Mary,' he said, 'like I knew you yearned to be.'

She could not deny it. She had never felt so much a woman and could understand why Jane had not been able to resist him. Some inner certainty told her that she was already pregnant but that it did not matter for there was nothing she wanted more that morning, than to give Reuben another child.

10

Reuben's ninth son was born on July twenty-fifth, 1869. He was a placid, chubby baby who gave Mary no trouble at all and they called him Albert, after Reuben's grandfather. Eliza adored him and George accepted him, just as he had accepted Johnny. But Johnny was jealous. His nose had been 'fair put out of joint' as Mrs Pugsley said and he was quite capable of giving Albert a sly pinch if Mary did not watch him.

For Reuben, Albert was the living proof of his love for Mary and she often surprised him gazing into the baby's cot as if he could not believe he was really a father again. She felt warm towards him then wondered why she had been so reluctant to marry him. During the months of her pregnancy they had never reached the same height of passion as on their wedding night but had settled into a regular pattern of mutual pleasure. People remarked on how well Mary was looking and how the carpenter seemed years younger.

All the same, it took Mary a while to adapt to managing Reuben's large household. Betsy Harding, the housekeeper, was given notice to quit as soon as Mary was properly installed and, although the young girl who helped with the heavy work still came in every day, there seemed to be a constant round of cooking and baking, washing and ironing to keep them all fed and clean and tidy.

Then Sally, who was always helpful, left the village school after her thirteenth birthday. Pleased with her progress, the vicar had recommended her to the governors of the Parish Church School in Barum which was approved for the training of pupil teachers. She would spend five years there, learning from the teacher to whom she was apprenticed and doing a certain amount of teaching herself. At the end of each year she would be assessed by Her Majesty's Inspectors and if she passed her final examination she would be awarded a Certificate of Merit.

She had to live in the town during the week so Reuben's eldest son, who was working for a local builder, found her a room in the house where he was lodging.

Reuben objected. He did not want Sally to leave home, especially as he would still have to support her while she was learning and only being paid a pittance.

'Seems to me 'tis a lot of hard work for nort,' he complained. 'I've lost one daughter already and I don't want to lose another.

Who's to know what bad company Sal might take up with in Barum?'

'Henry'll look after her,' Mary consoled him. 'And Sal's not like Em'ly.'

'But her's the only daughter I've got left now!'

Eliza clutched at his arm and smiled winningly up at him. 'You've still got me,' she whispered. Ever since he had saved her from the river, she had been Reuben's shadow, constantly striving to please him.

He ruffled her blonde curls. 'So I have, my beauty! You'm getting to be as much a daughter to me as Sally!'

Eliza was eight years old now and prettier than ever with her fair hair and bright blue eyes. Mary grew to rely on her help with the little ones when Sally left home. George and Reuben's Freddy had started school and Mary was grateful for that as she was still suckling Albert and trying to cope with the tantrums of three year old Johnny who was becoming more and more difficult to handle.

Reuben often lost patience with him and started smacking him hard on his bottom.

The first time this happened, Mary protested. 'He's still only a baby, Reuben. You'm too hard on him!'

'Well, you'm too soft! If you don't

master'n, Mary, your Johnny'll come to master you!'

They were cool with one another for the rest of that day and only softened, as they always did, in bed that night. But it worried Mary when Johnny began causing constant trouble between her and Reuben. He had always been the most demanding of her children and she blamed herself for spoiling him. He was John's last child and she could not help favouring him, despite his wilfulness.

Bert had a different reason for his behaviour when Mary and her mother met at her sister Anne's house one Sunday afternoon. Johnny was being so naughty, punching George and teasing Albert, that Bert grabbed hold of him and held him still. He laughed as the boy fought to break free. 'Y'know who this one takes after, Mary?' he asked. 'I can see the same glint in his eye as were in old Granfer Pugsley's! I used to think 'twas your Georgie took after'n, and so he do, in the face. But 'tis Johnny that's got his wild look, that free and easy gypsy look old Jack Pugsley had! You'd best watch'n, Mary, 'cos he could bring ee trouble!'

Trouble enough already! Mary thought, remembering how angry he often made Reuben.

'What's bred in the bone'll out!' her

mother said darkly. 'Tis a good job you've got Reuben Dark to help ee tame'n!'

Mrs Pugsley had suffered enough from her father-in-law's occasional brushes with the law and blamed her husband's early death on the worry of it. She had never forgiven him, even though he had made enough money to buy a big house and leave old Granny Pugsley in comfort.

She was failing these days. Mary called regularly to see her now that she was living next door but could not persuade the old lady to return the visit.

'I never put foot inside Reuben Dark's house when his first wife was alive,' she said, 'so I bain't going to start now! If he ever puts foot inside mine, 'twill be to measure me for my coffin. That won't be long now, 'cos I won't see this year out.'

True to her prophecy, she died early in March, leaving the bulk of her estate to be divided between Mary's mother and a daughter nobody had seen for years. Mary and her three sisters were each left ten guineas and all the children, except Albert, received a golden sovereign. Mary was hurt that he had been left out and that her grandmother had carried her dislike of Reuben to the grave. She put the three sovereigns in her box with her own legacy until Eliza, George and Johnny were old enough to appreciate them.

Granny Pugsley's death seemed to mark the end of an era. Change was in the air as Mr Gladstone had just been elected to form the first Liberal government and there was talk of all the reforms he meant to bring in. Nobody in Yarnscombe believed they would be much affected but Sally was indirectly, when Parliament passed an Education Act in 1870.

This was a drive to improve literacy and all the country's worst schools, up to then run privately or by the church, would be closed. Public schools would be provided out of the rates and local authorities given the power to compel children to attend. They could charge parents up to ninepence a week and fine them if their children played truant. The fact that more and better teachers would be needed gave Sally the incentive to work hard and even Reuben had to admit that she had perhaps made not such a bad choice of career after all.

Changes were also afoot in Barum. Ever since the arrival of the railway in 1854 the town had begun to prosper and Reuben came home after one of his trips excited by the news that some of the old cottages at the end of the High Street were being pulled down to make room for new buildings.

'There'll be plenty of carpent'ring needed,' he said, 'so I'm putting in a price. 'Twill be experience for James and Joey. They'll have to move on soon 'cos Charlie'll be leaving school at Christmas.' He frowned. 'Not that he seems too keen on the trade. He's hankering after farming 'cos one of his pals has been taken on at Westcott.'

'Westcott!' Mary started. 'With Farmer Blackmore?'

'Don't ee remember how Charlie helped with the haymaking down there in the summer?'

Mary had been so involved with her new baby she had hardly registered where Charlie was working, just that he had been delighted with the few shillings he earned. 'Josiah Blackmore's a hard man to work for,' she warned.

'Hard work never hurt nobody! If Charlie wants it, I won't stand in his way. Can't expect all my boys to take to the carpent'ring.' Mary had Albert on her lap and Reuben chucked him fondly under the chin. 'This little un's got the making of it, I reckon, and so's your Georgie. Needs a steady head and hand, does carpent'ring.'

Johnny came charging in at that moment with a furious Eliza after him and Mary saw

Reuben's expression change. He said nothing but it was clear that he had a different opinion of Johnny. But he'll change, she reassured herself. He'll settle down when he's older.

But Johnny showed no signs of settling down. Even when he started school he was always in trouble, teasing the girls or picking fights with the boys. Eliza came home nearly every day with tales of the things he had done and how Miss Baker had given him the cane for being cheeky. Even the vicar, who visited the school every morning to take the Scripture lesson and hear children's catechism, complained of him to Mary.

She despaired of Johnny and wept when Reuben beat him with his belt. He seemed to bring out the worst in her husband and she found it harder to absolve their quarrels in bed, often turning a stiff back on him when he would have held her close. Then he was cold with her for days and she remembered the lines in the poem Jane had marked. 'Thus to prevent my love from being cruel, My heart's the sacrifice as 'tis the fuel.' She thought she understood them at last and tried to repress her resentment until it overwhelmed her again the next time he beat Johnny.

She knew that Reuben had been just as

strict with his own boys and none of them bore him ill will. It was only Emily who had defied him and walked out. Nothing had been heard of her since the day she had accosted Mary and Reuben in the churchyard.

Then one Saturday evening in the Spring of '72, Sally and Henry came home with news. Like Walter, who was working in Torrington, they tried to spend Sundays with the family when they could. The lads were used to walking the long miles home, but if Sally was with him, Henry usually found a carter who would take them along the Exeter road as far as the turn off to Yarnscombe. Then it was only a couple of miles to the village.

It was when they were all sitting down to tea that day that Sally made her announcement.

'Em'ly's getting married,' she said and they all gaped.

'Married?' Reuben glowered at his daughter. 'How do ee know her's getting married?'

'Em'ly told me herself. I see her sometimes in Barum. She's working at the Pilton lace factory.'

Reuben's eyes darkened. He stood up and banged his fist on the table. 'So how long's this been going on — you seeing Em'ly behind my back?'

'Since I've been at the school. 'Tisn't often I see her. Henry knows that.'

Reuben turned his anger on his son. 'You've been seeing her, too?'

'Em'ly's my sister, Dad and I've no quarrel with her. I met her by accident first along — '

'Then you've both defied me! When Em'ly left this house I said her was never to come back. I finished with her then and so should you!'

'Hush!' Mary said. 'Henry's a man now and can make up his own mind who he sees. I'm glad Emily's getting wed. Who's her marrying, Sal?'

'Some chap called Bowden. Henry knows him.'

'Works in the iron foundry,' Henry said. 'He's got a good job, Dad.' He hesitated and looked at Mary for support. 'Em'ly wants me to give her away as her knows Dad won't.'

'Give her away!' Reuben nearly exploded. 'I wouldn't walk down the aisle with that on my arm if you gave me a hundred quid! Do this Bowden know what sort of a maid he's getting? Not that her be a maid now, from all accounts! Give her away! I'd sooner chuck her away and have done with it!'

'No!' Mary stood up, too. 'You'm not to speak like that about your own daughter! Think of Jane and what her would've wanted ee to do! You cut Em'ly off once. Do ee want to cut her off for ever and your grandchildren as well?'

Reuben glared at her. 'Grandchildren! I've enough to do with what I've got already, without grandchildren!' He rounded on Henry. 'You give her away, if you must! But don't come running to me for a job if you lose the one you've got! As for you, Sal, I expected better of ee than this. I never should've let ee go to Barum!'

'Em'ly wants me to be bridesmaid,' Sally said calmly, 'and I've said I will.'

Reuben's mouth opened and shut and the blood rushed to his face. For a moment Mary feared he would have a stroke. Then he left the table and stumped to the door, looking suddenly older. There was a shocked silence after he had left.

'I'd best go to'n,' Mary said.

'No.' Henry put a hand on her arm. 'Leave'n be. 'Twill take'n a while but he'll come to terms with it.'

Mary shook her head. 'He won't give Em'ly away.'

'Then I will.' Henry smiled at her. 'He don't know it yet, but I'm courting, too. 'Twill be a while before I've saved enough to get wed but I've found the maid I want.'

'Then bring her here one Sunday!'

'By'nby. Us'll let father get over this shock first. He's only just noticing some of us be grown up.' He grinned across the table at Walter. 'No use hiding your face, Walt! Us all knows you'm courting a maid in Torrington!'

'I didn't know!' Mary said.

The Dark boys laughed. 'Us did!' they chorused.

'You didn't tell me!,' Eliza complained, making Mary realise for the first time that although she and her children were apparently accepted by Reuben's family, there would always be some things from which they were excluded.

Even Reuben had not understood the strength of the ties that bound them to Emily. Henry and Sally would be at her wedding, Walter, too, it seemed, perhaps even James and Joey. They were all talking excitedly about it and Mary wished that she could be with them at the ceremony. That would not be possible unless Reuben changed his mind. Somehow she would have to make him see that his children were growing up and that he could not control them for ever.

He kept out of their way for the rest of the evening so she had no chance to talk to him until they were in bed that night. Then she snuggled up to him and slipped a hand under his night shirt. 'Reuben?' she whispered.

He pushed her hand roughly away. 'You won't get round me like that, Mary! I know what you'm up to!'

'Well, if you know, can't us just talk about it?'

'You've talked me out of too many things already! If 'twadn't for you, Sal wouldn't have gone back to school and her wouldn't be in Barum! I knowed 'twould come to no good!'

'No good — when Sal's soon to take her certificate and beginning to earn her keep? They'm all growing up, Reuben! Henry and Walter's both courting and I've seen the maids hanging round James and Joey. They'll be setting up on their own one day and wanting ee to come to their weddings! How's it going to look if you fall out over Em'ly's?'

'Em'ly made her choice when her walked out and broke Jane's heart. If her's made another choice I want no part of it. I don't want my family part of it, neither. If they'm fixed on going to the wedding, I can't stop 'em but I shan't ever forget they went against me!'

Mary drew away from him. 'You'm a hard man, Reuben Dark! I hoped I'd softened ee but I fear now that Em'ly might've been right.'

'Right?' He gripped her arm. 'You'll know who was right and why it pays to be hard when your own children grow up and turn against ee! The Lord knows I've tried to keep mine straight and I'll do my best by yourn, Mary. But I have to do it the only way I know!'

'There's gentler ways,' she whispered, 'ways you know how to show to me, Reuben. If you won't go to the wedding, can't ee try to forget what's past and give Em'ly your blessing? For my sake?'

He groaned. 'You'm asking too much, Mary.'

'For Jane's sake, then, or for your own comfort.' She reached up and stroked his cheek. 'So's you can live without this bitterness that's inside ee.'

''Tis only you takes that away,' he pleaded. ''Tis only you gives me that comfort.'

'Then take it now, Reuben! Take your comfort 'cos it comforts me as well!'

She drew him down to her and heard him sigh as she welcomed him and soothed his hunger the only way she knew and that Jane had discovered before her. He was not really a bad man. There was much good in him as she had once told Emily.

She lay awake for a long while after he fell asleep. Emily's marriage was forcing them both to look into the future. Reuben would soon be losing two of his sons and her own children were growing fast. She had no fears for Eliza and George who were both doing well at school and little Albert, the only one left at home, was running about happily now that Johnny was not there to torment him.

It was only Johnny who worried her. He was not interested in his lessons and was constantly in trouble. Always the first home from school, he headed straight for the barn where Reuben kept his horse. He had struck up an affinity with the animal and seemed to be only really happy when he was in its company. But what sort of man would he grow up to be if Reuben's beatings and her own reasonableness did not tame the wildness out of him?

Reuben did not relent over Emily's wedding. He would not speak of it even when the day came and went. Sally was bridesmaid, Henry gave her away and her three oldest brothers were in the church to support her. Mary was told how pretty Emily and Sally looked and how the Dark lads approved of Sam Bowden, the bridegroom. He had a responsible position at the iron foundry where there was a job going for a likely lad. Henry suggested it to Thomas who was leaving school in the summer and was not interested in becoming a carpenter.

'The iron foundry!' Reuben scowled at his

son. 'What sort of job's that for ee, boy, stuck inside all day in the heat and the smoke? Farming be better'n that!'

As for Eliza, she was dismayed. Tommy had always been her favourite and she could not bear the thought of his working in Barum. 'Don't go, Tom!' she pleaded with him. '"Twon't be the same here without ee.'

But Tommy went, just as Charlie had before him. Like the other lads, they tried to come home on Sundays. Charlie was nearest at Westcott, working in the stables there and returning with tales of Farmer Blackmore's fine team of horses.

Johnny listened avidly. Whenever he was missing, he could be found in the barn with Reuben's horse, talking to the animal or feeding it a handful of hay. He liked to help with the mucking out or the brushing down of the horse and gradually grew quieter, even earning some praise from Reuben.

'Happen us'll make summat of'n, after all, Mary,' he remarked one day. Mary nodded but said nothing, remembering, with dismay, how Johnny's great-grandfather had been a horse dealer and a rogue who had often brought shame on the family.

11

It was not Johnny whom Mary was soon to be concerned about but Eliza who became restless after Tommy left to work in Barum. She turned briefly to his brother, Philip for company. Nearer her age, he was a dreamy, quiet boy, fond of his books and more like his mother in his ways. When he left school, he made himself useful, helping his father with his time sheets and bills. Then he astonished everybody by walking into Torrington and finding himself a job in a seed merchant's office. That made Eliza want to leave as well and as soon as she turned eleven, she started clamouring to be allowed to get a job.

'Why can't I?' she demanded when Mary objected. 'I've passed Standard four so I could leave.'

'There be no need for ee to start work yet! Stay on a bit longer! Miss Baker's told ee you can be a monitor.'

'I don't want to be a school marm, like Sally! I want to make gloves, like you did. When us was in our own cottage you used to give me left over bits of stuff and cottons to make dolly's clothes. You said then I was good at sewing.'

'That don't mean you could make gloves! 'Tis trying work, Lizzie. And where would ee stay in Torrington?'

'Walter's getting married soon. He told me. He and Annie'd give me a room if I asked'n.'

Mary sighed. 'Well, wait till school finishes in the summer. If you'm still bent on it then, I'll take ee to Vaughan's and you can see what 'tis like. You'd only be an end tier to start with, like I was, and not earning enough for your keep. 'Twouldn't be fair on Annie and Walter.'

'P'raps Pa Dark would help me, like he helped Sally.'

Mary did not want to approach Reuben. She still had some savings from when she was working and had not spent the ten guineas left to her by Granny Pugsley. The money was all put away in her box, together with the three sovereigns she was keeping safe for Eliza and her brothers. If Eliza still wanted to learn the gloving, there would be enough to tide her over for a while.

That evening, Mary unlocked her box, a battered, tin affair that had belonged to John. As well as her money, which she counted carefully, it held her few treasured posessions — a couple of letters John had written to her when they were courting, a browning photograph of them outside the chapel on their wedding day and her first gold ring. There was also his penny whistle she had kept for George. He had shown no interest in it and she wondered now if Johnny might like it. It would be good for the boy to have something belonging to the father he had never known.

He was in the barn as usual, saying goodnight to Reuben's horse, so she waited until he came in to show him the whistle. He took it in his hands and stared at it, then put it to his lips and gave a tentative blow.

'Your father used to play tunes on it,' Mary said. 'He always kept it in his pocket. You can have it, if you want.'

The boy considered. 'Who's to learn me how to play?'

'You'll have to teach yourself, Johnny, like your father did. He used to play it out in the fields to the sheep or to call his dog.'

Johnny's eyes lit up at that. 'I could p'raps play it to Cap'n, then.'

''Twould be a good place to learn, in the barn.'

Mary watched as Johnny found the whistle's finger holes and began to experiment. His eight year old hands had a small enough span for the tiny instrument and she saw his pleasure as he began to blow a series of different notes. Then George and Albert ran in, attracted by the sound. Immediately, Johnny slipped the whistle into his pocket and began to saunter off.

'Keep it safe!' she called after him. He turned to grin and her heart went out to him as it always did. He might be difficult but he was John's last child and particularly dear to her.

Eliza could not be persuaded out of working at Vaughan's, even though John's brother, Will, came over from Atherington with the news that the rector's wife was wanting a girl to help look after her five children. Eliza was used to helping Mary with her little ones so Will had recommended her. She could live in and the Moores would be close at hand to keep an eye on her. But even the promise that she could come to see Toby whenever she liked, did not move Eliza. She wanted a proper job in a factory, like her mother, she told Will, so that she could always earn her own living.

Will laughed at that. 'You'll get married one day, Lizzie, purty little maid like you! Happen you've got a sweeheart already!'

'Tommy's Lizzie's sweetheart!' Johnny taunted.

Eliza stamped her foot. 'Tommy works in

the iron foundry and smells bad when he comes home!'

'And Philip's her sweetheart, too!' her brother teased. 'They was fighting over her last time they was here!'

'You're a liar!' Eliza cried. 'They'm my brothers now, or supposed to be!'

Mary stepped in to keep the peace and persuaded Bert to take her and Eliza into Torrington the next time he went delivering saddles to the town. Reuben did not approve of factory work for women and he was too busy, anyway, with work in Barum to take them. Every morning he drove off early with James and Joey. They had undertaken some of the wood replacement at the old Parish Church which was being restored, and were busy at the town's infirmary to which a new wing was being added. New houses were springing up in place of the old slums and there was money to be made in the town by those who were willing to work hard.

Walter was also doing well in Torrington. Ten years after Barum, the railway arrived there, making milk deliveries to London much easier. A new creamery was being built so Walter set up on his own to tender for some of the work and was soon employing a young lad to help him. Feeling more financially secure, he was planning to marry at the end of August, so after they had been to Vaughan's, Mary and Eliza called on him at his lodgings.

Eliza was full of what she had seen at the factory and launched into an excited description of the cutting room where the men worked and the machine room upstairs where the treadles whirred all day. Meg Connibeare was still in charge of the women and was astonished that Mary had a daughter old enough to start work. Out of consideration for Mary she offered to take Eliza on for a few weeks' trial.

'I can start next month,' Eliza told Walter, 'but I'll need somewhere to stay.' She looked at him hopefully.

He smiled. 'Annie and me can't afford a place of our own just yet, Lizzie, so us'll stay where us be for a bit. I daresay the missus could find a cheap room for ee, like her's done for Philip. You can eat with us, if you've a mind.'

Mary said, 'I can manage to pay for her keep, Walt, so her won't be a burden. Just so long's you'll all watch out for her. I know what them men from Vaughan's can be like!'

Walter laughed. 'Lizzie's a good maid, not like some of 'em. Her's got a lot of sense. Her'll be all right.'

So it was all arranged, despite Mary's

misgivings and Reuben's disapproval. Remembering how angry he had been when his sons went against him and attended Emily's wedding, Mary watched him anxiously as the time for Walter's approached. Surely he would not refuse to go? He kept her on tenterhooks until the week before the ceremony when he remarked grudgingly that he supposed he would have to hire a carriage to take them all to the church as there would not be room for everybody in the wagon.

''Twouldn't look well to turn up in that old thing, anyway,' Mary said. 'Will ee bring Sally and Henry back from Barum the night before the wedding, after you finish work?'

She held her breath as Reuben frowned. He had still not forgiven Henry for taking his place at Emily's wedding or Sally for being her sister's bridesmaid. At last he nodded. 'Can't bring one without t'other, seeing Henry's to be best man.'

Mary began to hope then, that whereas Emily's wedding had divided the family, Walter's might bring them together again. She felt proud of them all when they stepped from the carriage outside St Michael's church. They were a fine looking family, Reuben and his tall sons handsome in their dark suits, Sally and Eliza so pretty in summer skirts and blouses with flowers in their bonnets and her own three boys, clean and tidy for once and well behaved. Even Johnny seemed subdued by the occasion. Mary had bought fresh ribbons for her own bonnet and had stitched a new lace collar to her silk blouse but she wore the same jacket and skirt her mother had made for her own wedding to Reuben.

She thought about that during the ceremony and about her earlier wedding to John. She had embarked on the first light-heartedly, on the second with trepidation. Would she have made the same choices, she wondered, if she had known then what was ahead of her?

Walter and his young bride seemed to have no doubts. They clung to one another, smiling at everybody as they walked up the aisle at the end of the ceremony. When people began following them out of the church, the younger Dark boys hurried on ahead, clutching their bags of rice, eager to shower the couple. Mary saw Tommy stop briefly to speak to somebody in the back pew and realised, with a shock, that it was Emily. She was with a broad shouldered, stockily built young man who could only be her husband. When she turned to move out of the pew, the tell-tale bulge under her skirt showed that she was expecting a child.

Mary jerked at Reuben's arm and he glanced down at her in surprise.

'Emily's here,' she whispered. 'Don't make a scene, Reuben! Not today! Don't spoil things for Walter!'

Reuben stopped walking abruptly. They were already at the exit and Emily and Sam had disappeared outside. 'I won't see her!' he muttered. 'I'll bide in here. Who axed her to come? Walter?'

'If he did, 'tis only natural. Of course he'd want his sister to come!'

'I'd have stayed away if I'd known. Well, I bain't going no farther!'

'You must! You owe it to Walter. What would Annie's folks think if you didn't go down to their place afterwards?'

'You go then. I'll bide here till 'tis all over.'

'You'll do no such thing! Come outside, Reuben! Folks'll be wondering.'

She started propelling him forward until they were through the church porch and out into the sunshine. People were crowding around the bride and groom, showering them with rice and a photographer was setting up his camera on a tripod. Emily and her husband were laughing and talking with Henry and Sally and Reuben groaned when he caught sight of them.

'They'm all turning against me!' he

complained bitterly.

'No! 'Tis you that's turned against them! Come and meet Annie's folks and try to be pleasant! You've no need to speak to Em'ly if you don't want to. But look at her, Reuben! Can't ee see? Her's big with your first grandchild.'

' 'Twon't be a Dark!' he sneered.

' 'Twill 'ave Dark blood in its veins and might make ee proud one day! Forget the past for once and put on a smile! You must join the rest of 'em, 'cos they'll need ee for the photographs.'

The crowd was already drawing back from the bride and groom for the first picture to be taken. Walter and Annie smiled fixedly and held their pose when the photographer disappeared under his black cloth. For the second photograph they were joined by Henry, the best man and Annie's little sister who was the only bridesmaid. When the call went out for the parents, Mary pushed Reuben forward for the larger grouping with Annie's mother and father. He stood there awkwardly, grim faced and stiff backed, taller than everybody.

'You'd think he could at least manage a smile,' somebody said in Mary's ear.

It was Emily. Seen more closely she was older looking and more matronly than Mary remembered. 'At least he's here!' she said. 'Walter must be pleased you'm here, too, Emily, with your husband. How be keeping?'

'Pretty fair. Baby's not due till Christmas.' She hesitated. 'Sam'd like to meet Father and shake his hand. Would Father let'n, do ee think?'

Mary sighed. 'I don't know. He's still bitter.' She saw that Reuben was watching them. 'But I'd like to meet Sam, so p'raps us could manage it between us.'

Ignoring Reuben's baleful stare, she followed Emily to where Sam was waiting with Sally. His handshake was firm when Emily introduced them and Mary saw that his eyes were very blue. There was something about him she liked at once. 'I'm pleased to meet ee at last, Sam,' she said. 'I can tell you and Em'ly be happy together.'

'Us be well suited.' Sam was looking past Mary and when she turned she saw that Reuben was striding towards them.

His frown was ominous but she took no notice. 'This be Em'ly's husband, Reuben,' she said. 'He'd like to shake your hand. Sam — meet Em'ly's father.'

Reuben paused, nonplussed as Sam stepped forward smiling, with his hand outstretched. There was a taut moment when they all waited. Then Reuben took Sam's hand briefly and said, 'Pleased to meet ee.'

'I'll take good care of Em'ly, Mr Dark,' Sam assured him, 'and of the baby that's on the way.'

Embarrassed, Reuben turned to Mary. 'They'm all moving off now,' he said, 'if us be going down to Mill Street.'

Emily spoke then. 'I've told Walter us won't be stopping. I just wanted to see'n wed, like he came to see me. So us'll say goodbye now, Father.'

Mary saw the conflict in Reuben's eyes when he met his daughter's. Then he nodded, took Mary's arm and drew her away to join the others.

Knowing how much the gesture to Sam had cost him, Mary squeezed her husband's arm affectionately as they began following the wedding party to Annie's parents' house. It had not been much but it was a beginning, so perhaps things were going to be better at last.

Once Eliza moved to Torrington and settled in at Vaughan's, Mary only had the boys to worry about. Albert was at school, George was doing well and Reuben was looking to him and Freddy to carry on his trade when the older boys moved on. He liked to start them young, no older than twelve or thirteen. 'So long's they can read and write sufficient to fill out a time sheet,' he said, 'and can figure out costs and use a rule, they'll manage. I'll treat 'em both the same, Mary — six bob a week for the first year and a two bob rise every year after that till they'm out of their time.'

George and Freddy had been trotting into Reuben's workshop ever since they were small. They would sit under the benches where they were out of harm's way and play with pieces of wood in the sawdust. Now they began going in after school to watch what Reuben and his sons were making, doors and window frames, cupboards and cabinets or wheels for wagons and carriages. There were only a few months between the two boys so they left school together in the summer of '76 and began to make themselves useful.

At first they were only given mundane tasks, like sweeping up the sawdust and shavings, or turning the wheel of the grindstone for James and Joey to sharpen their tools. Then Freddy was put in charge of the glue pot to make sure it did not boil over and had plenty of water in it. George was entrusted with stoking the small forge Reuben used to heat the iron he shaped for the rims of the wheels he made and by the second week he was helping his stepfather clamp up a door.

By the third week he had sawn his first

piece of wood and boasted to Mary how Reuben had shown him how to start with a down stroke and put his thumb beside the saw to follow the line. 'I sawed'n straight, Ma,' he said proudly. 'Straighter than Freddy did his'n!'

There was rivalry between the boys from the start but George was better with his hands and picked things up more quickly. He was the first to be shown how to plane, using a jack plane and a trying plane to make sure the wood held straight. A few weeks later he was sent down to Westcott with Joey to help mend the weather boards on the farmhouse roof and the stalls in the shippen.

' 'Twas a terrible stink!' he told Mary. 'And it rained all the time us was on the roof so us didn't half get wet!'

'You'll have to get used to that,' she said, pleased that he was doing so well, especially when Reuben praised him.

'That boy of yourn'll make a craftsman, one of these days,' her husband said. 'You mark my words, Mary!'

Johnny never went near the workshop. He was only happy in the barn with the horse or playing his whistle and it irked him to be still at school when George and Freddy were working. One afternoon he did not come home and was still missing when it was nearly teatime.

Mary questioned Albert who admitted that Johnny had not been at school all day and had made him tell Miss Baker that he was poorly.

'So where's he been, Bertie?' Mary demanded.

The boy fidgeted. 'I wasn't to tell. He said he'd be home by end of school.'

'Well, he ain't. So you must tell me! He could be hurt somewhere.'

Albert began to cry. 'He'll hit me if I tell.'

'Your dad'll hit you if you don't! Come on, Bertie,' Mary wheedled. 'You can tell me. Then us can get'n home before your dad comes back.'

Albert rubbed his eyes. 'He said he was going down to Westcott to see the new foal. Charlie was telling us about'n on Sunday.'

Mary sighed in exasperation. 'I might've guessed! He'll 'ave forgot the time and gone off with Charlie somewhere. Just so long's he's kept out of trouble. Farmer Blackmore won't stand no nonsense!'

Johnny had still not appeared when Reuben and the other boys came home from Barum. By then, Mary was worried.

'Do ee think us should go down and fetch'n?' she asked.

Reuben shrugged. 'He'll come when he's hungry.'

'But s'pose something's happened to'n.'

'Us'd hear soon enough. Come on, Mary! Us wants our tea! So do you, I reckon. If the little beggar bain't here after that, I'll go and look for'n.'

They were in the middle of the meal when the kitchen door banged and Charlie burst in.

Mary's heart plummetted. 'What's happened?' she cried. 'Where's Johnny?'

'Maister's kept'n down to Westcott,' Charlie said. 'Told me to run and tell ee.'

'Kept'n? What do ee mean, kept'n? What's he done?'

Charlie squeezed in next to Joey at the table. 'Can I have a bit of pudding? I've missed me tea.'

Exasperated. Mary cut off a slice of roly poly and pushed it on a plate across to him. 'What's Johnny done, Charlie?'

Charlie grinned. 'Took the foal out of the paddock and tried to ride'n — got on his back but the foal shied and chucked'n off.' Charlie bit into the roly poly and continued with his mouth full. 'Then it took fright and broke through a hole in the hedge and got in with the cows. It was skittering about so, the cows started to run and the whole danged lot of 'em charged at the gate and got out into the lane. Took us best part of an hour to round 'em all up.'

The boys all started to laugh but Reuben banged his fist on the table. ''Tis nort to laugh at!' he stormed. 'What was you doing, Charlie, to let the boy behave like that?'

'I couldn't help it! I was harnessing the cart hoss and didn't see what he was up to.'

'But is he all right?' Mary persisted. 'Was'n hurt when he was thrown?'

'Not he! Johnny was the one that catched the foal, calmed'n down and led'n back to the paddock like he'd always done it. But Maister didn't half roar!'

'He had good cause,' Reuben said. 'Why's he keeping Johnny at Westcott?'

'He's put'n to mucking out the stables — says he wants two days' work out of'n for all the trouble he caused. Johnny don't care. He'd sooner be there than at school.'

'But he bain't staying longer than two days!' Mary said. 'He's only ten years old, with a lot to learn! Times be different now and school's important. If Johnny bain't home by Thursday, I shall walk down to Westcott and fetch'n back!'

Johnny did not come home. Mary knew, from the way he was always so happy to help with Reuben's horse that he would be a willing worker. She was convinced Josiah

Blackmore would exploit him, so that Thursday afternoon, when Johnny was still missing, she set off to walk the mile and a half down to Westcott farm.

It was the first time she had been that way since calling on Poll Potter to talk over her worries about marrying Reuben. Poll had come to her wedding and they had chatted once or twice in the village when Poll came up to shop but they had not had a proper talk for months. So Mary stopped off at the Potters' cottage before going to the farmhouse.

Poll was pleased to see her but Mary thought she did not look well. She was thinner, more lined in her face and her clothes were even shabbier than before. She insisted on making tea for Mary and guessed why she had come as the tale of Johnny's exploit had gone all round the cottages, becoming more exaggerated with each telling.

'I don't know what to do with'n, Poll,' Mary confessed. 'None of the others give me such trouble and he drives Reuben mad.'

'There's always one!' Poll said. 'Jacky be my worst. I miss Minnie since her went as scullery maid to the big house. Minnie could always handle'n. I hear your Lizzie's in Torrington, learning the gloving.'

Mary sighed. 'They'm mostly working now.

What about yourn?'

Poll shook her head. '"Tain't so easy these days, especially for the boys. Different times of the year they'm needed, then laid off. Billy talks of going to America or up north where wages be better.'

'America? What gave'n that idea?'

'Couple of the boys from Barton's went over last year — doing well from what they wrote back home. 'Tis making Billy restless.'

'They'm all a bit like that. I'm just glad Georgie seems settled with Reuben and likes the trade.'

Poll gave her a steady look. 'And what about you? Be you settled with'n.'

''Tis much as I thought 'twould be — better in some ways. I don't regret marrying'n, Poll. 'Tis just sometimes — ' She sighed and looked away.

Poll nodded. 'That's the way of things, Mary. Nothing be quite what us hoped. But if he's a good husband — '

'He's that all right — most of the time!' She laughed. 'Trouble only starts the few times he ain't!' She stood up to go. 'I'd best get to the farmhouse if I'm to fetch Johnny back. He won't want to come 'cos he's mad on hosses, but I'm keeping'n at school till he's reached his standard four, no matter what he says. Learning's going to be important, Poll, and them that don't have it, won't get nowhere!'

Mary discovered Johnny in the stables. He was filthy dirty, sitting on a pile of straw and chewing at a lump of cold bacon and a crust of bread. He grinned when he saw her.

'Maister said he'll give me a proper job when I've growed a bit,' he said. 'Want to see the foal, Ma?'

'I want to see you back home, boy! So run up to the farmhouse and tell Maister I've come to fetch ee! You should've been home today.'

Johnny stood up reluctantly. 'Will Pa Dark take his belt to me?'

'Not if I tell'n you've made amends.'

'Then will ee come with me to see Maister, so's you'll know I've done what he told me to?'

Mary hesitated. She had no wish to see Josiah Blackmore but she could not ignore the appeal in Johnny's eyes. So she nodded. 'So long's us be quick. They'll all be home soon and wanting their tea.'

The back door of the farmhouse was open and Mary could see the farmer's wife busy in the kitchen. When she knocked hesitantly, Mrs Blackmore came out and stared at her.

'Mary Moore? What be you doing here?'

'I've come to take Johnny home and to

apologise for the trouble he caused. Be Maister in?'

'Joe!' the woman called. She had put on weight since Mary had last seen her. Always buxom, she was now fat, her red face puffed and shiny. 'Lady to see ee, Joe!' she shouted and winked at Mary. 'That'll make'n come!'

Josiah Blackmore came stumping into the kitchen and leered when he saw it was Mary. 'Of course! You'm a proper lady now, Mary Moore — or Mary Dark as I 'ave to call ee. Done well for yerself, marrying the carpenter!' He grinned at Johnny. 'But you've got a chip off the old block there, I reckon. He've got the very devil in'n, just like old Jack Pugsley! You'll not keep'n away from hosses! The monkey tried to ride my foal on Tuesday.'

'I know. I'm sorry, Mr Blackmore. I hope he've done his best to make it up to ee.'

The farmer scratched his head. 'Well now, he've p'raps paid part towards his debt — '

'Two days, you said!'

'Two days? I don't remember saying two days!'

'He've missed school since Tuesday and can't miss no more!'

'There's always Saturdays! S'pose us said he comes down every Saturday for a month. How'd that suit ee, Johnny?'

'Yes, please, Maister,' Johnny said eagerly. 'I'll do that, Maister.'

''Tis taking advantage!' Mary cried. 'Like you always did!'

'I don't remember ever taking advantage of you, Mary!'

''Twad'n for the want of trying! I'll see what my husband has to say about it. Just 'cos Johnny's mad on hosses doesn't mean he'll work for you for nothing. You've had plenty out of me and mine already!'

Furious, she dragged the boy away with her and began hurrying him back towards the lane to Yarnscombe. But even as they made their way home she knew that one thing Josiah Blackmore had said was true. She would never be able to keep Johnny away from horses. Her children were already making up their own minds and she would lose them just as Reuben was beginning to lose his.

12

It was if the weddings of Emily and Walter set a fashion for during the next eighteen months Henry married his sweetheart, Harriet and set up house in Barum and Mary's sister, Becky, scandalised the village by running off with the blacksmith's son and marrying him secretly in Exeter. She said it was to save her mother the expense of a big family wedding but Mrs Pugsley felt hurt and ashamed.

'I never would've thought it of Becky,' she said, 'to let us all down like this.'

'At least her's married,' Mary consoled her mother. 'Jack Chugg's hard-working and in a good trade. After all, they've known one another for long enough!'

Becky and Jack had been courting for over three years, walking out on Sundays after church. Everybody assumed they would get married at St Andrews as Becky was working at the vicarage right up to the day of her sudden departure. When she came home with Jack to move into a poky cottage next to the blacksmith's forge, Mrs Pugsley refused to call on her for several weeks.

Like her mother, Mary had not expected

such behaviour of Becky. It made her wonder what her own children might be getting up to when they were out of her sight.

Eliza stayed on in the lodging house in Torrington after Walter and Annie found a cottage they could afford. Philip stayed on, too, so Mary was relieved that she still had company there. Almost seventeen now, Eliza had been promoted on to a machine of her own at Vaughan's and delighted in telling her mother all about the latest fashions in gloves when she was able to come home. She sighed enviously as she described the long, elbow length gloves made of fine net and lace the young ladies in London were wearing at their coming out balls. A young lady herself now, she was wearing her ringlets piled high and carefully braided. The older Dark boys were more attentive to her but she was cool with them for she had spent too many years growing up in their company to regard them as other than brothers.

Even her old favourite, Tommy, could not persuade her to walk out with him on Sunday evenings when they were both at home. 'I reckon Lizzie's got her eye on some chap in Torrington,' he grumbled to Mary. 'None of us be good enough for her these days.'

When Eliza began coming home less often, making the excuse that it was too far to walk and difficult to get a lift, Mary began to worry. She asked Philip if he knew how she spent her time off but he was so vague in his replies she felt he either did not know or would not say. The family's Sunday gatherings gradually became smaller. Reuben's married sons were infrequent visitors now that they had homes of their own and Sally and Tommy sometimes stayed on in Barum to spend their Sundays with Henry and his wife or, Mary suspected, with Emily and Sam. Charlie still walked home from Westcott but when James and Joey began courting local girls who were in service outside the village, there were sometimes only Mary's children and Charlie and Freddy around Reuben's large table on Sundays.

'They'm all leaving us, Mary,' he said gloomily. 'Us have 'em and rear 'em but they'm off like a shot once they gets the chance. Your Johnny'll be next, I'll be bound.'

Johnny had been clamouring to leave school ever since his tenth birthday but a second Education act compelling children to stay on until they had passed their standard four tests gave Mary an excuse to keep him there and made him work harder at his lessons. He was still spending his Saturdays helping in the stables at Westcott, earning a shilling a week now that he had completed his month of penance. Josiah Blackmore had promised him a job so Mary feared that she would soon lose him and hated the fact that it would be to the man who had caused her such heartache. Sometimes, when she heard the boy playing his father's penny whistle out in the yard, she was filled with such an urge to protect him, she could hardly stop herself from rushing out to hold him in her arms.

George, at least, seemed safe. He was the most undemonstrative of her children, plainer looking than the others but very determined. He knew what he wanted out of life. He was going to learn all he could from his stepfather and become a master carpenter in his own right. After eighteen months with Reuben he was regularly doing jobs without supervision and Mary remembered his pride the first time he was sent out on his own to put new sash cords in one of Mrs Pugsley's windows.

'Gran didn't think I could do it,' he boasted to Mary that evening over supper, 'but I knowed I could 'cos I'd done it before with Joey. Then I had to go next door to repair Widow Luxton's floor boards. I ripped up the old ones and fixed down the new uns all by meself. You wait, Ma! One o' these days, I'll be building houses!'

Mary laughed and turned to Freddy. 'So what about you, Fred,' she asked. 'Will you be building houses, too?'

Freddy grinned. 'I'll be helping George, I reckon.'

That made Reuben frown. 'You'll be helping yourself, boy, or I'll know the reason why!' he said. 'I bain't teaching ee the trade so's somebody else can reap the profit! Henry made that mistake.'

'Henry's firm's doing well in Barum, Dad,' James pointed out. 'They've got the contract to rebuild the cabinet works alongside the river after the old place burned down. Building's going to be important now, I reckon.'

'There'll always be room for carpenters and wheelwrights,' Reuben said stubbornly. 'You stick to the trade you know, Fred, and don't go hankering after moonshine!'

Although he made no direct criticism of George, Mary sensed a change in Reuben's attitude to him after that. He still worked the boy hard and taught him well but he began favouring Freddy in the allocation of jobs. George noticed this and resented it, but he said nothing as he was too dependent on his stepfather to object.

'Once I've done me time with Pa Dark,' he told Mary, 'I'll have to move on. There'll be no room here for me and Freddy, specially as there'll be Albert to think about.'

'Albert's only young yet!' Mary protested. 'You don't need to think of moving on for a long whiles!'

But Albert was already ten years old and each year the months seemed to pass more quickly. Johnny, after struggling on sullenly at school for another eighteen months, finally passed his leaving tests just before his thirteenth birthday, threw his books away and walked down to Westcott that same afternoon to claim his promised job.

When he came back he was almost in tears, punching the palm of one hand with the fist of the other and so incoherent with rage, Mary could get no sense out of him.

'That old bugger!' he choked at last. 'That old bugger! Said if he gived me a job he'd have to sack Charlie! After I've been working for'n every Saturday for a bob a week! Said I'd been paying'n back — not just for what I did but for what my father did, too! Dad didn' do nothing, did'n, Ma?'

Mary felt a hot surge of anger. 'Of course he didn'!' she said sharply. 'Your father took ill and died 'cos of trying to save Joe Blackmore's sheep! But two ewes got drowned and he's blamed'n ever since.' She put an arm around Johnny's shoulders. 'I'm glad you won't be working for'n. You'm well out of it. He's a hard man.'

'But what can I do now?' Johnny wailed. 'He promised me that job!'

'There'll be other jobs — other stables. Us'll ask around. Your Uncle Bert knows all the best places. Go'n talk to'n after you've had your tea!'

But Bert was not hopeful. Crop prices were still falling and money was tight on the farms. Horses were expensive to feed so the farmers of the neighbourhood were selling those they could spare, making one do the work of two whenever they could. Bert said he would make enquiries but he could not promise anything.

So for several months, Johnny was left to kick his heels with only the care of Reuben's horse to console him. He grew moody and started picking on on Albert again which only made Reuben angry. Mary tried to keep the boys apart, fearful that her husband might go back to beating Johnny and make him more rebellious or even drive him away as he had done Emily.

James and Joey were meanwhile working in Barum, renewing the floorboards of all the old almshouses in Church Lane. They came home one evening with the news that the town's brewery was in need of a stable lad to help with the care of the team of shire horses that pulled the heavy wagons loaded with beer barrels to the public houses in the town and out to the surrounding villages.

Johnny's eyes widened at the prospect. 'Shires!' he breathed. 'I'd give me right arm to work with they!'

Joey laughed. 'No need for that, boy! I've gived the manager your name and said you'm keen. Us'll take ee in to see'n on Monday.'

'A brewery!' Mary frowned. ' 'Twould'n be like working on a farm. The men there's sure to be rough, bad company for Johnny! And where would'n live?'

'They'd give'n a bed in the loft over the stables, as much food as he could eat and five bob a week.'

'No!' Mary was adamant. 'I'll not have'n go there!'

'Oh, Ma!' Johnny pleaded. 'I've never had such a chance!'

'You'm not working with a lot of drunken louts! Wait a bit longer, Johnny! There's bound to be a farm job soon.'

'I've waited weeks as 'tis! I swear I wouldn't touch a drop of drink, Ma, if that's what you'm feared of. 'Tis the hosses I want, not the beer!'

'Great hulking brutes!' Mary said scornfully.

'No! Shires be beautiful, not like the heavy hosses down to Westcott. I seed 'em once, that day us all went to Barum. A wagon was unloading at the Three Tuns and I went up to have a look at 'em.' Johnny smiled at the memory. 'They was all done up in ribbons and such 'cos shires be more than ord'nary hosses, Ma. They'm the kings of hosses, I reckon. Can't I just go in on Monday to see 'em?'

'If you see 'em, you'll want to stay!' But Johnny's eyes were so hopeful, Mary felt herself relenting. 'Wait till Pa Dark comes home,' she said, to gain time. 'Us'll see what he thinks.'

Reuben had been called out to measure the boot maker's five year old son who had died of diphtheria. It always upset him to make a coffin for a child as it reminded him of the baby Jane had lost, so he was morose when he returned. He ate his tea alone and in silence and was abrupt when Mary asked his advice about Johnny.

'Let'n go, Mary!' he said. 'Twill make a man of'n — knock'n into shape a bit.'

Mary was dismayed. 'I hoped you'd side with me over this, Reuben, 'specially as Johnny ain't easy to handle.'

'Let somebody else handle'n, then! You've done your share and so've I! Let'n knuckle down to some hard work and see how he shapes!'

"Tain't the work, Reuben! 'Tis the place! A brewery ain't fit for a young boy! If he won't shift from going in on Monday, I shall go in with'n, and see what 'tis like!'

Johnny was up before everybody else on Monday morning. He had already harnessed the horse to the wagon and was so eager to join James and Joey on their drive to Barum, Mary had not the heart to refuse him. In case he was given the job, she packed a bag with a change of clothes for him and a couple of meat and potato pasties to stave off his hunger. When she announced that she was going, too, Johnny's face flushed crimson and he glared at her.

'I'll look a proper fule if you come, Ma!' he protested. 'I can speak up for meself.'

'I daresay you can but you'm not going without me! I want to see where you'll be staying if you gets taken on.'

Johnny grumbled all the way into Barum but brightened up when he and Mary were dropped off at the Square. The brewery was just around the corner from it and they caught a strong smell of malt and hops when they walked into the yard. The place was busy and noisy with men in long aprons shouting directions to one another as they trundled out the barrels for loading on to the wagons. Johnny and his mother were ignored until

Mary asked the way to the manager's office and was pointed in the direction of a door in the main building. Once inside, they found the manager in a small room crammed with files of papers and order books.

He peered at them from behind his desk through gold rimmed spectacles. 'Yes?'

Mary pushed Johnny forward. 'You'm wanting a lad for the stables. This be John Moore that was mentioned to ee.'

'Ah!' The manager stared at Johnny. 'He's not very big for thirteen!'

'I'll grow,' Johnny said eagerly, 'and I'm very strong and used to hosses.'

'You are, are you?.' The manager raised his eyebrows and turned to Mary. 'You know the conditions?'

'I've been told,' Mary said. 'But I want to see 'em for meself before I let'n go. Johnny's a willing boy so I know he'll work hard. But if you give'n the job, I want to be sure he'll be looked after and not taken advantage of.'

'That's very commendable, missus,' the manager said. 'So if you'll follow me, I'll take you to the stables where you can meet Jeff King, our chief horseman. He knows best what he wants from a boy. If we all agree, I'll take your son on for a month's trial before deciding on a permanent job.'

The stables were apart from the main

building and the shire horses were just being led out, resplendent in gleaming bridles and horse brasses, their manes brushed and braided and their tails plaited high. Johnny caught his breath as he gazed at them. The man in charge, heavily built and bearded, bow legged in his breeches and leggings, doffed his cap when he saw the manager and stared curiously at Mary and the boy.

'Here's a new boy wanting to work with ee, Jeff,' the manager said. 'His name's John Moore.'

Jeff was watching Johnny who was not looking at him but at the horses, lost in admiration. 'Keen on hosses, be ee, boy?'

Johnny nodded. 'Specially them uns, Maister.'

'Not afraid of hard work?'

'Not with hosses, Maister.'

'He's been spending his Saturdays helping in the stables at Westcott,' Mary offered.

'Reckon he'll do, then,' Jeff said. 'Can'n start straight away?'

'Not till I've seen he'll be looked after.' Mary turned to the manager. 'You did say you'd show me.'

'Of course. Come this way.' The manager turned to move but Johnny lingered.

'You go, Ma!' he said. 'I'll stay here. That's if I can?' he asked Jeff.

'Ay. You can start by leading Major over to the wagons. I'll watch how you handle'n. Not afraid, be ee, boy?'

'No.' Johnny was used to the heavy horses at Westcott. He walked up to the huge shire, stroked his nose and spoke gently in his ear before taking the bridle and beginning to lead him away.

There was a lump in Mary's throat as she watched them go. 'I can't keep'n away from hosses,' she admitted.

Jeff King nodded. 'He'll be all right with me, missus. I'll make sure of that.'

The hay mattress and rough blankets Johnny would use were on the floor in a corner of the loft over the stables. Mary shook them out and examined them carefully. They seemed to be clean so she nodded.

'He'll be warm enough,' the manager said, 'with the hosses breathing down below. And he'll be on hand for when he's needed. I'll take you to the kitchen where the men eat and you can meet Mrs Stacey. She'll look after him.'

The kitchen was at one end of the main building and there was an appetising smell of cooking coming from it. Wooden tables and benches were lined against the longest wall and Mrs Stacey, a perspiring, red faced woman, beamed and winked at Mary when she was told about Johnny.

'I'll fatten'n up!' she said. 'And I'll keep an eye on'n, missus, 'cos I've got boys of me own.'

Mary turned to the manager. 'A month's trial, then,' she said reluctantly, knowing that Johnny was already lost to her. She left his bag with Mrs Stacey, finding Johnny in the yard when she went outside again. He was helping Jeff to back one of the shires between the shafts of a wagon and did not notice her until she called. Then he came running.

'Everything all right, Ma?' he asked anxiously.

' 'Tain't what I'd wish for ee, but 'twill do. You'm on a month's trial but you needn't stay if you don't like it.'

'Oh, I'll like it, never fear! Thankee, Ma!' He was already hurrying back to the horses.

'Your bag's in the kitchen!' she called after him.

And I've left part of my heart with it! she thought as she turned sadly away and left the yard to walk into the town.

She walked aimlessly for she had hours to kill before she could get a lift back to Yarnscombe and she had nowhere in particular to go. James and Joey would be working and Sally busy at her school. Henry and Harriet would be working, too, and so would Tommy.

She drifted into the Hight Street where most of the shops had just drawn back their shutters and stared through the bow fronted windows at the goods on display inside. A pottery shop with an array of decorative dishes held her attention for a while, as did a chemist's with its large jars of coloured potions and its tins of cure-alls.

She was gazing into it when somebody touched her arm. 'Mary? What be you doing here, all on your own?'

It was Emily. She was carrying a baby slung in a shawl from her left shoulder and holding a little boy by the hand. News had reached Reuben that he now had two grandchildren but he still refused adamantly to see them. Mary knew that Sally and Henry and even Tommy often paid them a visit but it came as a shock to see Emily with children of her own.

'I've just left Johnny,' Mary said. 'He's starting at the brewery stables.' She glanced down at Emily's little boy. 'Don't seem but yesterday he was the size of yourn.' To her consternation, she began to sob uncontrollably. Ashamed, she fumbled in the pocket of her skirt for her handkerchief and mopped her eyes. 'Can't think what came over me,' she choked.

'It must be hard to let 'em go,' Emily said. 'I can see that, now I've got two of me own. So would ee like to come back to my place for a cup of tea, Mary?'

'Oh, I don't want to hinder ee if you'm shopping.'

'I can pick up what I want on the way back.' She pushed the little boy forward. 'This is Alfred — called after Sam's dad. And this — ' she pulled back the shawl from the baby's face, ' — this is Jane, called after my mother.'

'Jane!' Mary peered at the little pink face. The baby's eyes were tightly shut. 'Your mother would've been pleased. Your father ought to be pleased, too, 'cos that's what he called the baby your mother lost. She wanted to call her Em'ly, 'cos she thought she'd lost you for good.'

'I wad'n really lost,' Emily said. 'Neither's your Johnny, unless you want it so. Will ee come for that cup of tea, Mary? No sense in wandering around on your own.'

Mary knew what Reuben would say if he found out. But Emily seemed so welcoming, she nodded and walked along with her, taking Alfred's hand when they stopped for the shopping. Their little cottage was in one of the back streets of the town. It was sparsely furnished but clean and tidy and Mary was glad to sit down and hold the baby while Emily brewed a pot of strong tea. The little boy came to lean against her knees, staring curiously at her. She stared back at him and then down at the baby. These were Reuben's grandchildren and her stepgrandchildren. She wondered if they would ever learn to call her Gran.

She smiled at Alfred. 'You'm a big boy,' she said, 'and you've got blue eyes just like your dad. What colour eyes have Jane got?'

He grinned and peered at the baby, then shook his head.

'I know her's asleep,' Mary said, 'but I'm sure you can tell me. Can't ee?'

'He don't say much,' Emily said, 'but he's fly enough, watches all what goes on.'

'Green!' Alfred suddenly said. 'They'm green,' and he burst into a peal of laughter.

'They'm not green, you monkey!' Emily scolded. 'They'm brown, like mine.'

Mary laughed, reminded of when Eliza and George were small in the cottage at Westcott and how Eliza had often made her and John laugh at the things she said. It would be even better with grandchildren and yet Reuben was obstinately denying himself the pleasure of these two.

She did not mean to stay long but once she and Emily began talking the time flew past.

Like Mary, Emily planned to go back to work as soon as she had stopped feeding the baby, as Sam's mother would mind the children while she was at the lace factory.

'I bain't landing meself with one every year like my poor mother,' Emily said. 'Sam knows that. You was lucky you only got caught once with Father.'

Mary flushed. 'He's not so young as he was. If more had come, they'd have been welcome. But Albert's the apple of his eye and I've tried to do my best for the rest of 'em.'

'Oh, you've been a good mother to 'em all,' Emily conceded. 'I'll give ee that, Mary. I never thought you'd stick it, knowing what he's like.'

'He's softened of late,' Mary said. 'I wish you and him could see eye to eye again.'

'Takes two for that! Sam tried once before.'

'But if your dad could only see your little ones, it might change'n. Would ee bring 'em to Yarnscombe, if he said you could?'

Emily shrugged. 'Sam would bring 'em if he thought they'd be welcome. He don't like trouble in fam'lies. I'd do it for Sam, but not for Father.'

'I'll ask'n, then. I'll ask'n tonight!'

Reuben was not in a good mood when Mary, James and Joey returned home late that afternoon. A cart on its way to the village had tipped into a ditch, breaking a rear wheel and axle. Reuben had been forced to make his way to it on foot as his wagon was in Barum. With only Freddy and George to help him, he was feeling hard done by.

So Mary waited until they were in bed that night. As soon as she mentioned that she had been to Emily's cottage and had met his grandchildren, his face contorted with rage.

He sat bolt upright in bed and turned on her. 'You went against me!' he shouted. 'You'm like all the rest of 'em, Mary! You don't care how much suffering that maid caused my poor Jane!'

'But these be your gran'children, Reuben! They had nort to do with any of that!'

'They'm no gran'children of mine! I disown 'em, like I disowned her that's borne 'em! They can all keep away from this house! D'you hear me, Mary?'

She shook her head sorrowfully. 'I hear ee, Reuben, but I don't understand ee. There's another little Jane, waiting in that cottage to capture your heart if you'd only let her!'

He looked so fierce Mary feared he might hit her. Then he turned his back, thumped his pillow fiercely and slumped down into the bed without another word.

He didn't even ask about my Johnny, she

thought, and felt a great loneliness as a tear trickled from the corner of her eye. It was a long time since she had wept for her first husband but she wept for him then and for the son he had never known that she had left behind in Barum.

13

As the year turned, so did the decade, bringing its troubles with it. Philip, who read the newspapers, regularly came home, excited about what Parnell was doing in Ireland or the Boers in Africa. He set the menfolk arguing but such things did not worry Mary as she was more concerned with what was happening in the family.

She sensed a new restlessness and the first to be affected by it was James. Working so often in Barum had opened his eyes to the changes taking place in the town. Although he sometimes sounded envious of the wider experience Henry was getting by working for a building firm, nobody expected him to leave his father and accept a job there himself.

'You'll wish yourself out of it!' Reuben warned him. 'You'll 'ave some jumped up young boss breathing down yer neck all day, telling ee what to do!'

'No more'n you do now, Dad!' James said. 'I'll have to move on sometime and I'll be getting a lot better pay.'

'Finding a lot more to spend it on, too!' Reuben sneered. 'I s'pose 'tis this fancy maid you'm courting that's put ee up to it!'

James glared at his father. 'Her name's Jessie, as you know full well! And her had nort to do with it!'

He stormed out, leaving Mary to pacify Reuben. She knew how he depended on James who was a good workman with a clever head for figures. He had already relieved his father of most of the costing of jobs and the working out of the bills.

'You've still got Joey,' she comforted, 'and there's Freddy and George. James bain't far off thirty now. He can't wait for ever to be wed.'

'I bain't so young as I was, neither!' Reuben complained bitterly. 'They none of 'em thinks of that!'

'Aw, come on, Reuben!' Mary put an arm round him and gave him a squeeze. 'You bain't sixty yet! There's plenty of life left in ee still. Us both knows that!'

All the same, she had to acknowledge that he was looking older, as she was herself. Her fortieth birthday had just passed and she was beginning to feel obliged to dress in darker colours. When Eliza came home from Torrington one weekend she scolded her for conforming to what was expected.

'You're as old as you feel, Mother!' she said. 'You don't look forty so there's no need to dress like Gran! You should see the fashion pictures of the ladies in Lunnon — as old as you be, some of 'em, and dressed to kill!'

Eliza looked blooming and there was an air of suppressed excitement about her. She was wearing a new pair of Vaughan gloves and when she peeled them off and held out her left hand for Mary's inspection, it was to display a ring on her third finger, a simple gold ring with one tiny ruby.

Mary gaped at it. 'Be that — ?'

'An engagement ring!' Eliza danced around the kitchen. 'All the girls at Vaughan's be green with envy!'

'But — but who — ? You naughty maid, you've never said a word!'

'I know and I'm sorry. I waited till I was sure. But you'll like'n, Mother. His name's Simon — Simon Tucker. His father's farming over Black Torrington way.'

'A farmer's son!' Mary's eyes widened.

'He's the youngest. There's two older brothers before Simon so us can't expect much from the farm. But I don't care about that! He's so tall and handsome and he says I'm the only maid he's ever fancied. I meet'n when he comes into town on Saturdays.'

'So how old is he?'

'Twenty-one. Old enough to be wed!'

'But you'm only nineteen, Lizzie! Plenty of time for ee yet!'

'You was wed before that!' Eliza pointed out. She sighed. 'Us'll have to wait, anyhow, till us have saved a bit. Can I bring'n home next weekend, so's he can meet you and Pa Dark and me brothers?'

'Course you can bring'n home! I want to see what he's like!' Impulsively, Mary pulled Eliza to her and kissed her on the cheek. 'I'm glad for ee, Lizzie! I was beginning to wonder, when you didn't come home so often.'

'Philip told me you were asking. I made'n keep it quiet.' She frowned. 'He don't seem too struck on Simon. But Walter and Annie like him well enough.'

'So they've all met'n before me! You'm a dark horse, Lizzie!'

Mary could not rest until she had made enquiries of her own about the Tuckers. Bert knew all the local farmers and he assured her that they were a respectable family who had been farming for generations. He had met Simon but could not tell her much about him except what Mary already knew, that he was the youngest son.

Reuben shook his head when he heard that. 'Any trouble on a farm always comes from the youngest,' he said. 'Course, this one might be different. Us'll have to wait and see.'

As soon as the news went round the family that Lizzie was engaged to be married and was bringing her intended home the following Sunday, all the Dark boys who had been sweet on her from time to time, contrived to be in the carpenter's house that day. Her brothers were also there as Johnny came home from Barum. So, to Mary's delight, did Sally. She was a rare visitor these days as she was busy with her school work after being awarded her certificate and being put in charge of a class of her own. She had lost her early prettiness but had developed into a handsome, rather severe looking young woman, plainly but stylishly dressed with her hair swept back into a bun. Eliza admired her but Reuben despaired of her ever getting married.

'I told ee her'd turn into an old maid once her went school teaching,' he complained to Mary. 'I should've put a stop to it when I had the chance!'

'Sal's doing what her wanted,' Mary said, 'and what Jane wanted for her. 'Tis no use trying to make their minds up for 'em once they'm grown. Us've both found that!'

She sighed as she thought of Johnny. He had been taken on permanently at the brewery and had grown four inches over the year as a result of hard work and Mrs Stacey's cooking. He was now almost as tall as Charlie and boasted to him that Sunday about his prowess with the shires which were so much more exciting than the horses at Westcott. He had just been to Barum fair where he had met some of the gypsy horse dealers and become obsessed with the idea of breeding horses himself and running a stable of his own one day.

'You keep away from them rogues!' Mary ordered sharply. 'They was nearly the downfall of your great-granfer Pugsley!'

Charlie only laughed at him. 'You wouldn't make much headway breeding hosses now, Johnny! The farmers be selling 'em, not buying 'em. I've heard of two more stable hands round here that lost their jobs last week. They'm off to America soon's they've raised the fare. They've heard tales of the prairies and the ranches in Texas and fancy themselves as cowboys! 'Twouldn't suit me — too wild, I reckon.'

But Johnny's eyes gleamed. 'America! I hadn't thought of that!'

'Then don't think of it!' Mary said. 'I don't want to lose ee to foreign parts or to the gypsies! The brewery's better'n that!'

They were all ready and waiting when Eliza and Simon Tucker arrived in style later that morning. He had borrowed his father's horse and trap for the occasion and they were both looking smart in their Sunday best. The September days were still warm so Eliza was wearing her flowery straw bonnet and a light shawl over her pretty blouse and skirt. Simon was bare headed, his thick dark hair a little tousled from the breeze. Apart from his flamboyant necktie he looked a typical farmer's son in his jacket and breeches and well polished boots.

Mary remembered her own embarrassment the first time she met Reuben's large family and was prepared to sympathise with him. But Simon Tucker stepped into the carpenter's house with no hint of shyness. He shook Reuben's hand heartily and nodded deferentially to her. She could see at once why he would appeal to Eliza as he was certainly handsome with bold features and striking dark eyes. She took his hand and murmured a greeting, then watched him as he moved from one to another of the family, chatting with ease. Eliza hung on his arm, glowing with pride and so clearly in love, Mary's heart ached for her. She turned away to busy herself with getting the Sunday dinner on to the table. Don't let him hurt her! she thought.

For the first time for weeks nearly

everybody was at home. Once they were all settled, Reuben beamed around his crowded table and took up his carving knife and fork to begin attacking the leg of mutton which had been cooking slowly all morning in the big pot with the vegetables. The meat was almost ready to fall off the bone and when Mary handed him the plates she thought, this is what he likes, having all his family around him!

She doled out the vegetables and the potatoes which had browned nicely in the side oven, piling up the plates as they all had good appetites. They had a lot to talk about, too, as this was the day of the week when they always exchanged news. The presence of a stranger did not deter them as Simon had as much to say as anybody and plenty of opinions of his own. Like Philip, he read the newspapers and was soon involved in a heated argument with him over whether Mr Gladstone had been wise in giving the Boers the freedom to form an independent republic in the Transvaal.

'Kruger won't stop there!' he maintained when Philip tried to put the case for the Boers. 'There'll be all out war over there soon, you mark my words. Us'll have to finish off the Boers like us finished off the Zulus, 'specially as South Africa's going to be the place where a chap could make money. If I had the means, I'd be off there meself.'

Eliza looked alarmed. 'South Africa? You don't mean that, do ee, Simon?'

'The world's a big place, Lizzie. South Africa, Australia, they'm all opening up and lots of chaps be emigrating now times be bad.'

'And America?' Johnny asked eagerly. 'Do ee fancy America?'

'I fancy anywhere I could be my own maister. Land — that's where the money'll be and there bain't enough of it in this country. 'Tis all parcelled up and in the hands of a wealthy few that don't care what happens to it!'

'I see you'm a bit of a radical,' Reuben said. 'What do your father say about such ideas?'

'Oh, Dad! He's content to be a tenant farmer all his life! S'long's he can pass on the tenancy to one of me brothers, that's all he bothers! But I bain't going to hang around, tacky-lacking for one of they all me life! I want better'n that for me and Lizzie!'

'Good luck to ee, then!' Reuben said. 'I've gived most of my lads a trade so's they can make their own way in the world. None of 'em's thought of going so far as South Africa or America, though! Or not yet!'

'I have,' Philip said unexpectedly and they

all stared at him. 'I'd like to see the world. I don't want to emigrate but I wouldn't mind trying the army.'

Everybody laughed, even Mary, at the idea of quiet, easy going Philip contemplating army life. His face reddened and he said no more but there was a determined set to his mouth. Mary wondered if he had perhaps been serious and how serious Simon was. Eliza was looking troubled and was whispering in his ear.

After the meal, the two girls helped Mary to clear everything away and wash the pots. The menfolk wandered off, Reuben and Joey to show Simon the workshop and Charlie and Johnny to compare the merits of the Tuckers' horse with theirs. Shouts and bumps from the yard suggested that some of the younger boys were kicking a ball around.

Sally laughed. 'They never grow up, do they?'

'Some of 'em do.' Mary sighed. 'Too quick for my liking. Seems like only yesterday, Lizzie, you was playing with your old rag doll.'

Eliza looked anxious. 'You do like Simon, though, don't ee, Mother?'

''Tain't what I like, 'tis what you like! He seems a nice enough boy — had plenty to say for hisself!'

'That's because he was nervous, meeting everybody. He ain't like that with me.'

'I'spect you've got better things to do than talk! Just go careful, though, maid! Don't get carried away, 'specially not so far as South Africa!'

Eliza gave her a hug. 'I bain't going nowhere and neither be Simon. He's just looking around, that's all.'

Mary was only partly reassured. When she and Reuben were in bed that night, she asked him, 'So what did ee think of young Tucker?'

Reuben yawned. 'A bit too big for his boots but he'll learn. Comes of being the youngest — has to show off a bit.'

'I wouldn't want'n to take Lizzie somewhere abroad.'

Reuben rolled over towards her and cuddled her to him, the way he always did when he was ready for sleep. 'I don't s'pose Lizzie'd go with'n, anyhow,' he said. 'Her wouldn't go off and leave her Ma.'

Comforted, Mary snuggled into him. A sudden memory came to her of four year old Eliza, the day that John was buried, promising solemnly that she would look after her mother when she grew up. I'm worrying over nothing, Mary thought, and closed her eyes with a sigh of relief.

But things were changing. Albert left

school the following Easter and came obediently to work with his father. Like Freddy and George before him, he never questioned what he should do. Always placid and goodnatured, he proved willing enough, if not as ambitious as George to whom he most often turned for instruction. Mary was pleased that George, the most dependable of her sons, had taken him under his wing.

So it was a shock when George was the next to surprise her. After James left, he was regularly sent out with Joey to tackle the more difficult jobs in the neighbourhood. That April, they set off in the wagon to a large house in the village of Dolton where extensive carpentry was needed to replace the main staircase which had become dangerous. It was going to be a big job, taking several days. Once they had made the necessary measurements, Joey drove back to the saw mills at Torrington to fetch the wood they would need, leaving George to start dismantling the original staircase. He was offered a bed for the night so that he could continue with the work the next morning before Joey returned.

Exactly what happened that night, nobody in the family ever properly found out. According to Joey, when he arrived the next day, George and the young maidservant,

Hannah, had struck up such a close relationship, he could hardly prise them apart. 'Wherever he was working,' Joey told Mary, 'that maid was hanging around. And when I couldn't find George, he'd sloped off to the kitchen. Must be love at first sight!'

'So what's her like?' Mary asked, astonished. Although George had run around after some of the village girls he had never shown any serious interest in a girl before.

'Oh, her's a fine looking maid — quite tall, as tall as George. Thin's a rush, though and quiet spoken — a bit shy with me.'

'But not with George?'

'Well, her didn' have much to say to'n — just watched'n all the time, like he kept staring at her. They'm both smitten, I reckon.'

'Then 'tis a good job you'll soon be finished over there! How much more do ee have to do?'

'Once us've done the main staircase, us have to look at the back one — and there's flooring in one of the bedrooms that needs seeing to. Could be there a week or more yet.'

Time enough for George to make a fool of himself! Mary thought and watched him carefully when he came home the next day. He was eighteen now, still stocky and sturdily built with an even more determined jut to his jaw. George usually knew what he wanted and if he wanted Hannah, she thought he would be sure to get her. Still, Dolton was a good nine miles away and distance did not always make the heart grow fonder. Once the job was finished and he became involved in the next one, she was sure that George would forget young Hannah.

But Mary had reckoned without her son's persistence. George had a good pair of legs and was not afraid of walking. After he and Joey completed their job in Dolton, he set off every Sunday morning after breakfast to trudge the nine miles to visit his sweetheart and did not return until after nightfall. Mary grew anxious that his constant presence might annoy Hannah's employers but it seemed the girl had a few hours off on Sunday afternoons which they spent in wandering the lanes or visiting her parents in the village.

'So when be ee going to bring her to see me?' Mary demanded after several weeks of this.

'If Pa Dark'll lend me the horse and trap, I'll fetch her over next Sunday,' George said. 'Can't expect Hannah to walk all that way.'

Reuben grumbled that his horse worked hard enough during the week without having to turn out on Sundays as well. He gave way to Mary's pleading eventually, only insisting that George should collect Hannah on the Saturday evening, if she should get the time off, and take her back the next afternoon, giving the horse a good rest in between. This arrangement delighted Mary as she would be able to see more of the girl.

She made up a bed for her in Eliza's old room and awaited Hannah's arrival with trepidation. But as soon as she saw her she had the curious feeling that she had met her before. What was it about this tall, slim girl with gentle eyes and a shy manner that disturbed a memory? There was an air of refinement about her that she could not place until she discovered her the next morning in Jane's old sitting room, reading the titles of the books in the bookcase.

'Be ee fond of reading?' Mary asked.

The girl started for she had not heard Mary come in. 'When I get the chance,' she said. 'Maister's got a fine library at the house and he lets me borrow a book sometimes if we're not busy with visitors.'

'You must borrow some of these, then! They belonged to my husband's first wife but I'm sure he wouldn't mind. Here!' Mary reached for the poetry book Jane had given her. 'This one's mine that was gived to me. Do ee like poetry?'

'I haven't read much, 'cept at school.'

'I didn't understand a lot of this,' Mary confessed, 'but you might. Take it and see!'

The eager way Hannah took the book and began leafing through it made Mary realise that, of course, the girl was like Jane! Perhaps George had not made a fool of himself after all!

She smiled at her. 'How old be ee, Hannah?'

'Seventeen next month.' The girl blushed. 'I've never walked out with a boy before George but Mother likes'n and Father said he seems steady.'

'He's steady all right!' Mary said. 'And I'm sure he's picked a good maid in you, Hannah. But you'm both young yet. Plenty of time to think about settling down.'

'I know. George said he wants to make his own way in the trade before us thinks of getting wed.'

'Did'n tell ee that?' Mary frowned. 'Nothing's been said about'n moving on. He's well set here with his stepdad.'

Hannah flushed. 'P'raps I spoke out of turn, then.'

'No. Later on, I daresay he'll move. I 'spect that's what he meant.'

But Mary began to wonder and when Hannah offered to help her with the Sunday dinner she probed gently as they worked together. The girl lost most of her shyness and began chatting about her family, how she had a brother and a sister, both married, and that her father was a shoemaker and her mother a seamstress. So Mary told her how she had been a glover and that Eliza was following in her footsteps.

'You'll like Lizzie,' she said, 'and you'll like Sally, my stepdaughter. Sal's clever — school teaching in Barum.'

'George told me 'twas a big family,' Hannah said, 'but that I wasn't to be scared, meeting 'em all.'

'They'll be about presently but some'll go to church. Did George say what he'd be doing this morning?'

'He said he'd take me for a walk after he's been to church with Mr Dark but I was to stay and talk to you.'

'Oh?' Mary was astonished as George rarely went to church. 'You didn't want to go with'n, then?'

'We're chapel. I'd have gone but George said 'twas best I stayed so's you and me could get to know one another.'

And so that he could talk to Reuben? Mary wondered. Perhaps it was true, then that he was ready to move on. But where? Had he already found a job like Henry and James? If so, that was probably because of Hannah. He would want to better himself now that he had found her and Hannah was the sort of girl who would encourage him. But what was Reuben going to say if George was also planning to leave him?

14

Nothing was said by either Reuben or George when they and the rest of the family came home from church. Mary tried to judge from their expressions what might have passed between them but their faces gave nothing away. It was not until after the Sunday dinner when George had taken Hannah out for her promised walk and the other boys had dispersed to their various activities, that Reuben confided in Mary.

He sat slumped in his fireside chair, puffing broodingly at his old black pipe, waiting until she finished clearing away after the meal. When she took her usual seat opposite him, he removed his pipe from his mouth and said, abruptly, 'Seems your George've got hisself fixed up in Barum.'

'Fixed up?' Mary feigned astonishment. 'What do ee mean, fixed up?'

'Seeems he met up with Bill Luxton, the builder, when he and Joey were on that job last week. Luxton said he was short of a carpenter and offered to take George on.'

'So what did George say?'

'Told'n he'd have to have a word with me first.'

'I'm glad he had enough sense to say that! What sort of chap be'n, this Luxton? Do ee know'n?'

Reuben took a pull on his pipe. 'Oh, I know'n all right — helped'n out a few times when he had more carpentry work than he could handle. 'Tis a small firm but they'm well thought of. Luxton's a bit too well known, I fancy. He likes his drink, does old Bill! Spends too much time in the Rising Sun.'

'That don't seem much of a chap for George to work for!'

'He could do a lot worse. Luxton knows his trade and he does a good job when he's sober. A steady young chap like George could be just what he needs.'

'And you'd let George go to a man like that — after all you've done for'n?'

Reuben shrugged. 'I've done what I promised ee, Mary. I've gived'n a trade. If George wants to go, that's his look out. He'll have to move on sometime. I've Joey and Fred and Albert to think about. There won't be enough work to keep us all going.'

Mary was silent. Enough work for your sons, she was thinking, but not for mine! She knew she was being unreasonable, as Albert was her son, too. But she could not suppress a suspicion that Reuben was secretly relieved that George was leaving.

'That's that, then!' she said. 'When's George going to start in Barum? Did'n say? And where's 'n going to live?'

'You'd best ask George that when he's finished his courting.' Reuben gave a sly grin. 'He won't be able to do so much of that when he's working in Barum!'

This was true enough, making Mary wonder if the move might finish the affair between George and Hannah.

But once again, she had reckoned without her son's persistence. He had it all worked out, she discovered, when he and Hannah came back from their walk. He had already found a lodging house in Barum where he could get a cheap bed. So if Mary would bake him enough bread and pasties to help him through the week, he would walk into Barum on Sunday evenings and back to Yarnscombe after his week's work on Saturdays. On Sunday mornings he would walk to Dolton as usual to visit Hannah before trudging back to Barum. Some days he might get a lift in a cart, but if not, he had a good pair of legs and a strong pair of boots.

Mary was dismayed. 'You'll wear yourself out with all that walking! You can't tramp all them miles and do a good week's work as well!'

'I told'n that!' Hannah said. 'I told'n I didn't want'n to kill himself for me.'

George's mouth set in a stubborn line. ''T'won't be for long — just so long's it takes me to save up enough for Hannah and me to be wed. After that, I'll find a place for us to live in Barum.'

'Then I'd never see ee at all!' Mary cried.

''Course you would! Us'd come over to Yarnscombe sometimes, or you could come into town with Pa Dark or the boys. 'Tain't as if I won't have family about. Johnny's there and Henry and James — '

'And Sally!' Hannah said eagerly. 'You said us could call on Sally once us was settled.'

Mary shook her head. ''Tis all so sudden,' she complained. 'And you'm just like Lizzie, George! You never said a word about what you was thinking!'

'That's 'cos us didn't want to worry ee before time! You knew I'd have to move on some day and this be my chance. Luxton's bain't a big firm but I know I can make my mark there, more'n I could if I stayed with Pa Dark. I told ee I aim to build houses and this is how I'll learn. You wait! In a few years I'll be taking ee to see the very first house built by George Moore. And that's a promise!'

There was such determination in his eyes, Mary saw that George meant every word. Hannah was watching him with the same pride and adoration as Eliza had watched Simon and Mary hoped that they would neither of them be disappointed. She wondered what John would have thought of his children now — Eliza engaged to be married and George and Johnny both striking out on their own, all so full of expectation and promise. She and John had started out like that but who knew what life might bring? A cold feeling of uncertainty gripped her suddenly, making her turn away from the two confident young people so that they should not see her doubt. She was glad that Reuben came in at that moment, demanding to know when George was taking Hannah home to Dolton as his horse had to be rubbed down and stabled before dusk that evening.

'Joey'll need'n in the morning for that job over to Alverdiscott,' he said. 'I'll send Freddy with'n. Then you can take yerself off to Barum and tell Bill Luxton you can start straightaway.'

'Tomorrow?' Mary was dismayed. 'I won't have time to get his clothes ready and bake'n some vittals to take.'

George put a hand on her arm and faced his stepfather. 'That'll suit me fine,' he said.

'I'll set off early. If you pay me my week's wages, I'll have enough to get by. No need to fret, Ma!'

Reuben glowered. 'No doubt your ma'll find ee summat,' he grunted, 'like her always do!' He stumped out of the room, leaving an awkward silence behind him.

'Well!' Mary said. 'Seems he could be taking it hard.'

'Harder than I thought,' George admitted. 'He didn't seem to mind when I told'n, first along.'

'He's come to rely on ee,' Mary said, 'like he did with James. I hope you'm doing the right thing, George, taking up with this Luxton. Seems he bain't all that reliable.'

'That's mostly talk! I've seed the houses he's built and they'm still standing! I'll take from Bill Luxton what I need, just as I have from Pa Dark. You'll see!'

Mary gazed at him, troubled by this streak of ruthlessness. 'He's gived you a lot, George,' she said quietly, 'more than you know. I hope you've said thankee to'n. If you haven't, will ee do it now, for my sake?'

George frowned. 'I've worked hard for Pa Dark and I've earned every penny he's paid me. Still, since you must've married'n for my sake, Ma, and for Lizzie's and Johnny's, I'll do it for you.' He turned to Hannah. 'You fetch your things and I'll take ee back to Dolton soon's I've spoken to'n.'

Mary was left momentarily speechless. Had George really believed she had only married Reuben for the sake of her children? She thought back to her other reason, to the strong physical attraction that was was still not quite spent. Without it, she would never have married for a second time.

Hannah was watching her. Reading sympathy in her eyes, Mary said, 'George don't always see eye to eye with his stepfather. You mustn't take too much notice of what he says.'

'He told me how you were left widowed young with three little ones. That must've been hard.'

Mary nodded. ''Twas hard. But 'twas a long time ago, Hannah. My little ones be growing into men and women with minds of their own. They don't remember the past. I don't think of it much meself nowadays, till summat brings it back.'

'Like what George just said?'

Mary was astonished at the girl's perception. Even in this, she resembled Jane who could always understand without needing everything spelled out. She reached out to take Hannah's hand. 'I'm glad George've found a good maid like you. You'll be a great help to'n. He's got such big ideas.' She sighed. 'I wouldn't like'n to be disappointed.'

'I'll help'n if I can,' Hannah said, 'and I'll wait for'n till he's ready to wed, even if it takes a year or two.'

'Oh, George won't want to wait that long!' Mary warned her. 'Once he's made up his mind, nothing stops'n! Soon's he's found his feet in Barum, he'll be sending for ee, Hannah.' She gave a wry smile. 'But you'd best fetch your things, like he said. He'll want to be back before dark and I must look out what I can for'n to take tomorrow.'

As well as a change of clothes and such food as she could spare, there was something else Mary wanted to give George. The sovereign he had been left by old Granny Pugsley was still in her old tin box. Eliza had made good use of hers when she started at Vaughan's and now it was time for George to be given his. He would have to pay rent for his room in Barum and might need to buy extra tools. He already had quite a collection, built up during his time with Reuben and Mary remembered his pride when he first went off on a job with a toolbag of his own.

Upstairs in the room she shared with Reuben, she dragged her tin box from under her skirts in the wardrobe and unlocked it. She took out George's sovereign, added one from what she had over from the ten she had been left and put them both into a little drawstring bag. Johnny's stayed safely where it was. He was careless with money and she had not felt able to trust him with his when he started at the brewery. His bed and food were provided and he was earning a few extra shillings now that he was more experienced with the horses. He had plenty enough to spend and would be glad, one day, that she had kept his sovereign for when he really needed it.

She sighed when she looked at the photograph of herself and John outside the chapel on their wedding day. It all seemed so long ago. She slipped his ring on her finger for a moment. Then George's words came back to her, that she had only married Reuben for the family's sake. With a feeling of guilt, she pulled off John's ring and dropped it back into her box. I did what I thought was right, she told herself, and because it was what I wanted. It's been hard sometimes but I don't regret any of it.

She looked out a set of clean clothes for George and went downstairs again, only to discover that he had already left for Dolton with Hannah. Reuben was sitting in his old armchair, sucking at an empty pipe.

'They'm gone,' he said. 'Couldn't even wait

to say goodbye to ee.'

'Well, George knew you wanted'n back before dark.' Mary tried to judge her husband's mood. 'What did ee think of Hannah, then?'

'Seems a nice enough maid. Bit too skinny for my liking!'

''Tis the fashion, Reuben! All the young maids hanker after an eighteen inch waist.'

'I prefer summat I can get a hold of!' He reached out and patted Mary's plump bottom. 'Still, if her's what George wants, good luck to'n. I told'n not to be in too much of a hurry to get wed. They'm young yet and he needs to make his way a bit first. I've paid'n his wages and told'n he can take my spare jack plane to add to his tool bag.'

'That was good of ee, Reuben!' Mary gave him a hug. 'I was feared he might've upset ee, by going off to Luxton's.'

'No.' Reuben pulled her on to his knee. 'The boy came and thanked me for what I'd done for'n. That be more'n my own sons have done, Mary. They've just took it as a right and gone off without a word.'

'I'm sure they'm grateful. They just haven't thought to tell ee so.'

Reuben sighed. 'I s'pose 'tis no more'n I deserve. I struck out on me own after Father died and never thought to say thankee to

Uncle Will. I've been sat here, thinking about that and about other things I should've done and didn't. 'Tis all a lot too late now.'

'No!' Mary rubbed her cheek against his. ''Tis never too late if there's things that can be put right. I'm glad George spoke to ee. You've been a good father to'n — to all my children.'

'And you've been a good mother to mine, even speaking up for the one I cast out. Do ee think — ?' He hesitated and Mary could see he was struggling with himself. 'Do ee think Emily and Sam Bowden would bring their little uns to see me if I changed me mind and let 'em come? I bain't getting any younger so p'raps 'tis time I saw my grandchildren before I've missed me chance.'

'Course they'd bring 'em! And you've plenty of time left! Us could send a message by George when'n goes to Barum tomorrow. I'm glad you want to see Emily's children, Reuben. They'm beautiful, 'specially little baby Jane!' She put her arms round her husband and kissed him warmly on the cheek. 'You'll not regret it, I promise ee!'

She was elated. All this because she had told George to thank Reuben! Such a small thing, yet with such unexpected results! Don't let him change his mind! she thought and before he had the chance, she wrote an invitation to Emily and persuaded him to sign it. When George returned that evening she gave him the note and told him to deliver it to Emily as soon as he could find the time.

He was more interested in his sovereign which he had forgotten about as he had been so young when old Granny Pugsley died. 'With this and the one you've given me I'll have a good start and can begin saving right away,' he said. 'I don't want Hannah to have to wait too long.'

'Hannah won't mind waiting. Her's a good maid. You just make sure you treat her right and don't go running after them flighty maids in Barum!'

He grinned. 'Fat chance I'll have, working all week and tramping to and fro on Saturdays and Sundays!'

He set off jauntily the next morning before the others were up, carrying a sack of clothes and food over one shoulder and his tool bag over the other. Mary had risen even earlier to make his breakfast and she went outside to wave him on his way, waiting until he turned the corner towards the road to Barum. They had all gone now except Albert and she was overwhelmed with loss when she went back into the kitchen and stared at Reuben's long table which had always been so crowded. The room seemed to echo with emptiness instead of the chatter and banter of the family.

Then Joey and Freddy and Albert came clattering down the stairs, followed at a slower pace by Reuben and she was busy again, doling out porridge from the big iron pot and slicing into a cottage loaf, the last of her baking. She would have to make more that morning as she had packed two loaves and a couple of pasties for George, keeping just enough for Joey and Fred to take to Alverdiscott where they would be working all day. Only Reuben and Albert would join her for the midday meal. She knew the others would return when they could and that there was no need to feel gloomy but she could not shake off her despondency.

After the menfolk left for work she sat for a while at the table with her chin in her hands, wondering what she was doing there, all alone in the big, echoing house. She thought back to the little cottage at Westcott she had shared with John, then to her cramped quarters in her mother's house and the cottage next door she had managed to rent. What had it all been for? She was haunted by a premonition that one day everybody she cared about would be gone and she really would be completely alone.

Only the arrival of the girl who helped with the heavy work shook her out of her brooding and made her start clearing away the breakfast dishes and prepare for her baking. That afternoon, when all her work was done, she walked out of the carpenter's house and called on her mother, her sister Becky and her sister Anne and caught up on all the village gossip. She felt better afterwards. Of course she was not alone and never would be while there was family nearby!

A few days later a letter arrived by post, addressed to her and Reuben. It was from Emily. She and Sam would bring the children the following Sunday afternoon, just for a couple of hours. She hoped that would be convenient. It was a cool little note but Mary was delighted. Reuben read it with a furrowed brow and threw it down on to the table.

'Don't seem her's all that eager to come,' he grumbled.

'Well, what do ee expect, after all these years? Just be glad they'm coming and try to put on a smile!'

They arrived by pony and trap, bringing Sally with them. Mary hurried to greet them and when they all crowded into the porch, she thought at first that Sally's presence was to help ease the situation between Emily and her father. But she soon realised that Sally was a great favourite with the children.

Alfred, who had grown into a sturdy six year old since she had last seen him, clung to his aunt's hand when Reuben appeared, a tall, fierce looking, bearded figure who stared down at his grandson without a word. Little Jane, three years old now and no longer a baby, hid her face in her mother's skirts.

When Emily said nothing, it was left to Sam Bowden to break the ice. He moved forward and gripped Reuben's hand, just as he had at Walter's wedding. 'Pleased to meet you again, sir,' he said. 'Alfred's been looking forward to coming to Yarnscombe, 'cos Em'ly's been telling him all about you.' He beckoned to the boy. 'This be your grandad, Alfie, the one who makes wheels for carriages and carts and all sorts of useful things like cupboards and window frames. Come and say hello to'n.'

Sally slipped her hand from Alfred's and gently edged him foward. He looked up at his grandfather solemnly. 'And did ee make a great big table,' he asked, 'for Ma and Aunty Sally and all their brothers to sit around?'

Reuben smiled. 'That I did!' He crouched down to the boy's level. 'Do ee want to see it?' Alfred nodded. 'Then come on! You shall sit at it next to me when us all have tea.'

Alfred put his hand in Reuben's and the pair of them disappeared towards the kitchen, leaving the rest of the family astounded.

'Well!' Mary said. 'I never thought to see Reuben won over so easy! Your Alfred's a real charmer, Em'ly.'

'Father always did favour the boys,' Emily said. 'He never had much to say to Sal and me unless us did wrong!'

'Well, come on in!' Mary urged. 'Some of your brothers are here already. Charlie's up from Westcott and Joey and Fred be somewhere about. My Johnny turned up from Barum with George last night — walked most of the way. He'll see to the pony, Sam. You'll be glad of a cup of tea, I'll be bound.'

She bustled them all into the kitchen where she had already laid the table with plates of scones and bread and butter, a large cooked ham, dishes of jam and cream, a blackberry and apple pie, plates of buttered lardy cake and yeast buns and a huge seed cake, resplendent on a cut glass stand. The heavy kettle was steaming over the fire and she moved it to one side because the ladies were excusing themselves to visit the earth closet at the bottom of the garden. Reuben and Alfred were nowhere to be seen but Joey put his head round the door to tell her that his father had taken the little boy out to show him his workshop.

Mary sighed in exasperation. 'Well, you tell

'em to be quick and get your brothers and Johnny inside! There be folks here wanting their tea.'

But she was pleased that Reuben was taking such an interest in Alfred and later on, when his big table was crowded again and she saw his pleasure in having so many of his family around him, she knew that she had done the right thing by encouraging him to settle his differences with Emily.

Not that everything could be forgiven at once. She knew that. Emily said little to her father and they avoided one another's eyes. It was Sam and Sally who did most of the talking and the Dark boys and Johnny who chimed in when they had a chance. The children seemed overawed by so many people but Mary could see that Alfred was taking everything in. When his grandfather made a remark he looked at him and nodded. Mary thought he seemed too wise for his years and wondered what it would be like when she had grandchildren of her own.

They were all laughing and she realised she had missed a joke. It was Johnny they were teasing because he had gone to Barum fair and challenged one of the boxers in the booths in the hope of winning ten shillings. Instead, he had been knocked out for his trouble and was boasting a ripe black eye.

'You keep away from them gypsy rogues!' Mary scolded him. 'I told ee before, they'll only get ee into trouble!'

She could tell that Johnny did not care, that he would go his own way regardlesss. He was still full of ideas about going to America to make his fortune and she wished that Simon Tucker would not encourage him with such talk. He and Eliza had not been to visit them for several weeks and she was beginning to wonder if something had gone wrong between them

All the same, she was not prepared for Eliza's turning up alone that evening after the visitors had left. She was disshevelled and footsore because she had walked all the way from Torrington and, as soon as she saw her mother, she burst into tears.

15

Mary hurried Eliza into Jane's old sitting room, out of the way of the rest of the family. 'Whatever's the matter, Lizzie?' she asked, alarmed to see the girl's distress.

Gradually, between sobs, it all came out. There was a ship sailing from Plymouth to America in six weeks time at the end of August. One of Simon's hunting friends, a farmer's son like himself, was travelling on it, going over to join a cousin in Oregon who had set up a sheep farm a few years before. He was making money fast and needed extra hands. Simon's friend had persuaded Simon to ask his father for the money to buy a passage for himself, so that they could travel together. To Simon's delight and Eliza's dismay, his father had agreed. Now he had his booking and was all set to go.

'But what about you?' Mary asked. 'Is he expecting you to sail with'n?'

'No.' Eliza sniffled miserably. 'He said he'd send for me when he's settled 'cos they've a long way to go across America. Seems they have to head west and take the Oregon trail, wherever that be. I could kill that Jim Barrow for putting such ideas in his head!'

'Simon had plenty of his own before that!'

'But I was trying to talk'n out of them! I've tried all I know but he won't listen to me. Why did'n buy me a ring, if all the time he was itching to be off? He can't care a fig for me, Ma!'

Eliza started crying again so Mary put an arm round her. 'Have ee broke it off, then?'

'No.' Eliza choked. 'He wouldn't hear of that.'

'Well, then, he can't be leaving ee for good.'

'But I don't want to go to America! I told'n so today. I thought that might stop'n going, but it didn't make a bit of difference. We had a terrible row. Oh, how can I bear it? I might never see'n again and that would break my heart.'

Mary held her close. 'Don't fret yourself, Lizzie! Your Simon thinks too much of ee to leave ee for good. If he do, he won't be worth crying over! Now, you bide here where 'tis quiet and I'll go and make a cup of tea. You must stay in your own little room tonight.'

She hurried into the kitchen where Reuben was dozing by the fire. He looked up at her sleepily. 'Did I hear somebody come, Mary?'

Mary nodded and banged the kettle on to the smouldering coals. ''Twas Lizzie — walked all the way from Torrington.'

'Walked? This late? Summat up, then?'

'Simon Tucker's off to America in six weeks. Her's taking it hard.'

'Bain't her going with'n, then?'

'No. He's s'posed to be sending for her when he's settled and has earned some money.'

Reuben whistled. 'How's'n got the money to go, then?'

'Seems his father's paying his way.'

'Old man Tucker?' Reuben grinned. 'Glad to get rid of'n, I bet. Don't do to have too many sons on a farm, 'specially when the youngest has such big ideas. Saved hisself a passel of trouble, old Tucker have!' Reuben yawned and leaned back in his chair. 'I'll have a mug of tea, Mary, if you'm making a fresh brew.'

''Tis for Lizzie, to calm her down!' Mary scolded. But she poured him a mugfull when the tea was made. 'Her'll have to sleep here tonight,' she said, 'and her won't be back for her job at Vaughan's in the morning. Can't send 'em word, neither.' She clicked her tongue. 'I had a feeling this Simon Tucker'd upset the apple cart! I've never seen Lizzie in such a state.'

However, Eliza had stopped crying when Mary took the tea in to her. She poured them both a cup and they sat together on Jane's old sofa, sipping without speaking for a while. Then Eliza said, 'I'll have to get back tomorrow. 'Twon't do to lose my job at Vaughan's if I'm to end up an old maid.'

'Don't talk such nonsense! If Simon Tucker give's word there's better men than he, only too glad to take ee for wife! But he haven't done that yet so us must give'n a chance. I'll make up the bed in your old room so's you can get a good night's sleep. Things'll seem better in the morning.'

Mary was up early the next day but Eliza was down before her, already dressed and ready to leave.

'Where do ee think you'm going,' Mary demanded, 'without a bite to eat?'

'Walking back. I'll be late enough as 'tis.'

'You'll do no such thing! Sit down and have a proper breakfast! The boys'll be taking the wagon out and 'twon't be much out of their way to give ee a lift to Torrington.'

'Pa Dark wouldn't hear of that!'

'You leave Pa Dark to me! I won't have ee turning up at Vaughan's in a state like you was in last night. 'Tis bad enough when George and Johnny have to walk to Barum. 'Tis a lot worse for a young maid like you.'

'I've done it before with Philip!'

'Philip bain't here! I'm surprised he let ee come all that way on your own.'

'I didn't tell'n.' Eliza looked down. 'I don't see so much of Philip these days, not since I've been courting Simon. I didn't want'n to know we'd had a row.'

Mary regarded her keenly. 'Philip thinks a lot of ee, Lizzie.'

'I know. He thinks too much! That's why I didn't tell'n, in case he thought — ' She broke off. 'What do it matter, anyhow? He'll know soon enough.'

Mary moved to the fire and tried to coax a flame from the embers which had burned low during the night. She handed the coal scuttle to Eliza. 'Here — make yourself useful and fetch a few coals and sticks from the back while I see to the porridge! The boys'll be down soon, wanting their breakfast.'

Then I'll ask Reuben to help Lizzie with a lift to Torrington, she thought. He can't refuse her a small thing like that.

But Reuben had other ideas when he came down. The wagon was needed for Alverdiscott, he said. Eliza could be given a lift to the cross roads but she would have to walk the rest. In vain Mary pleaded. Joey spoke up for Eliza but was over-ruled and the argument was getting heated over breakfast when Albert thought he heard somebody outside in the yard.

He ran out to look and came back

grinning. 'Simon Tucker's here for Lizzie,' he said. 'I asked'n to come in but he said he'd sooner bide outside.'

They all turned to Eliza whose face was aflame. 'How did'n come?' she asked.

'By pony and trap — said he guessed you'd be here when he couldn't find ee at your lodgings and he knew you'd want to get back.'

'Well, he needn't think I'm going back with him! I'd sooner walk.'

'Now, Lizzie!' Mary pleaded. 'He's come all this way out of kindness. You can't just leave'n outside without a word! Go and ask'n in for a cup of tea!'

Eliza's mouth set in a stubborn line. 'You ask'n if you must! He didn't give much thought to me when he bought a ticket to go to America!'

Mary sighed. 'Us'll both ask'n, then. I don't want hard feelings between us and Simon Tucker.' She rose from her place at the table, then waited until Eliza got up, too, and followed her grudgingly to the door. The boys rushed to the window to watch, nudging one another in anticipation, but Reuben hacked into the loaf for another slice of bread and sat on, unmoved.

Outside, Simon was standing at his pony's head, holding the bridle. He looked uncertain when the two women approached, then doffed his cap politely to Mary.

'Won't ee come in, Simon?' she asked him. 'Us be just having breakfast. I'm sure you must be wanting a cup of tea.'

He shook his head. 'I'm wanting Lizzie more, Mrs Dark! I couldn't rest till I knew her was safe.' He turned to Eliza and his eyes were pleading. 'Won't ee come back with me now, Lizzie? I didn't mean the things I said. I can't do without ee, you know that.'

'You'll do without me well enough when you're in America!'

''Twill only be for a time! I've told ee that. We'll have a better life over there than we could ever have here. I'm only doing it for you.'

'You're doing it for yourself!'

'It's for both of us!' He looked to Mary for support. 'You understand, don't ee, Mrs Dark? You've got sons of your own so you know how hard it is for a young man to get started in this country.'

'Perhaps I do,' Mary said. 'But I know a lot less about the chances in America! 'Tain't me you have to convince, Simon, 'tis Lizzie here. I'd be sorry to see her go so far from me but I'd never hold her back if 'tis what her wants. Now — be ee coming in for that cup of tea or not?'

Simon hesitated, his eyes on Eliza. 'I thought you'd want to get back for your job,' he said, 'but I'll come in, if you like.'

'No!' Eliza suddenly made up her mind. 'I'm ready to go if you are. 'Twill be quicker than walking.' She would not look at him when he gave her a hand up into the trap and she edged away when he took his seat beside her. He shook the reins to get the pony moving and smiled at her but she sat stiff-backed, staring straight ahead.

'Come and see us again when you've more time!' Mary called after them. Simon waved but Eliza stayed rigid and Mary felt despondent when she went back into the kitchen.

'There's trouble brewing there,' she said.

Reuben was on his feet, ready to leave. 'Could blow over. If it don't, there bain't much you can do about it, Mary. Leave 'em to settle it themselves!' He reached for his cap from the hook on the door. 'Us must be off 'cos there's work to do. Pour yerself another cup of tea and stop worrying!'

But Mary worried about Eliza all that week and was not reassured by Philip when he appeared the following Sunday. He was his usual reserved self and had not much to say about the situation between Simon and Eliza. He knew that she was upset but thought they were still seeing one another even though Simon had not changed his mind about going to America.

'If'n goes, do ee think 'twill finish it between them?' Mary asked.

Philip shrugged. 'Depends how long they'm apart and if he keeps in touch. Once he's over there where everything's new he could forget Lizzie altogether.'

'Or Lizzie could find somebody else!'

Philip looked away. ''Twould take a special sort of chap to turn Lizzie from Simon Tucker, the way her feels about'n now.'

'She hardly gived'n the time of day when he fetched her last week!'

Philip smiled wryly. 'But she still went with'n!'

Mary could see that he was having difficulty discussing Eliza and she understood why. How much simpler things would be, she thought, if Simon Tucker disappeared for good and Eliza took up with Philip instead. He was a good, steady boy, gentle in his ways and unlikely to take Eliza away from her family.

Then a new consideration struck her. 'You haven't thought any more about joining the army, have ee, Philip?'

'I still have it in mind but I'm in no hurry. I'm biding me time, to see if summat better turns up.'

This left Mary as worried as before. Soldiers' wives followed their husbands so even Philip could not be relied upon to keep Eliza nearby. She could lose her only daughter whatever happened.

She comforted herself with the thought that George, at least, was settled in his job and would hardly leave Barum once he and Hannah were wed. He tramped home regularly each weekend, bringing his washing and taking back clean clothes and a batch of fresh baking. Every Sunday he visited Hannah, except for one memorable day when her mother and father borrowed a pony and trap and brought her to Yarnscombe for a visit instead. Mary liked them both and even Reuben remarked that they seemed decent, respectable folk. No, Mary was not worried about George. She looked to him to keep an eye on Johnny who was unpredictable with a preference for the wrong sort of companions she feared might lead him into trouble.

Almost a month went by before she heard from Eliza again. Then a letter arrived, telling her that she and Simon were coming to Yarnscombe the following Sunday so that he could say goodbye to them all before he sailed for America. She hoped that plenty of the family would be there to give him a good send-off. It was a cheerful enough letter with no hint of her earlier distress.

Mary showed it to Reuben. 'What do ee think?'

He squinted at it as his eyes were beginning to bother him for close work. 'Seems they must've made it up, then. But what's her expecting us to do — kill the fatted calf?'

'No! Just to be friendly and wish the boy well. I'll put on a good tea. Could be the last time us'll see'n.'

Reuben regarded her quizzically. 'Sounds as if you'm hoping 'twill be!'

'No!' But Mary could not disguise from herself a sneaking hope that Simon Tucker might disappear from their lives for good so that they could all settle down again.

He brought a large map of America with him and spread it on Reuben's table for Johnny and the rest of the boys who had come home to scrutinise. He showed them New York where the ship would dock and traced with his finger the long trek across America he and Jim Barrow hoped to take towards Oregon where there were forests and prairies and great stretches of virgin land just waiting for adventurers like them and Jim Barrow's cousin to open up. There would be mountains to cross and rivers to navigate but they were ready for all that and for any dangers they might meet. The Dark boys and

Mary's sons listened open-mouthed as Simon held forth about his plans for the future.

'Caw!' Johnny breathed. 'I wish I was coming with ee!'

Mary was watching Eliza who sat quietly. There was a new calm about her as if she had accepted the inevitable and had no more will to fight it. Her eyes were constantly on Simon except for once or twice when his flights of fancy became so outrageous she looked down at her clasped hands and shook her head sadly.

'So how be ee going to manage for money when you'm crossing America?' Reuben asked. ''Tis one thing to get there but a journey like you'm planning'll need a lot of cash.'

'Jim and me'll work our way across,' Simon said. 'Folks over there be only too glad to help new arrivals from the old country. Or so I'm told. Neither of us be afraid of hard work or fussy about what us'll do. 'Twill be hard at first. That's why I can't take Lizzie with me. But 'twill be worth it in the long run.'

'How long do ee think it'll take ee to get settled?' Mary enquired.

'Oh — a couple of years — p'raps three — '

'Years?' Eliza stood up so suddenly she sent her chair flying. 'You didn't tell me that!

Twelve or fifteen months you said!'

He looked embarrassed. 'One year — two — what's it matter so long's us'll be together some day?'

'It matters to me!' she cried and looked as if she might burst into tears.

Alarmed, Mary went to her. 'Come on, Lizzie!' she said. 'Us'll get the tea on the table. They can shift their old map some place else. 'Tis all talk,' she comforted as she bustled her daughter away. 'If things don't work out for'n, he'll be back home again before you've hardly missed'n.'

'But he didn't tell me!' Eliza mourned. 'He led me on and didn't tell me the truth!'

'Well, try not to take it so hard! You don't want'n to remember ee with a sour face. You'm usually so lively.'

To Mary's relief, things became more cheerful over tea and afterwards Reuben astonished her by producing a bottle of port and insisting that they should all drink a toast to Simon's success and good health in America. He rarely drank himself so she knew he must have bought the bottle especially for the occasion and she felt grateful for his forethought. By the time the young couple were ready to leave, Eliza's face was flushed and her eyes were bright. She smiled and waved when the family came out to cheer them on their way and Mary sighed in thankfulness.

She took Reuben's arm as they made their way back into the house and gave it a gentle squeeze. 'Thankee, Reuben,' she whispered. ''Twas good of ee to get the port for Simon.'

'I did it more for Lizzie's sake and yourn, Mary,' he said. 'If that young rogue lets her down, he'll have me to answer to. Lizzie's always been a good maid, not like some.'

Mary knew he was thinking of Emily. They had not seen her since she and Sam had brought the children to Yarnscombe. Mary hoped to persuade Reuben to visit them one day as they had an open invitation but she knew from past experience that he could not be pushed. He had to find his own way through his problems. Yet he could still surprise her as he had done that day and she felt a rush of affection for him. Everything would surely be all right while she had him by her side.

News filtered through to Yarnscombe a few days later that Simon and Jim Barrow had left for Plymouth and later on that the ship had sailed. Mary knew that it would be several weeks before Eliza could hope for a letter telling her that they had arrived safely and feared she would be moping for Simon. She thought she might come home sometimes when she was feeling down but Eliza stayed away. It was Philip who eventually brought the news that the two young men were in America and planning to take the railroad through Pennsylvania on the first lap of their journey.

'What about Lizzie?' Mary asked. 'How's her taking it?'

Philip hesitated. 'She don't say much — keeps to her room a lot writing letters. Trouble is, she can't post 'em till Simon sends her a fixed address.'

Mary shook her head. 'Tell her to come home next Sunday if her can get a lift! 'Tain't natural to be cooping herself up like that.'

Still Eliza stayed away. After several more weeks Mary could stand the waiting no longer. 'Summat's up,' she told Reuben. 'If her don't come home this Sunday I'll have to go down to Torrington to see her. If you bain't going that way, I'll ask Bert to take me the next time he's buying leather from Chapple's yard.'

'Joey'll have to fetch wood from the saw mills next week,' Reuben told her. 'He could drop ee in the town and pick ee up again on his way back. What will ee do, call in at Vaughan's?'

Mary frowned. 'Lizzie mightn't like me to hinder her at work. They'm usually busy this time of year, stocking up for Christmas.'

However, when Eliza did not come home that Sunday, Mary decided she would have to take the chance of a lift to Torrington with Joey. She set off in the wagon with him the following Thursday and went straight to Vaughan's as soon as he left her in the town.

The glove factory was humming with activity and upstairs in the machine room, Meg Conibeare greeted her with astonishment. 'Mary? What be you doing here?' she asked.

Mary was scanning the lines of busy women for Eliza. 'I was in town so I thought I'd call in on Lizzie.'

'Oh!' Meg hesitated. 'Lizzie bain't been in for a couple of weeks, her's been so sick.'

'Sick?' Mary felt a cold hand clutch her heart.

'I told her to take some time off till her was over the worst of it,' Meg said. 'I thought you'd know.'

Mary shook her head. 'I've been worried about her 'cos her didn't come home. What — what be the matter, then?'

Meg's eyes were sympathetic. 'The usual, Mary. Her's in the family way. The first three months are always the worst but I've told her the job'll be waiting when her feels well enough to come back.'

For a moment, Mary felt so sick herself she thought she might faint. Then she managed to mumble, 'That's good of ee, Meg. I'll — go to her then and see how her be.'

She stumbled to the door, down the stairs and out into the street where she took a deep breath of the cold air to steady herself. Eliza was pregnant and hadn't told her! Why hadn't Philip said, or hadn't she told him, either? She felt a surge of hatred against Simon Tucker who had gone off to America so unconcernedly, leaving Eliza in such a state. But perhaps he didn't know yet if Eliza couldn't contact him.

Then another more disturbing thought struck her. Whatever was Reuben going to say?

16

'Why didn't you tell me?' Mary demanded.

Eliza was sitting on the bed in her lodging house room. There was a pad on her knee, a pen in her hand and an inkwell on the little table beside her.

She did not answer but looked down with a frown at what she had just written. Her face was pale and Mary thought it seemed thinner while her usually tidy hair was escaping in wisps. 'Be ee writing to Simon?' she asked more gently. 'Have ee told'n about the baby?'

Eliza shook her head. 'What'd be the use?'

'The use? It might bring'n back again!'

'No! He must do what he wants to do. Plenty of time to tell'n about the baby when it happens.' She stared at her mother. 'Who told you, anyhow?'

'Meg Connibeare — made me feel a proper fule! Your own mother and the last to know! How could ee, Lizzie?'

Eliza grimaced. 'I didn't want to shame ee with Pa Dark, knowing how he was with Em'ly.'

'But you must've known us'd find out sometime!'

'I was putting it off.'

'Oh, Lizzie!' Mary sat beside her on the bed and put an arm round her. 'There be a lot worse things than having a baby! 'Tain't as if you bain't engaged to Simon!'

'But what'll Gran say? You know how her was when Aunt Becky ran off without telling her!'

'Your Gran'll come round. They all will.' Mary looked around the room with distaste. 'But you can't bide boxed up in here all on your own! Why don't ee come back this afternoon with Joey and me and bide a while till you'm past the sickness. Us don't need to tell Pa Dark why, or not yet. I'll break it to'n later on when I catch'n in a good mood.'

'I can't come back! Simon wouldn't know where to write if I went to Yarnscombe.'

'Do'n write regular, then?'

'I've only had two letters,' Eliza confessed. 'They take a long time coming and he's travelling. But he writes when he can.'

Mary clicked her tongue in exasperation. 'I don't know why he went off in the first place, specially leaving ee the way you be! How be ee managing for money if you'm not working? Meg said you was taking time off.'

'Just for a week or two till I'm over the worst. Simon left some money with me that's supposed to be towards my passage to

America. I'll use that if I have to.'

'By the time you go, there'll be two of ee! Oh, Lizzie, I never thought you'd be so foolish!'

'I'm sorry. But he was going away! I couldn't let'n go without — ' Eliza's voice broke into a sob. 'He was so sweet and gentle. I never thought I'd get caught — not so quick.'

Mary pulled her closer. 'I know. 'Tis hard to refuse 'em when they mean so much. But if you won't come home with me you must take care and eat proper meals for the baby's sake. And you must send a message by Philip if you ever want me to come down. Have ee told Philip yet?'

Eliza shook her head. 'I think he guesses but he hasn't said. I didn't want'n to know in case he blamed Simon.'

'There'll be more'n Philip'll do that!' Mary said. 'The boys'll be ready to take a horse whip to'n when they find out!'

'Then you mustn't tell 'em! I'm as much to blame as he is. Don't tell 'em yet, Ma!'

'You won't be able to hide it much longer. Still, you should be all right for a while. But promise me you'll come home for Christmas Day. They'll all wonder if you don't.'

Eliza hesitated, then nodded slowly. 'Just for Christmas, then. I don't want to be away from here for more'n a couple of days in case there's a letter.'

With that Mary had to be satisfied. But she was preoccupied when she travelled back to Yarnscombe alongside Joey. The wagon was weighted down with the planks of wood he had bought at the sawmills so their progress through the deep lanes was slower.

'Lizzie all right, then?' Joey asked.

'Moping a bit for Simon but her's coming home for Christmas.'

'Good. There won't be so many of us this year. Walter's Annie's near her time and Harriet's expecting, or so Henry told me when I was in Barum. They won't be coming. The rest of 'em'll be there, I reckon. James wanted to bring the little maid he's courting but her can't get time off from her place. Seems they'm expecting a housefull. What's George doing?'

'Hannah can only get the afternoon off so he's going over to Dolton to her folks.' Mary glanced at Joey. 'What about you? When be you going to bring a sweetheart home?'

He laughed. 'Plenty of time for me! You and Dad have enough to be going on with already!'

Which is true enough, Mary thought. All these weddings and sweetheartings and all these grandchildren for Reuben! Soon she would be a grandmother herself and would probably have to help Eliza in bringing up her baby.

Her heart was heavy but she tried to answer Joey cheerfully. 'Well, however many come there'll be room round your Dad's table and plenty to eat. I've made the plum puddings and enough mincemeat for dozens of pies. There's a side of pork salted and a couple of geese promised from Atherington. I've told the boys to gather in some holly to deck the place up a bit. 'Tis cold enough for snow so us could have a white Christmas and then the sledges'll come out again.'

Joey chuckled. 'Remember the time Dad gave ee a ride down the church field? James and me guessed then that he was sweet on ee!'

'Get away with ee, Joe!' But Mary blushed. ' 'Twas just a bit of fun, that's all!'

'Turned out all right, though, din't it, for all of us? Best thing Dad ever did, to marry ee after Mother died.'

This was the first time any of Reuben's children had commented favourably on his second marriage. Mary's spirits rose at once. 'Thankee, Joe,' she said. ' 'Twas the best thing I did, too. Your dad's been very good to me and mine.'

But what will he say when he hears about

Lizzie? she wondered. What will Mother say? She had tried to reassure her daughter that they would come round eventually but she was not very confident that they would.

She pushed the thought from her. There was no need for anybody to know yet. Christmas came first. She had a lot more to do for it and did not want anything to spoil the family festivities. When Reuben enquired after Eliza she said only that she was missing Simon but would be home for Christmas Day. After that she threw herself into her preparations. This could be the last Christmas we're all together, she realised with a pang, so I must make it the best ever.

Most of the boys walked home on Christmas Eve, Charley from Westcott and James, George, Tommy and Johnny from Barum. They were greeted with whoops of delight from Joey, Albert and Fred who insisted on dragging them out again to go carol singing around the village. They protested that they could not walk another step but it seemed that Johnny was needed to accompany them on his penny whistle. When they came back they were merry as several people had invited them in and pressed them to take a glass or two of cider.

Sally arrived more sedately the next morning as she had hired a pony and trap. In anticipation, Reuben had laid in extra feed and made more room for stabling in his barn. The last to arrive were Philip and Eliza and Mary was beginning to feel anxious when they appeared just before noon as she was basting the pork and the geese in the side oven.

'You've never walked, have ee?' she asked for they both looked weary and pinched from the cold.

'Only the last couple of miles,' Philip said. 'We got a lift nearly to Westcott. 'Twas slippy underfoot coming up the lane, though.'

'Well, get your things off and come nearer the fire!' Mary urged. 'You look frozen, the pair of ee! Your father'll soon be back from church, Philip, with your brothers. Sally's here already.'

'I saw Johnny outside, seeing to her pony,' Eliza said. 'But where's George?'

'Halfway to Dolton by now. He's spending the day with Hannah's folks and coming back tonight. They'll all be glad to see ee, Lizzie.' She looked more closely at her daughter. 'How be feeling now?'

Eliza flushed. 'I'm all right!' she said sharply. ''Twas just a bit of cold I had.'

Mary could have bitten her tongue. 'Well, why don't ee take a jug of hot water upstairs and have a wash before dinner? That'll warm ee.' She filled a tin jug from the steaming kettle over the fire, wrapped it in a towel so that Eliza would not burn herself and handed it to her. 'You'm sharing with Sally in your old room,' she said. 'Her's just gone up so you can have a word with her before the boys all come in.'

She watched Eliza walk out of the kitchen and was turning back to her basting when Philip said, 'I reckon 'tis a bit more'n cold that's ailing Lizzie. Have her told ee yet?'

Mary was taken aback. 'What do ee mean? What's her been saying, Philip?'

'Nort to me. I heard it from one of the maids at Vaughan's. They all know there her's in the fam'ly way.'

Mary drew a breath of dismay. 'Well, don't let on to the rest of 'em!' she begged. 'Lizzie told me when I went to see her but her don't want your dad or the boys to know yet. I just pray Simon Tucker'll come back and marry her.'

'If he don't,' Philip said, 'there be one here that will. I'd never stand by and let Lizzie be the butt of a lot of loose talk.'

Mary stared at him. 'You'd take on another chap's baby?'

'I'd take on Lizzie's if her'd have me.'

Mary shook her head in amazement. 'You'm a good man, Philip. Not many would go so far. Lizzie's a lucky maid to have ee for a friend.'

More than a friend, she thought, as she read the steadfastness in Philip's eyes and realised just how much he cared for her daughter. He would not let her down. It might be all for the best if Simon Tucker stayed in America and never sent for Eliza. Relief flooded through Mary with the hope that she might not lose her after all and she returned to her basting feeling more contented than she had done for weeks.

Then Reuben and the boys all came home from church and the kitchen became full of their noise and banter until she shooed a couple of them out to fetch water from the pump and coal and logs for the fire. Sally and Eliza came downstairs to help lay the table and light a row of candles in the middle of it while Reuben fussed about making a bowl of punch. Mary's mother, who was joining them for dinner, arrived red-nosed from the cold and had to be warmed up with the first taste of it.

At last everybody was present and all seated around the festive table under the branches of holly and ivy the boys had hung from the beams. Mary felt a glow of satisfaction as she looked at them all. Their faces were rosy in the candlelight which made even Eliza look less wan. Reuben was waiting, impatient to carve so Sally helped Mary to lift out the heavy baking pan from the side oven and everybody cheered when the sizzling pork and geese were carried to the table. Eliza passed the plates to her stepfather to fill while Mary unhooked the big pot hanging over the fire in which two plum puddings in their cloths sat atop the steaming vegetables. She left them on a tray to keep warm while she doled out the vegetables. Sally went round with the potatoes and parsnips until everybody was served. Mary was perspiring and flushed by then but had hardly time to finish her own helping before the boys were passing up their plates for more.

'Leave room for the puddings and pies!' she warned them, glad that they had such good appetites, especially the young ones who were working away and rarely so well fed.

Another cheer went up when she carried the puddings to the table and fetched a large bowl of clotted cream from the cool of the larder. There was hardly a crumb left between so many. A plate of mincepies went as well and a large box of sugary sweets Sally had brought as her contribution.

'That was the best Christmas dinner I ever ate!' Johnny said and patted his stomach. He fished in his pocket for his penny whistle and began playing 'Good King Wenceslas.'

They all started to sing and when Mary looked at Reuben she saw that he had joined in, too. Perhaps Christmas might, after all, be the time to tell him about Eliza, he was in such a good mood. But she did not want anything to spoil his pleasure. Later, she thought. There's no need for anybody to know just yet.

After the meal, when the women had cleared the table, the boys brought the cards out and began playing gin rummy for halfpennies. It was not long before a roar went up that Johnny was cheating, using a few tricks he had learned from his gypsy friends. Reuben was brought in to adjudicate and banned Johnny from taking part unless he played fair.

Mrs Pugsley was helping Mary and the girls to wash the dishes. She shook her head. 'Your Johnny don't improve, Mary!' she commented. 'He'll get hisself in trouble one of these days, you mark my words! He never should've gone to Barum, working in that brewery!'

'He's good with the hosses,' Mary protested, 'and he's earning more now — promised another rise after he's seventeen in March.'

''Tis a good job George be so steady and that young Albert takes after'n.' Mrs Pugsley turned her eyes on Eliza. 'But you bain't looking too good, Lizzie. Have ee heard from that young man of yourn lately?'

Eliza's face reddened so Mary broke in to rescue her. 'Simon writes regular when he's somewhere he can post a letter,' she said, noticing that her mother's shrewd glance was travelling over Eliza's body. When it lingered on the bulge under her apron, she added hastily, 'Us be pretty well finished here now, Mother. So why don't ee go into the sitting room where 'tis quieter? I'll bring ee in a nice glass of port.'

Another roar from the table made Mrs Pugsley put down the cloth she was using in disgust. 'I'll get a splitting headache if I bide in this racket!' she said. 'Thankee, Mary. I'll be glad of a glass of port.'

Mary caught Eliza's eye and read her relief as Mrs Pugsley left them. 'The port'll send her to sleep till her goes over to Bert and Anne's,' Mary confided. 'They've asked her for tea with Becky and Jack and Lou's family.'

She poured out a generous drink and took it into Jane's little sitting room where her mother had already made herself comfortable on the sofa. She took an appreciative sniff of her port, then looked slyly at Mary. 'Lizzie looks as if her could be in the fam'ly way,' she remarked.

Mary tried to laugh. 'You'm imagining things!'

'Us'll see! I've watched too many go that way in me time. I hope for your sake her bain't, your man being so strict and God-fearing, Mary. 'Tis a crying shame young Tucker went off and left her the way he did.'

'Lizzie'll be all right. No need to worry, Mother! No need to start spreading rumours, neither!'

Mrs Pugsley looked affronted. 'Nobody could accuse me of being a gossip! 'Specially not about me own fam'ly!'

First Philip, Mary thought, and all the girls at Vaughan's and now Mother! Too many people were getting to know already. She felt worried when she went back to the kitchen. The girls were finishing the washing up and the boys had tired of cards. They were clamouring to pick sides for pass the button. Joey had been nominated as one captain and Philip as the other and they were already facing one another across the long table.

'One girl in each team,' Joey said. 'That's fair!'

'Lizzie, then!' Philip called before his brother could draw breath and he beckoned Eliza to sit next to him.

'Over here then, Sal!' Joey said.

Philip chose Charley, James and Albert, leaving Joey with Fred and Johnny. 'We're one short,' he complained. 'You'll have to join in, Dad.'

But Reuben had already settled down with his pipe and could not be budged. So Mary, who had come to the table with a button for the game was captured, protesting, and pulled down next to Johnny.

'Us've got the button!' Joey gloated. 'So us'll start.'

'That bain't fair!' Charley yelled. 'You should've tossed for it!'

'Too late!' Joey said. 'Hands down!'

The hands of his team disappeared under the table top and there followed a lot of shuffling and giggling as the button was passed from one to another. 'Hands up!' Joey called and up came five pairs of clenched fists.

Albert was the first of Philip's team to try to find the button. He did well at first, saying 'Take it away!' to most of the hands he thought had nothing hidden until he was left with only three. Then, 'Tip it!' he cried and tapped Johnny's left fist.

Johnny jeered as he showed his empty palm.

'One to us!' Freddy cried, revealing the button.

The hands of Joey's team went down again, and again, three times until it was Philip's turn to find the button. Mary had it and, although she tried to keep a straight face, she lost it to him.

Then she had to try to get it back so she watched carefully as his team began passing it along under the table top. Eliza was sitting between Philip and Charley and Mary could tell from her expression that more was going on out of sight than just the passing of the button. She jerked once or twice and blushed.

'Board's the button!' Charley cried for the button was on the floor.

He scrabbled for it and the game continued. Mary could see that Eliza was uncomfortable so she tried to get the button back but guessed wrongly for Philip had it.

'One to us!' he cried. 'Hands down again!'

'No!' Eliza stood up suddenly. 'This is a silly game! I don't want to play any more.'

They all stared at her. 'Why?' Philip asked. 'What's the matter, Lizzie?'

Johnny laughed. 'Charley was tickling her under the table!' he said. 'I seed'n.'

'No, I wadn',' Charley said and grinned sheepishly. 'I was just trying to pass her the button.'

'You had a funny way of doing it!' Eliza snapped and walked away from the table.

There was an awkward silence until Mary stood up, too. 'You won't need me now you'm equal numbers,' she said and followed Eliza out of the kitchen into the sitting room where Mrs Pugsley was already fast asleep. Eliza was in tears.

'Now, Lizzie!' Mary rebuked her. 'A little thing like that ain't worth crying about!'

'But don't ee see?' Eliza sobbed. 'Charley'd never have done what he did before — '

'Before what?'

'Before I fell for the baby! He was feeling up my legs. He must think I'm no good now — just a common slut!'

'But Charley don't know about the baby! Do'n?'

'He must've heard somehow. 'Tis all over Torrington and he's often in town from Westcott. I feel so ashamed! I used to like Charley.'

'And he likes you. All the Dark boys like ee, Lizzie. They'd never wish ee harm. Why only today, Philip said — ' She broke off.

'Philip? What's Philip been saying? Do he know, too?'

'He's heard summat. But he'll stand by ee, Lizzie, like us all will.'

'I don't need anybody to stand by me! I've got Simon and he won't let me down.'

''Course he won't!' Mary gave her a hug.

'But he ain't here so us'll have to think what's best to do till'n turns up again. Be ee back working at Vaughan's?'

'I started last week, they was so busy before Christmas.'

'Then you'm all right for a bit. But once you get nearer your time you'll have to come home, Lizzie. 'Tis no good thinking you can have a baby in that lodging house and look after'n proper.'

'What if Pa Dark won't have me?'

'Then he won't have me, neither!' Mary said firmly. 'But come on, m'dear! 'Tis Christmas and I'm sure Charley didn't mean to upset ee.' Mrs Pugsley suddenly gave a loud snore making them both start. Mary smiled. 'Put on your jacket and bonnet and walk your Gran down to Uncle Bert's. They'm expecting her for tea and 'twill give ee both a breath of air.' She shook Mrs Pugsley's shoulder. 'Time to wake up, Mother! Lizzie here'll walk ee down the hill.'

'Can I stay with Gran at Uncle Bert's?' Eliza asked. 'I haven't seen 'em for a while.'

'Well, they'll have a housefull and they bain't expecting ee —— '

'I'd rather,' Eliza said, 'if you don't mind. I'll come back in time to see George.'

Mary realised that she did not want to face all the Dark boys again or to risk Johnny's teasing. So she nodded. 'Pa Dark and me be asked over for a Christmas drink later on, so us'll fetch ee back then.'

The button game was still in progress when Mary, Eliza and Mrs Pugsley went back to the kitchen. If the others were surprised when Eliza put on her outdoor clothes to escort her grandmother down the hill, nobody commented. It was only later, after they had all had tea and Mary found herself alone with Reuben on their way to Bert and Anne's cottage, that anything was said.

'What was up with Lizzie this afternoon?' he asked. ' 'Tain't like her to get so upset over nothing.'

Mary hesitated. ' 'Tis only natural. Her's missing Simon. Once her knows he's settled, her'll stop worrying.'

Reuben grunted. 'Then 'twill be your turn to start, if her goes off to America with'n!'

It's my turn to worry already, Mary thought, because I know I should tell you about the baby before somebody else does. But I can't find the words.

17

Christmas passed and the new year roared in, wild and stormy. Although she was not usually superstitious, Mary felt this was an omen, that 1883 was going to bring trouble. Reuben was run off his feet, repairing damaged roofs and barns and wrecked farm gates so she still did not find the right opportunity to tell him about Eliza.

Then her worst fears about the year were confirmed when a message came from Barum that Walter's Annie had lost her baby, a little boy who had lived only a few hours. Annie was distraught and Walter so upset he had not felt able to come to tell his father. He and Annie had been married for almost ten years and this was their first child.

'You must go and see 'em, Reuben,' Mary said. 'Walter'll need ee now.'

Reuben pulled at his beard. ''Tis more a woman's job,' he muttered. 'Will ee come with me, Mary?'

They went by horse and trap the next day and found a sad household. Annie was in bed, looking deathly pale and she burst in tears when she saw them. She clung on to

Mary's hand as if she would never let it go, reminding Mary of Jane when she had lost her baby.

'I wanted a boy for Walter,' Annie sobbed.

'There'll be time yet,' Mary comforted.

But Walter had taken his father downstairs and told him in confidence of the doctor's warning that Annie was unlikely to bear another child. Reuben was cast down by the news and gloomy on the drive back to Yarnscombe. Mary sat silent beside him, aware that Jane was in both their thoughts. She was also worrying about Eliza, wondering how she would fare. She wanted to share their worries but realised it would be too cruel to tell him that she would soon have a grandchild when he had just lost one of his own.

So the opportunity receded again and it was over a month later that Reuben came home late for his tea with a face like thunder. He flung his cap on to the table and glared at her. 'Why've ee been hiding things from me, Mary?' he demanded.

Mary's heart lurched. 'What — what things?' she faltered.

'Things ever man Jack in Torrington seems to know about your Lizzie! Joey and me've been down to the saw mills for wood. How do ee think us felt to hear the men there, sniggering behind our backs? 'Twasn't till Joey faced 'em that us found out!'

Mary held on to the table as her knees had suddenly weakened. 'I was going to tell ee — ' she began but he interrupted angrily.

'So how long have ee known? How long have ee been making a fule of me?'

' 'Twasn't like that, Reuben — '

'How long, woman?'

Mary flinched. 'Since — ' Her voice broke. 'Since — just before Christmas.'

'Christmas! Hah!' He gave an ironic laugh. 'Now us finds out! Now us knows why Lizzie got herself so worked up over Charley! Her must've let Simon Tucker do a lot more than just tickle her!'

'That bain't fair, Reuben!'

'Fair? After I've brought her up like one of me own and now can't look folks in the eye? I've always kept a God-fearing, respectable house and won't have it smirched by that young baggage! So you can tell your Lizzie to keep away from here!'

Mary gasped. 'You can't mean that, Reuben?'

'I meant it before and I mean it again! I'd never have let Em'ly back in this house if it hadn't been for you and your wheedling ways!'

'You wanted to see your grandchildren,'

Mary reminded him, 'just like I'll want to see mine!'

'Then you can see Lizzie's brat some place else!'

'But her's engaged to Simon Tucker! He's sure to send for her soon — '

'Young Tucker?' Reuben sneered. 'Her won't see him again — not when he finds out there'll be two mouths to feed! He's away making his fortune and won't want to be dragged down by the likes of Lizzie! He's got his eye on the main chance, has Simon Tucker!'

Because Reuben was voicing her own fears, Mary stared at him in dismay. She had not expected him to be so hard. Disapproving, yes, but not so cold and unbending or so cynical about Simon. Suppose Simon did not send for Eliza and she turned to Philip instead? Mary hardly dared to imagine how Reuben might react to that.

She licked her lips nervously, trying to find something to say that would pacify him. She was saved by Joey, Freddy and Albert coming in for their tea and when she caught Joey's eye she saw him take in the situation.

'Fire could do with a couple of logs,' he said. 'You fetch some in, Bertie, while I check over these invoices with Dad. Seems to me us've been charged for more planks than us've unloaded.'

He spread the bills on to the table in front of his father who sat down with a frown and began examining them. Mary escaped to start dishing up the meat and vegetables for their tea, aware that things could not be left as they were. But she had lived with Reuben for long enough to know that she would have to give him time and would need to move carefully if she was going to persuade him to help Eliza.

He hardly spoke over tea and went out straight afterwards to re-check the wood they had bought. Albert, always eager to help his father, followed with the oil lamp, leaving Mary with Joey and Fred. She was clearing away the dishes when Joey put a hand on her arm.

He looked embarrassed. 'I just want ee to know us don't think no worse of Lizzie,' he said. 'I gived one of them chaps at the sawmills a bloody nose today and I'd've gived Simon Tucker a worse one if I could've got hold of'n.'

'He'd best not show his face round here again!' Fred said stoutly.

'Do ee all know, then?' Mary asked. 'Even Albert?'

Joey shook his head. 'I only told Fred — thought it best you should tell Albert — and George and Johnny when they come home, seeing as they'm Lizzie's brothers. The rest of 'em'll get to know soon enough.' He hesitated. 'Father's taking it hard. But he's always had a soft spot for Lizzie. Us all have. The Dark boys'll stick up for her, never fear!'

Mary felt so touched she could have wept. 'You've been just as good brothers to her as her own,' she said. 'Lizzie knows that. Her'll come through this bit of trouble even if Simon Tucker lets her down. 'Tis just — your father — ' She broke off, not wanting to speak against Reuben to his son.

Joey looked at her keenly. 'What's'n been saying?'

'Well — you know your dad. He's a good man, but strict, like he was with Em'ly — '

'He bain't turning Lizzie out, too?' Joey scowled.

'No. Leastways, he threatened. But I 'spect he'll come round.'

'He'd better! None of us'd stand for that! We're men now and too big for'n to take his belt to us!'

Joey looked so angry, Mary was anxious. 'Don't say anything to'n!' she begged. ''Twould only make things worse. Lizzie's all right where her be for a while yet. Once her can let Simon Tucker know about the baby us can work out what's best to do. He might send for her straightaway.'

'But Lizzie can't travel the way her be now!

From what Tucker said when he was here, it could take'n a couple of years to get settled. The baby'll be walking by then!'

Mary was silent, realising that this was true. Lizzie would be her responsibility until Simon Tucker made a move and there was not much she could do without Reuben's support.

In bed that night he turned his back on her and when she snuggled up against him the way she always did, his spine stiffened. She knew then that it was too soon. She pretended not to notice and yawned sleepily, closing her eyes. Gradually he relaxed against her as he drifted into sleep but she lay wide awake, wondering how she could help Eliza if Reuben did not change his mind.

Her only other hope was her mother who would also have to be told so Mary called on her the next day. Mrs Pugsley regarded her with suspicion. 'What be you doing here on a Wednesday?' she asked. ''Tis always your baking day.'

'I've made a start and left the girl to keep an eye on the oven.' Mary sat down. 'I've something to tell ee, Mother, before you hear it from some busybody.'

Mrs Pugsley sat down, too and folded her arms. 'So which one of 'em's in trouble — Johnny or Lizzie?'

Mary flinched. 'Why've ee always got it in so for Johnny? He's working and doing his best!'

''Tis Lizzie, then. In the fam'ly way, be her? I spotted that at Christmas.'

Mary sighed. 'I should've told ee then — and told Reuben, too. 'Twould've saved a lot of trouble.'

'So what's her going to do? Have her told Simon Tucker?'

'Not yet. She's waiting for an address to write to.'

Mrs Pugsley sniffed. 'I had me doubts about that young man from the start. Too cocksure for his own good! When's the baby due?'

'Sometime in May. Lizzie's still working but her won't be able to stay in that lodging house when her time comes. I hope her'll be able to come to me if Reuben'll have her.'

'What if he won't? He's a hard man, your Reuben!'

'I can usually talk'n round. Only I wondered — if I can't — ' She looked hopefully at her mother.

Mrs Pugsley shook her head. 'No! I've done me best for you and yourn, Mary! I had ee all here when John died and then you upped and left me soon's you thought fit. I'm too old to go through all that again. Lizzie's made her bed so her'll have to lie in it! If Simon Tucker bain't man enough to marry her, her'll have to manage on her own, like all the other silly maids who get caught. You gived her too much her own way, Mary, like you did Johnny!'

Mary stood up, incensed. 'If that's what you think — '

'I do! You spoiled 'em both, letting Lizzie go to Vaughan's and Johnny to that brewery. If they've got into bad company, 'tis no use crying over spilt milk now! No use running to me for help, neither!'

'I'll go, then!' Mary said. 'Lizzie and me'll manage somehow, even if I have to go back to work to help her bring up the baby!'

She stalked out of her mother's cottage, angry and despairing. Now that her mother knew, so would all the Pugsleys and the rest of Yarnscombe. There could be no more secrecy.

That evening she took Albert aside and told him gently about Eliza. He was nearly fourteen now and growing up but he still reddened in embarrassment and could not meet Mary's eyes. He mumbled something about being sorry and escaped as soon as he could to join Joey and Fred in a game of shove halfpenny.

Mary sighed as she watched him go. Always

a placid baby, he was growing into a plump, equally placid young man who did his father's bidding without question. Reuben said he had the makings of a good carpenter but she wondered sometimes if people might not too easily take advantage of his good nature.

That could never be said of her husband! The subject of Eliza hung like a cloud between them, marring their relationship. She did not venture to bring it up again with him but told George and Johnny when they walked home from Barum together at the weekend.

She waited anxiously for their reaction and for a moment, neither of them said anything. Then, to Mary's astonishment, Johnny laughed.

George rounded on him at once. ' "Tain't funny, you fule! I hope I'd never leave Hannah in such a situation!'

'That ain't likely,' Johnny mocked, 'your Hannah's so straight laced! 'Tis Simon I'm laughing about — has his bit of fun and then buggers off to America! Good luck to'n, I say!'

'Johnny!' Mary scolded. 'How can ee talk like that about your own sister? Simon'll send for her, Lizzie knows that! 'Twill just take'n a bit of time, that's all.'

Johnny grinned. 'America's a mighty big

place to get lost in!' he warned and sauntered off.

'He don't care a fig!' Mary said, hurt and disappointed. 'I can't make'n out these days.'

'Take no notice!' George advised. 'He just tries to be clever. But what's Lizzie going to do? Will her come here to have the baby?'

Mary shook her head. 'I don't know, George. Pa Dark won't hear of it yet. I'll have to try to talk'n round.'

'Do ee want me to speak to'n?'

'No. There's plenty of time before May. A lot could happen in between.'

But they were almost into March before encouraging news came. Mary received a letter from Eliza, telling her that Simon was now in Iowa. He and Jim Barrow had been taken on at a cattle ranch not far from the Mississipi where they intended staying for a few months, working to earn enough money to continue their journey farther west. He had sent Eliza a post office address to which she could write.

Mary was so relieved, she read the letter to Reuben who listened without comment. 'He means to do the right thing by her, you can see that now!' she said. 'But I'd best get down to Torrington to make sure Lizzie writes to'n to tell'n about the baby. 'Tain't no use waiting till 'tis born.' She looked at Reuben.

'Be there anything you want me to say to her?'

He shrugged. 'What should there be?'

'I thought you might've changed your mind about letting her come here.'

'No.'

Mary took a deep breath. 'Then when Lizzie's time comes, you won't find me here, neither! I shall go to Torrington to be with her and I'll get me old job back at Vaughan's to keep us both till Simon sends for her or Lizzie can manage on her own.' She stared at Reuben defiantly.

His eyes darkened. 'You'd never shame me like that, woman!'

'I would! My mind's made up, too. If you cut off my daughter like you cut off your own, you'll be cutting me off as well!'

'Then you needn't think you can come crawling back here when Lizzie goes off to America!'

'I wouldn't come back, Reuben! If I go, I go to stay.'

They confronted one another, eye to eye, and Mary would not let him out-stare her. Her heart was thumping but she was determined not to be brow beaten. At last his eyes flickered and he turned from her with a grunt.

'Have it your own way, then!' he muttered.

'You mean — ' Mary was shocked. ' — you'd let me go to Torrington?'

'Don't seem I could stop ee, do it?'

'But — ' Mary's head was in a whirl at the turn of events. ' — how would ee all manage without me?'

'Us managed before. I daresay Betty Harding'd come back as housekeeper if I asked her.'

'Reuben — you wouldn't!'

He shrugged. 'A man without a wife has to make do with what'n can get!'

Mary's face flamed. 'Is that why you married me, after Jane died — 'cos I was all you could get? The truth's coming out now, I see! 'Tis a good job I'll be leaving ee, then!' She flung away from him and made for the door.

Before she reached it he came after her and swung her round to face him. There was an agonised expression on his face. 'No!' he cried. 'You know why I married ee, Mary. 'Twas 'cos I was burning to have ee for wife. Us lit a fine flame between us then that ain't quite burned out yet. It still flickers in me when I come home from work and find ee waiting, or when I turn to ee for comfort in bed of a night.'

'Oh, Reuben!' Mary put her arms round him. 'Why be us quarrelling, then? I don't want to leave ee! 'Tis just I'm so worried about Lizzie. Her's all alone. I have to be at her side when her gives birth!'

He sighed heavily. 'I see I can't refuse ee, Mary. Never could! Best go to her, then. Tell her to come here when her time comes but after that her must shift for herself. What Lizzie's done goes against me conscience but p'raps 'tis me Christian duty to help her through.'

It was a concession of sorts and Mary was grateful for it, just as she was happy to thank him that night in bed. As she was drifting off to sleep, cradled in the crook of his arm, she seemed to sense Jane nearby, smiling in sympathetic understanding.

The wagon was not going to Torrington for a while but Mary was able to get a lift from Bert a few days later. She found Eliza looking blooming, happy now that she had an address for Simon and prettier than ever in the full smock she had made to hide her pregnancy. She listened to Reuben's grudging invitation with a wry smile and said she could probably fix herself up with one of her married friends at Vaughan's if that would make life easier for her mother.

'You'm not to think of it!' Mary said. 'You'm coming home now he's said you can. Have ee written to Simon and told'n yet?'

'I've written,' Eliza said, 'but I haven't told'n and I don't intend to till I have the baby safe. 'Spose something happened and I lost it like poor Annie lost hers? Simon might think I'd been having'n on.'

'Oh, Lizzie! You should've warned Simon! 'Twill be a shock when he knows.'

But Eliza was adamant and Mary could not persuade her. She did manage to extract a promise that she would come home a few days before the baby was due as Philip had said he would hire a pony and trap to bring her. After that, it was just a question of waiting.

May came in warm and sunny and the roses were budding in the little patch of garden at the back of the house that Mary had claimed for her own when the pony and trap arrived unexpectedly early.

'Have ee started?' Mary cried, alarmed to see that Eliza was already in pain. 'Why didn't ee come sooner?'

'I must've reckoned wrong — thought 'twould be next week.' Eliza clutched at her back and gave a moan.

'Help me get her upstairs, Philip!' Mary ordered. 'Then fetch Ma Shaddick! Tell her 'tis urgent! You should've come sooner!' she scolded as she and Philip helped Eliza to bed.

Her pains were coming so fast she was

clearly well into her labour and Mary was thankful that Reuben and the boys were working in Atherington and safely out of the way. She could have done without Philip, too, whose face was creased with worry when he came home with the midwife. He hovered about as anxiously as if he had been the father and kept asking, 'Will she be all right? What can I do?'

'Put the kettle on,' Mary said, 'and make us all a pot of tea! Then take yerself off for a walk and don't come back for a couple of hours! Lizzie's in good hands and doing well.'

She was proud of her daughter who bore her pain without complaint and only cried out during the last agonising push that sent her baby slithering into Ma Shaddick's waiting hands.

''Tis a boy!' the midwife cried. 'As fine a boy as I've ever seed!'

'Give'n to me!' Eliza begged and held out her arms. The sweat was shining on her face and wilting her fair hair but Mary thought she had never looked more beautiful. She smiled as she took her baby and whispered to him, 'Hello, Simon! Your daddy's going to be proud of you one day.'

But when will that day be? Mary wondered as she bent over to greet her first grandchild. His eyes were open and he seemed to stare straight at her. For a moment it was as if John was looking back at her from a long time ago and she felt a sense of shock. Then the baby yawned, squeezing his eyes shut. The moment passed but Mary knew she would always remember it.

'You can write to Simon now,' she said and was unexpectedly flooded with resentment. This was the man who would take her beautiful grandson away from her! She tried to suppress the hope that he would not send for Eliza. That would be too distressing for her. All the same, when Philip came back she greeted him warmly and sent him into the bedroom when he asked if he could see the baby. Then she watched hopefully from the doorway as he cradled her grandson and smiled down at her daughter with undisguised love in his eyes.

18

Eliza wrote to Simon the same day, sitting up in bed with a pad propped on her knees. When the Dark boys came home from work they were amazed and charmed by the baby that had arrived so unexpectedly. Even Reuben's face softened as he looked down into the crib Mary had rescued from the attic. Visitors arrived as the news spread — Mary's sisters and their families and a tight-lipped Mrs Pugsley who came out of curiosity but found her disapproval melting when she held her great-grandson in her arms.

'Well, he looks healthy enough!' she said. 'Takes after your John a bit, Mary.'

Mary smiled, hiding her fear that John's first grandson might soon be stolen from her. She busied herself during the next few days with all the tasks that had to be done for Eliza and her baby, enjoying their company while she could. She knew that Reuben would expect them to move on as soon as her daughter was on her feet again.

Eliza had already made her plans. She was going back to Torrington. While she was feeding the baby, she would follow Mary's example and take in home work from the glove factory. 'You managed,' she told her mother, 'and so will I. I won't be beholding to nobody till Simon sends for me.'

She seemed so confident, Mary did not dare to ask what she would do if he did not send. She was pinning her own trust on Philip who promised to look after Eliza when she returned to the lodging house and to send word if she ever needed her mother. He came with a pony and trap to collect her when she was fit enough to leave and Mary watched them set off together with hope in her heart.

Reuben came outside to see them go and frowned when Philip helped Eliza carefully into her seat and handed her the baby. 'Seems to me Philip's a dang sight too interested in that maid of yourn,' he growled. 'By the way he fusses over that baby you'd think he was the father. I hope he bain't thinking of making a fule of hisself if Tucker gives word!'

Mary glanced warily at her husband. 'Philip's been like a brother to Lizzie,' she said. 'Would ee mind if he wanted to be more'n that?'

'Mind?' Reuben glared at her. ''Course I'd mind if a son of mine tied hisself to a maid with another chap's bastard!'

Mary flinched. 'I don't think of little Simon

like that! And nor should you!'

'Why not? 'Tis true enough!' He swung away from her with a grunt and stumped back to the house.

'That's my grandson you'm talking about!' she called after him but he paid no heed.

Because she knew that his opinion of Eliza was the same as that of so many in the village, Mary's heart ached for her daughter. Let something good happen soon! she prayed.

But it was not until late in August that Eliza had a letter from Simon in answer to her own. He and Jim Barrow were about to move on to Nebraska, he told her, so she was not to try get in touch until he sent her another address. He seemed surprised to hear about the baby but did not question that it was his and was pleased he had such a healthy son. He suggested that she should contact his father at the family farm if she needed assistance because it would be a year or more before he was settled enough to ask her to join him. He sent her his best love and hoped that she and the baby were well.

Eliza showed the letter to her mother when she was visiting her in Torrington. 'What do ee think?' she asked.

Mary read the letter twice. It seemed to her cold and stilted but she did not say so in case she upset her daughter. 'At least you know

now where you stand,' she said. 'Have ee been to Tucker's farm?'

'No, and I'm not going! They know about the baby. 'Tis common talk round here and they've never so much as asked after us. Simon didn't get on with his father. That's why he went off to America.'

'Have ee showed his letter to Philip? What do he think about it?'

'Oh, Philip!' Eliza shook her head. 'I know what Philip thinks and what Philip wants but I won't let'n say it! 'Twouldn't be fair. I've waited for Simon and I'll go on waiting so long as I have to. He's the father of my child and the only man I've ever wanted.'

Despite her brave words, Mary thought that Eliza's confidence seemed now more like defiance and she went home feeling depressed. Even the pleasure of spending the afternoon with baby Simon had not lifted her spirits. The summer days were shortening into Autumn and she knew that some of her gloom was because George had told her that the gypsy caravans were already in the West Country and moving towards Barum for the annual fair. Each September Johnny became more excited by the tales of the horse dealers and their easy ways of making money. He was seventeen now and earning more at the brewery. She was afraid he might squander some of his money in a reckless venture that would get him into trouble.

When he did not come home with George as usual a few weeks later, she feared the worst. 'Where's Johnny?' she asked. 'Fair opening bain't till Wednesday.'

'Last I heard he was down at North Walk helping his pals set up their shooting alleys. You won't see'n this week, Ma, nor next. He'll be at the cattle market for the horse sales and at the fair every night, trying to win a prize or two.'

Mary clicked her tongue. 'I told'n to keep away from all that!' she said crossly.

She knew too much about the seductive charms of the fair — the noise and colour of it under its flaring lamps, the persuasive patter of the cheapjacks, the cries of the gypsy women entreating the gawping locals to buy from their stalls of sweetmeats or cheap jewellery and lace, and the shouting of their menfolk who took charge of the darts, the coconut shies and shooting alleys. Best of all there were the fortune tellers who lured the young girls into their caravans and spun them romantic yarns that turned their silly heads.

Yes, Mary knew all about the fair! It was on one warm, September evening there that John had first kissed her and bought her her a box of fairing. They had shared the sugary sweets away from the crowds, walking along the river bank, staring down at the dark shimmer of the Taw.

She sighed as she remembered. 'I thought you'd want to take Hannah to the fair next Saturday,' she said.

George shook his head. 'She can't get time off. Hannah and me have got better things to spend our money on, anyhow. I'll be twenty-one next birthday and us don't want to wait too long to get wed.' His eyes gleamed. 'Bill Luxton's put me in charge of a big job for the Bridge Trust, Ma — some renovating work at the Bridge Buildings. Could get me a rise.'

'You don't regret going to work for'n, then?'

'Best thing I ever did. Old Bill can't keep going for ever. I'll be in the right place to take over from'n when he gives up.'

'Albert still misses ee. You used to show'n what to do when you were out on a job.'

'He's got Joey and Fred for that! Albert'll be all right 'cos he's a Dark. I have to make my own way, Ma.'

Mary could see that George still felt some resentment against his stepfather for not regarding him in quite the same way as his own sons. Yet Reuben had given him a trade and had done his best for him.

'You'll be all right, too, George,' she told him. ''Tis only Lizzie I worry about and young Johnny. I wish I could see 'em both settled.'

But Eliza was kept waiting while Simon travelled across America and Johnny did not come home after the week of the fair or for several weeks that followed. George reported that he had failed to turn up at the brewery and that nobody knew where he was. Mary was frantic with worry and desperate for news of him until the middle of October when he arrived home one Saturday evening on horseback.

He swaggered in looking dashing in breeches and leggings, boasting how he had followed the fair around the West Country, working with the gypsy horse traders to pick their brains. He had won enough money on cards to buy a young gelding which he would sell once he had broken it in.

''Tis a start, Ma,' he said. 'Next fair time I'll buy a couple more 'cos there's money to be made in hosses.'

'But what about your job?' Mary cried. 'What did 'em say at the brewery?'

Johnny grinned. 'Jeff King growled a bit but he knew I'd come back 'cos I'd be missing the shires. He's letting me stable Prince at the yard till I sell'n and reckoned

I'd got meself a bargain. Come out and see'n, Ma! He's a bit frisky yet but old Cap'n might steady'n down.'

Prince was getting acquainted with Captain at the water trough when Mary went out to meet him. He was certainly fine looking, a sleek, glossy chestnut with a fiery eye. She moved to stroke him but Johnny restrained her. 'He bain't used to women,' he warned, 'and he's nervous yet — nearly threw me when us met a wagon on the hill coming up to Yarnscombe. Still, 'twas easier riding than walking! I'll get'n rubbed down and fed and into the barn for the night.'

'S'pose Cap'n don't take to'n?'

'Cap'n bain't fussy, be ee, old boy?' Johnny blew into Captain's nose and the old horse snorted back in recognition He was Johnny's first love, his silent confidante when the boy had so often been in trouble when he was younger.

Not that he's much better now! Mary thought as she watched her son. She wondered what Reuben would say when he discovered a strange horse in his barn. But he was remarkably tolerant, saying only that he hoped Johnny would contribute to the cost of the animal's feed if he was going to make a habit of riding home.

The year rolled on and suddenly it was

Christmas again. To Mary's relief, Reuben made a concession and let Philip bring Eliza and her baby home for the gathering on Christmas day. She had heard from Simon Tucker who had left Nebraska where he and Jim Bowden had worked for a few months and they were now heading for Oregon.

'But when's'n going to stay put?' Mary asked. The Christmas dinner had been eaten and the dishes washed and she was relaxing with some of the family around the fire. 'When's'n going to sent for ee, Lizzie? 'Tis eighteen months now since he left.'

Eliza's mouth set in a stubborn line. 'He'll send when he's ready,' she said, 'and when he sends I'll be just as ready to go!'

Philip was sitting next to her, bouncing her chuckling baby on his knee. When he heard what she said he glanced sharply at her, got up and passed the baby over to Sally. Then he walked away from the others towards the window where he stood, looking moodily out.

Reuben had been watching him playing with the baby and Mary could tell from his scowl what he has thinking. Now he left the group and joined his son. He put a hand on his arm and said something to him. Whatever it was made Philip fling off his father's hand and Mary could only guess from their furious, muttered undertones that they were quarrelling.

She knew it would be about Eliza and watched anxiously. Then Philip spat out a loud, 'No!' He swung away from Reuben and marched out of the kitchen. After a moment the door to the yard banged.

Mary bit her lip, wondering how much the others had noticed. But Sally was cooing over the baby who was seven months old now and in danger of being spoilt as the women passed him from hand to hand, from Sally to Harriet, then to Annie and finally to his great-grandmother. As for the younger Dark lads, they were all playing cards and oblivious to anything else.

So Mary went over to her husband and asked him quietly, 'What have ee been saying to Philip, Reuben?'

'Warning him, like any father would!'

'Against Lizzie?'

'Against falling into a trap! Seems the young fule's offered for her!'

Mary caught her breath. 'Offered? So what did her say?'

'Turned'n down! But he bain't giving up. He thinks Tucker'll give word and then Lizzie'll take'n on the rebound. Got'n on a long rope, your maid have!'

'But that ain't Lizzie's doing!' Mary

protested. 'Her can't help it if Philip's fond of her!'

'Hah! Lizzie could wind all my boys round her little finger — first Tommy, then Charlie, now Philip — '

'They'm like brothers to her, Reuben! 'Tis only Simon Tucker that Lizzie wants!'

'Then the sooner he sends for her, the better I'll be pleased! 'Tis unsettling Philip, having her around.'

But as the weeks went by and Eliza still waited, Mary watched her daughter's eyes beginning to lose some of their hopeful sparkle. It was not until February that the news came that Simon and Jim Bowden were at last in Oregon, settled in the centre of the state where Jim Bowden's cousin had the sheep ranch that would provide work for them both until they were ready to branch out on their own.

Eliza waved the letter triumphantly at her mother. 'And he says there'll be a place for us to live — nothing fancy but a start. And he's coming back to fetch me so's us can be wed before us sail and so's he can look after little Simon and me on the journey. I told ee, Ma! I told ee Simon wouldn't let me down!'

Mary stared at the letter, feeling astonished and dismayed. She was visiting Eliza in Torrington and had not expected such news.

'So when's 'n coming?' she asked.

'Not till the end of the year, probably September if he's saved enough for the fare. He can't say definite but he'll let me know in good time to fix the wedding.' Eliza cuddled her baby to her and gave him a smacking kiss. 'Your dada's coming, Simon!' she cried. 'Won't he be surprised to see you'm such a big, fine boy!'

Little Simon laughed, caught up in her excitement. But he quickly wriggled free because he knew that his granny would have a bag of sweets for him in the deep pocket of her skirt.

When he scrambled over and came fumbling for them, Mary asked, 'Have ee told Philip Simon's coming back?'

Eliza's face clouded. 'I've told'n but he said he'll believe it when it happens. Why's he got it in so for Simon?'

'You should know that better'n me! Pa Dark said Philip made ee an offer.'

'But I told'n all along 'twas no use! Even if Simon didn't come back I wouldn't have wed Philip just to give my baby a name! 'Twas different for you, Ma, left with the three of us. That must've been hard.'

Mary said nothing. So Eliza, like George, thought she had only married Reuben for the sake of her children! Probably most people in

Yarnscombe thought the same. She clung to the memory of her other reason, that unexpected passion that had given her Albert. Sometimes, when she looked at her youngest son, she marvelled at his difference from the others.

'Well,' she said at last. 'I hope 'twill all work out for ee, Lizzie. I'll be sorry to lose ee to America and to miss the growing of little Simon. Still — if 'tis what you want — ' She sighed. 'Will ee be married in Yarnscombe?'

'No. 'Twould make too much talk. Simon wants it done quietly in Torrington with just a few family. We'll be married from the farm.'

'Tucker's farm? But — I thought — '

'I couldn't get married from Pa Dark's! You know that! I don't 'spose he'll come to the wedding, anyhow.'

'He'll come if I have to drag'n there!' Mary said.

Eliza laughed. 'He wouldn't come if I was marrying Philip!'

Which is true enough, Mary thought. Reuben, at least, would be pleased that Simon Tucker was making an honest woman of Eliza and taking her off his hands. But she worried about Philip who still seemed unable to accept that Eliza would never be his. Perhaps he would only believe it when she and Simon were actually married.

It was August before Eliza heard that Simon had booked his passage to England and to expect him late in September. Barum fair came and went before he arrived and Johnny, who had been horse trading again, was cock-a-hoop because he had sold his first gelding at a profit and had set up a mysterious deal that was going to make him a lot of money.

'You be careful!' Mary warned him. 'Them gypsies've been trading hosses for generations. 'Tis in their blood. They won't take kindly to somebody like you queering their pitch. You could end up with a knife in your back!'

Johnny laughed. 'There's no flies on me, Ma! I can keep upsides with the best of 'em. So could Great-granfer Pugsley, from what I've heard.'

'You don't want to follow after him, boy!' Mary said. 'He brought a lot of trouble to our family. You just stay clear of it!'

She knew he would take no notice of her but because she soon became caught up in the excitement of Simon Tucker's arrival, Johnny and his horse trading slipped to the back of her mind. It was Philip who brought home the news that Simon was at last in the country. He had been to Torrington and swept Eliza and her baby away from the lodging house to his father's farm. Philip had not seen them since.

Mary gaped. 'So what's Simon looking like?' she asked.

Philip's lips twisted. 'Burned brown from the sun and dressed to kill — dolled up in one of them big cowboy hats and leather breeches. Little Simon was scared of'n.'

'And Lizzie?'

Philip looked away. 'Lizzie couldn't take her eyes off'n so I left 'em to it. I've been to Barum today, to the recruiting office. They'm wanting volunteers for the Devon Regiment so I've signed up to join the fourth battalion.'

Mary gasped. 'Oh, Philip, no! Why've ee done that?'

'You know why. I've had it in mind for a while but I waited to see if Lizzie needed me. Now her don't, so there's nothing to hold me back.'

'Yes, there be! There's your family — your father! What's 'n going to say?'

''Tis too late for'n to say anything 'cos 'tis done. Soon's they send me my papers I'll be off.'

'Where to?'

'Barracks first for training, then wherever I'm needed. Ireland, perhaps or India.'

'Oh, Philip, I'm so sorry!' Mary clasped one of his hands in both hers. 'If 'twas up to me, I'd sooner you had Lizzie than Simon Tucker! She's a silly maid not to see what's best for her!'

'Lizzie's made her choice, so that's an end to it. Father did warn me but I wouldn't listen. I won't stop to tell'n what I've done 'cos I can't face'n just now. You tell'n I'll come and say goodbye before I go.'

He began moving to the door but Mary called after him, 'You can't leave me to tell'n! What can I say? 'Twill break his heart!'

'You'll find the words — better'n I could.'

He went and Mary sank down into a chair and put her head in her hands. She knew what would happen when she told Reuben. He would blame Eliza and then, inevitably, herself. But if he was losing a son, she was losing a daughter. Surely they could somehow find the means to comfort one another?

He was late for his tea and she was giving a stir to the stew pot over the fire when he and they boys came in together. He did not give her his usual smile when she nervously greeted him and the boys all seemed subdued.

'Heard a bit of talk today, Mary,' he said.

'Talk?' Instantly she thought of Philip and dropped her spoon. 'What sort of talk? Where've ee been?'

'Atherington — finishing that barn job for

Farmer Joplin. He told me your Johnny's heading for trouble.'

'Johnny?' Mary clutched her heart. 'What's 'n done?'

'Seems he took money from a couple of gentry old Joplin goes hunting with to buy cheap hosses for 'em. That was weeks ago and they've never seen hide nor hair of'n since. They'm only giving him another week before they take'n to court.'

'Oh!' Mary cried. 'I told'n not to trust them gypsies! They'm behind it, you mark my words! What can us do, Reuben?'

'Nothing.' Reuben settled himself calmly at the table. 'I bain't throwing good money after bad! If your Johnny's got hisself in trouble, he must get hisself out of it!'

'But — ' Mary looked wildly at the boys. ' — can't one of ee at least go to Barum and talk to'n,' she appealed, 'and find out if 'tis true?'

Joey and Fred looked uncomfortable but Albert spoke up. 'P'raps he'll come home on Sat'day, Ma, then you can ask'n yourself.'

Mary slammed the plates down on to the table and began slopping out the stew. 'If he don't, then I'll get to Barum somehow, even if I have to walk all the way!' she declared.

She was angry with Reuben who seemed not to care but she was even angrier with

Johnny. He had not only disregarded her advice, he had also made it impossible for her to tell Reuben calmly about Philip. She did not want to make the mistake of hiding the news from him, the way she had hidden Eliza's pregnancy, but if she told him now he might think she was comparing his son to hers, to the advantage of neither.

So she waited, burdened with a double load of anxiety and going about her household tasks in an automatic fashion. She was so distracted when she and Reuben were getting ready for bed that night that he asked, 'What be the matter, Mary? You've not been yerself all day. Be ee really worried about that rascally son of yourn?'

He was not usually observant and spoke so kindly she could not stop herself from bursting into tears. Concerned, he drew her to him. 'Don't fret! Your Johnny can always talk his way out of trouble. You know that.'

''Tain't only Johnny!' she sobbed. ''Tis Philip.'

'Philip?' He frowned. 'What about'n?'

She told him then between sobs and snuffles and he listened until she had finished. She expected a storm but none came. Instead, he put her quietly from him, finished undressing and got into bed. When she joined him there, he was lying flat on his back, staring up at the rafters. She wished he would say something but when he spoke at last, his words cut her to the quick.

'Philip was Jane's favourite,' he said. 'He was always more like her than the rest of 'em. Now your maid have probably sent'n to his death.'

'No!' Mary cried. 'You mustn't think that! He may never go to war!'

She would have put her arms round him but Reuben turned his back and shut her out of his private grief while she lay as stricken as he, not knowing how to comfort him.

For days afterwards, he was cold with her, outwardly polite but distant. He did not mention Philip's name or Eliza's and Mary did not dare to speak of the wedding or to ask him if he would take her to it.

When Johnny did not come home at the weekend, she was distraught, especially when George arrived with the news that his brother had gone missing again and was probably with the gypsy horse traders, following the fairs as he had done before.

'But what about the trouble he's in?' she cried. 'What about the money he took?'

'He won't come back till he can pay it off,' George said. 'You know Johnny!'

'But there's Lizzie's wedding! 'Tis a week on Sat'day and I want ee all there!'

George grinned. 'Johnny won't miss that if he can help it! You wait and see!'

Because Reuben had distanced himself from all the preparations, Bert arranged for a carriage to take the Pugsleys and Mary's family to Torrington. George was going to give Eliza away and the wedding would be a quiet affair in St Michael's Church, followed by a meal for the guests at Tuckers' farm. Mary knew that some of the Dark boys were planning to travel down in the wagon, in defiance of their father but as the day approached, she felt more and more apprehensive. She hated the thought of appearing without Reuben and feared she might break down when she saw Eliza at Simon's side, knowing she would be losing her for ever.

Then the night before the wedding, Sally arrived unexpectedly from Barum. She kissed Mary and held her close. 'I thought you could do with some support tomorrow,' she said. 'And I couldn't let Lizzie get married without me!'

Mary was so overcome she clung to her. 'Thanks, Sal!' she whispered, feeling her eyes wet with tears. 'I'll be glad of your company since your dad won't be there. And I know Lizzie'll be pleased to see ee.'

Ignoring her father's disapproval, Sally joined Mary's family and the Pugsleys in the carriage to travel to Torrington. There had been no sign of Johnny but Fred and Joey and Charley followed on in the wagon. Just as they were all drawing up in the lane outside the church, there was a sudden commotion as a rider on horseback scattered the gathering crowd. It was Johnny, as reckless as ever, who leapt from his horse, tethered it to the gate and ran to join his mother.

He laughed when he saw her face. 'Right on time, Ma!' he cried. 'Allow me to take ee in!'

Mary's heart lifted at once. With her head held high, she walked proudly into the church on Johnny's arm with Sally and Albert following them. George waited outside for the arrival of the bride. When the organ started up the wedding march and Eliza came down the aisle on her brother's arm, looking radiant in blue velvet and carrying a posy of Christmas roses, Mary was able to smile through her tears. She forgot Reuben and thought only of John, wishing he could have been there to see his beautiful daughter married.

The ceremony passed her by in a haze and there was such a crowd afterwards at Tuckers' farm, she could not have said who had been there. She was introduced to this one and that and plied with food and drink, her face aching with the effort of constantly having to smile. But Eliza kissed her and little Simon found her and clung to her hand, refusing to leave her for the whole of the time. He seemed nervous of his father who looked handsomer than ever and held the company spellbound with tales of his travels and the wonders of Oregon where there were mountains and forests, the great Columbia river and vast stretches of land as yet unclaimed. He boasted of how he was going to make his fortune there while Eliza listened and worshipped him with her eyes.

Mary saw that Johnny was hanging on his every word and when it was all over and people were beginning to depart, he came over to his mother, his eyes alight with excitement.

'I've been talking to Simon,' he said. 'He thinks he might be able to get me a passage on the ship going back to America if I can raise the cash. They'm off at the end of March and I could travel with 'em! I know enough about hosses now to make me way and I'll stand a better chance over there than in this country. What do ee say, Ma?'

Mary's head spun and she felt faint. Oh, no! she cried inwardly. Not you, too, Johnny!

She put a hand on his arm to steady herself

and her smile was more like a grimace. ' 'Twill need thinking about,' she said, 'and talking over. It can't be decided in a hurry. And if you'm just running away from trouble, boy, no good'll ever come of it!'

19

Mary was very quiet on the drive back to Yarnscombe. Sally sat next to her in the carriage and squeezed her hand once. 'Don't worry!' she comforted. 'Lizzie's a sensible girl. She'll be all right. Simon Tucker seems to have everything planned and you can see he thinks a lot of her and the little one.'

Mary nodded, her heart too full for speech. She had extracted a promise from Eliza that they would all come to see her before they set off for Plymouth and she had begged Simon to think again about taking Johnny with them. She hoped he would not be able to raise the money for his passage, then remembered guiltily that she still had his sovereign from old Granny Pugsley in her tin box. He can only have it to help pay off what he owes! she vowed, knowing all the time that if he came begging, she would not be able to refuse him.

Reuben was in this workshop when they reached Yarnscombe, fuming because his boys had all left him on his own to finish off a pair of cart wheels ordered for Ley farm. He came out and glowered at Albert when he and

George walked into the yard. 'So you'm back!' he said. 'Too late to change out of your Sunday best, boy, and give me a hand!'

His lip curled into a sneer when he turned to Mary and Sally. 'So — be ee all starving or did that old skinflint. Tucker, feed ee at the farm?'

'They put on a good spread,' Sally said, 'and the wedding went well, Father. You should have been there.'

'I was best out of it!' He looked at Mary, taking in her dejected expression. 'From the looks of ee, you'd have been better off staying at home! Too much for ee, was it?'

Mary flinched and Sally put an arm round her shoulders. 'We're just tired, Father,' she said quietly, 'and in need of a cup of tea.'

'Then get inside and put summat on the table! I've had to shift for meself all day.' He stumped grumpily back to the workshop with Albert hurrying after him.

'Don't mind him!' Sally murmured in Mary's ear as they and George went into the house. 'Take off your bonnet and shawl and put your feet up while I find us something to eat.'

'There's plenty of cold ham and pickles in the larder,' Mary said, 'and I left him a couple of pasties. He didn't have to go hungry.'

He was punishing her, she knew, not just

for leaving him to go to the wedding but because Philip had come home the day before to tell them that his papers had arrived and that he was on his way to report to the barracks in Exeter for training.

Reuben had been abrupt with him and they had parted coldly. He was regretting that, she could tell, but because he would not turn to her for consolation, she felt powerless to help. Now she was suffering too, yearning for some hint of compassion while she faced what was going to be a double loss.

The other Dark boys arrived home soon afterwards in the wagon and, by the time they all came in for their tea, she and Sally had the table spread. Reuben stood staring down at it for a moment, pulling at his beard. Then he looked directly at her. 'What's all this I hear about Johnny?' he asked.

She realised that the boys must have told him. 'Seems he wants to go to America too,' she said and felt her throat ache as she forced the words out.

'And you'll let'n go?'

'How can I stop'n? He's a man now, or thinks he be.' Her voice broke and her lips trembled.

There was a pause, then Reuben said, ' 'Twill be hard for ee, Mary, to lose Johnny as well as Lizzie.'

'Ay. Even when they'm trouble, 'tis still hard to see 'em go.' Something in Reuben's concerned expression made her snap at him. 'Oh, do ee sit down, Reuben! You said you was wanting your tea!' But her eyes were blurring so when she reached for the teapot that she caught it with the back of her hand and tipped it over, sending a stream of scalding tea across the tablecloth. Albert jumped back with a shout and Sally ran for a cloth but Mary just stood as if stunned.

Then she gave a gasp of pain and fled from the kitchen, through Jane's little sitting room and up the stairs to the bedroom she shared with Reuben. Here she flung herself on to the bed and gave way at last, her body racked with dry, shuddering sobs.

She did not hear him coming up the stairs or realise he was in the room until he touched her on the shoulder. Startled, she jerked round and looked up at him, her eyes so full of misery he sat down on the bed beside her and wrapped her in his arms.

'Oh, don't ee take on so, Mary!' he pleaded. 'I can't bear to see ee so troubled. Your Johnny has wits enough to look after hisself and Lizzie'll be all right now her's wed. Us'll just have to get used to letting 'em go.'

'I'm sorry,' she wept, her voice muffled

against his shoulder, 'sorry for being such a fule and for Philip and all the trouble I've brought ee — '

'No! Not trouble. 'Tis mostly joy you've brought me, Mary! If this be a bad patch, us've been through worse.'

'Then don't turn from me, Reuben!' she pleaded. 'That's what hurts, when you turn away. I need ee more than ever now.'

'Us needs one another,' he admitted. 'I know that, even when I'm being a stubborn old mule! You should be used to me by now, m'dear.' He pulled his old red handkerchief from his pocket and mopped her tears with it. It smelled of glue and she gave a watery smile. 'That's better!' he approved. 'Now — be ee coming down for your tea before them boys clears everything off the table?'

'Sally wouldn't let 'em do that!' Mary said.

Reuben chuckled. 'No. Her's too much the school marm these days!'

He stood up and held out a hand to Mary. She took it with relief. It was a strong hand, roughened by hard work but warm and reassuring. She leaned against him as they walked out of the bedroom and down the stairs together. They were all right again and she was thankful. Whatever happened, she would be better able to bear it if Reuben was at her side.

Christmas was quiet that year. Simon and Eliza spent it at Tuckers' farm and George preferred to be in Dolton with Hannah. Johnny arrived home on foot on Christmas Eve. He had sold his horse to raise the money for his passage and had been on a winning streak with his gambling but he was still short of what he needed.

'What about the money you took for them hosses you never delivered?' Mary demanded. 'That should be paid back first!'

Johnny grinned. 'I've paid part over to the court and promised the rest in a couple of month's time. I should be in America by then.'

'Johnny! That ain't fair!'

'Fair enough! Old Joplin's fancy friends won't miss it. They'm rolling in money.'

'But 'twill give the fam'ly a bad name!'

'That'll die down once I'm gone. If any of 'em comes asking, tell 'em I'll pay 'em back when I've made me fortune!'

Mary gazed at him in dismay. 'You'll find yerself behind bars one of these days!'

'Not me! I'll be free as the air, riding with the cowboys over the range! You heard what Simon said at the wedding. 'Tis a man's life in America. All I need is a little more cash to get me there.' He glanced at Mary out of the corner of his eyes. 'George was telling me how you helped'n to get started in Barum with some money Great-granny Pugsley left. He thought p'raps you might do the same for me.'

'George should keep his mouth shut!' Mary said. 'I've been keeping that money safe for when 'twould do ee most good.'

'That's now, Ma! 'Twill do me more good now I'm starting out on a new life than when I'm too old to make best use of it!' His eyes gleamed. 'Think of me in America with me own ranch in five or ten years time! Think of the next generation of Moores growing up over there! I could make our name one to be reckoned with if I have the chance!'

Mary shook her head. 'You could just as easy make it a byword the way you behave, boy! Your poor father'd turn in his grave if you ended up a cheat and a rogue.'

'I promise ee, Ma,' Johnny said solemnly, 'that I'll be honest from now on if you'll help me. Just give me the chance and you'll see!'

Mary regarded him steadily. 'Don't let your father and me down then, boy! Come upstairs and I'll let ee have your share of what Granny Pugsley left.'

He followed her to the bedroom and watched while she took her tin box from the bottom of the wardrobe. She put his own sovereign and one extra into his eager hands just as she had done for George and then showed him the photograph of herself and John on their wedding day.

'You never knew your father,' she said, 'but he was a good man, even if he didn't make his fortune. That old tin whistle I gave ee was about the only thing he ever owned.'

'I've kept it safe, Ma, and I often play it.'

'Then take it to America to remember'n by and play it to your own children one day, like he played it to Lizzie and George. He used to sing, too. He had a lovely voice. He died singing, Johnny, sitting up in bed singing "Gentle Jesus."'

The memory made her choke and Johnny put an arm round her. 'I wish I'd known'n,' he said. 'And I wish I could take ee with me, Ma.'

'I'm too old for that, now. Just remember the things I've taught ee and keep yourself straight! And stay close to Lizzie 'cos you'll be all the family her've got in America.'

'I'll stay close,' Johnny promised. He pocketed his sovereigns and kissed his mother on the cheek. 'I'll be seeing Lizzie tomorrow 'cos I'd best get down to Tuckers' farm to tell Simon I can pay me way.'

'Tomorrow? But that's Christmas Day! I wanted ee here for the last time!'

'You'll have Albert and all the Darks

— plenty to keep ee company!'

But no Lizzie and no George and not even Johnny now that he had what he came for! It seemed to Mary that all John's children were deserting her. If 1883 had been a bad year, she feared that 1885 was going to be even worse.

At the beginning of March, Simon and Eliza arrived unexpectedly with the baby to say goodbye. They were leaving that weekend, taking the train from Torrington to Barum where Johnny would join them at the Junction station to catch the train to Exeter. They would change again for Plymouth and their ship would sail from the Baltic Wharf the following Wednesday.

Mary hugged Eliza and kissed little Simon, laughing and crying all at once, begging them to write as soon as they landed and to take care. 'But where's Johnny?' she kept asking. 'I didn't know 'twould be so soon. Why ain't Johnny come to say goodbye?'

'I believe your son has some unfinished business in Barum,' Simon said drily, making Mary's heart jerk in alarm.

'But he'll come, Ma!' Eliza reassured her. 'He'd never go without seeing ee.'

'I'd never forgive'n if he did!' Mary said. 'But do ee sit down, while I get the tea! Why didn't ee let me know you were coming?'

'"Twas only decided last minute,' Eliza explained, 'there's been such a lot to do.' She moved to help her mother who began bustling about, laying the table and bringing cold meat and pickles from the larder and a large yeast cake to slice and spread with butter.

While they worked Eliza told Mary how they had been told what clothes they should take for the journey which would last about a month — six shifts and six pairs of stockings for herself as well as two pairs of shoes, two flannel petticoats and two gowns. Then she would need several changes for the baby and a warm shawl to wrap him in when it was cold.

'Simon knows what to take 'cos he's done it before,' Eliza said, 'and he's told Johnny he must have six shirts and six pairs of stockings, two sets of outdoor clothes and a change of shoes. They look in our boxes before we sail and check everything's clean with no vermin. They might even make us strip and have a good wash before letting us on board!'

'Oh, my!' Mary said. 'I never thought 'twould be like that! Do ee think Johnny's got all he needs? What about food? Do ee have to take that?'

'No. That's provided and Simon says 'tis sufficient. I just hope I won't be sick if the weather's rough.'

Mary looked at her. 'You bain't — ?'

'No. Not so far's I know!'

'Then be careful, maid! You've enough to be going on with without another baby!'

Reuben looked in when they were in the middle of their preparations. He stood staring at the visitors. 'I thought it must be you when I seed the hoss and trap,' he said. 'Be ee off soon, then?'

'On Saturday,' Simon said. He stood up and offered his hand to Reuben. 'We sail next Wednesday.'

There was a moment's hesitation before Reuben took his hand. 'I'd better wish ee luck, then,' he said. 'Not that I'm in favour of all this traipsing off to America. There be good land and better in this country, I reckon.'

'But not enough of it, Mr Dark!' Simon said. 'Not if a chap wants to get on.'

'Splitting up fam'lies!' Reuben grumbled. 'Taking young maids away from their mothers! You mind you look after Lizzie when you'm over there with all them Injuns and wild men us hears about!'

Simon laughed. 'Not so wild where we're going, Mr Dark! I'll take good care of Lizzie and little Simon, never fear!'

'You'll answer to me if you don't,' Reuben threatened, 'seeing as Lizzie's own father bain't here to speak for her. And watch out for that Johnny! If anything happens to either of 'em, 'twill break their mother's heart.' He glowered at Simon. 'Well — I've said what I meant to say and I've still got work to do. So I'll leave ee all to it.'

He was making for the door when Eliza ran over to him and, to Mary's surprise, flung her arms round his neck and kissed him. 'Goodbye, Pa Dark,' she murmured. 'I won't forget ee. You saved me from the river, else I'd never have met Simon or had his baby. I'm sorry if I shamed ee but 'twas never meant. Look after Ma when I'm gone!'

Reuben seemed momentarily lost for words. He patted Eliza's shoulder and cleared his throat. Then he said gruffly, 'I'll look after her. You'm a good maid, Lizzie. I never really thought different.'

He went and Mary felt tears beginning to well up in her again, not from sorrow now but from gratitude that Reuben had made his peace with Eliza. To cover her confusion she hurried to the fire where the kettle was steaming and made the tea in her old brown pot. Eliza came to take it from her mother and smiled. 'I'm glad he said that,' she murmured. 'I feel better about leaving ee with'n now. But if you ever want to come away, just let me know. Simon and me'll get ee over to us somehow!'

'I'd never leave Yarnscombe,' Mary said, 'and all me family!' Or Reuben, she realised, feeling an upsurge of tenderness for him. When he and the boys all came in for their tea she presided as usual at his table, happy that there was still a place for her in the carpenter's house.

Johnny appeared on Friday, shamefaced because he had spent a night in the cells at Barum for not honouring his debts. 'I'll be glad when I'm out of this country!' he grumbled. 'A chap don't stand a chance!'

'You'd stand a chance if you kept to your word!' Mary scolded him. 'Make sure you behave yerself in America. They might string ee up over there!'

'Don't go on, Ma!' Johnny pleaded. 'I've walked all this way to say goodbye to ee and I'll have to walk all the way back again tonight! Give me a kiss and wish me luck, won't ee? I don't want to leave on a sour note.'

'Then come here!' Mary clasped him in her arms. 'I only want the best for ee, boy! I'd sooner you stayed but if you won't, then I wish ee all the good fortune any mother'd ask for her son!'

Johnny winked. 'I'll p'raps send ee a diamond brooch one day, Ma!'

'You just send me a letter now and again! That'll be enough for me.'

After he left that evening she sat alone for a while in Jane's little sitting room. Hannah had returned the poetry book Jane had given her so she began leafing through it, looking for the puzzling lines Jane had marked so long ago. As she read the whole poem through again, Mary began to see that perhaps it was love itself the poet had meant was cruel. Love was often the cause of heartache because you could not have one without the other, yet even pain could be treasured if it grew out of love. 'Not a sigh, nor a tear, my pain discloses,' she read, 'But they fall silently, like dew on roses.'

Dew on roses! That was a beautiful picture. It did not lessen the pain she felt at losing Lizzie and Johnny and little Simon but it somehow made it more bearable. When Reuben came looking for her she was able to smile at him.

'What be you doing, sitting in here all on your own?' he asked her.

'Coming to terms with things,' she said.

'You bain't making yerself miserable again, be ee? Crying over Lizzie and Johnny won't bring 'em back!'

'I know that so I bain't crying!' She stood

up and took his arm. 'There be plenty left for us, Reuben, if us holds fast.'

'Then that's what us'll have to do, m'dear,' he said. 'Us'll have to hold fast while us have one another!'

20

It was weeks before Mary heard that Eliza, Simon, Johnny and the baby had arrived safely in America. The sea journey had been uncomfortable, Eliza wrote, the accomodation cramped and the weather so rough at one time she had to tie little Simon in the berth with her. She had been very sea-sick but he had loved the excitement of it all and she was sure he had grown an inch already. There had been plenty of food — flour, rice, oatmeal and biscuit, sugar and treacle and two ounces of tea for each passenger. There was even a boiler and an oven for baking in the hold and sometimes the sailors caught fish which they cooked. They had seen whales and lots of other ships but Eliza was thankful when they sailed into New York harbour.

'It was wonderful, Mother,' she wrote. 'Everybody rushed up on deck to cheer when we caught sight of the Statue of Liberty which is quite new. It is a beautiful, gleaming statue of a woman holding a torch and Simon told us it was given to the people of America last year by the people of France to celebrate their two revolutions. He said it represents freedom and he held little Simon up to see it and told him never to forget that he had come to the land of the free. There were dozens of other ships and hundreds of little boats in the harbour and crowds of immigrants like us when we docked on Long Island. We all had to report at a place called Castle Gardens before we were allowed into the country so that took a long time and we are weary now and glad of a rest. I am writing this in a cheap lodging house not far from the docks and in sight of the Hudson river. It is a rough place where the seamen stay but we shall move on soon and set off west, first by the railroad, Simon says. I may not be able to write again until we reach the ranch in Oregon but I gave you the address before we left so I hope to have a letter from you soon. Always your loving daughter, Eliza.'

Mary wrote at once so that her letter would be waiting to welcome the travellers when they arrived. She showed Eliza's with pride to Reuben and the rest of the family and then put it in her old tin box with the rest of her treasures. Every week after that she wrote, sending her daughter all the latest news of the family.

She knew she would be delighted to hear that George and Hannah were planning to marry at the end of August. One Sunday he brought Hannah over from Dolton and told his mother that he had found a house in Barum to rent and that he would take them both to see it if Pa Dark would lend him the horse and trap. It was a terrace house, not far from the centre of the town and it had the new gas lighting installed, a mains water supply and a flushing lavatory in the backyard.

Mary tried to suppress a feeling of envy that Hannah would have so many advantages but she could not help being charmed with the house when she saw it. It had a porch and a parlour, a large kitchen and back kitchen, a yard with a shed at the end of it and three bedrooms. She and Hannah lit the gas lamps, delighted with their gentle glow and they measured the windows for curtains. Mary promised to help make them on her old sewing machine. Then there was all the excitement of preparing for the wedding which would be in the chapel at Dolton, so much going on and to think about, she sometimes forgot about Eliza and Johnny for hours at a time.

Then a letter arrived from Eliza that awakened all her worst fears. Eliza and Simon and the baby were safely installed at the ranch but Johnny had left them before they reached Oregon. He had met up with a bunch of cowboys who were heading for California and had gone off with them because he wanted to be a cattle man rather than work on a sheep farm. 'You remember how he always said he wanted to ride the range,' Eliza wrote. 'Simon and I begged him to stay but he would not. He said he would send word when he found work but so far we have heard nothing. I hope he will write to you, Mother, and let you know where he is.'

Mary gave a cry when she read this. She was all alone as Reuben and the boys were at work. Distressed, she snatched up her shawl and ran down the hill to her mother's cottage, desperate to share her trouble with somebody.

Mrs Pugsley shook her head when she read the letter. 'Well, there's nort you can do about it, Mary. You let'n go so now he'll have to find his own way. 'Twill be a rough life, I reckon, but he's fly enough.'

'He said he'd stay close to Lizzie!' Mary cried. 'He promised me he'd stay close!'

'Promises are made to be broken,' her mother said, ''specially your Johnny's!'

'But I don't know where he is now! If he don't write, I never will!'

'The less you know, the less you'll have to worry about! You'll hear soon enough when he's in trouble! Oh, sit yerself down, Mary and I'll make a pot of tea! At least your Lizzie seems well enough.'

This was some comfort and all Mary had to cling to. Reuben was no more reassuring when she turned to him that evening. 'Your Johnny'll either end up a rich man or at the end of a rope!' he said. ''Tis up to him which it'll be so you'd best put'n out of your mind, Mary!'

Mary could not do that. She watched every day for a letter that never arrived and even George's wedding, a happy family occasion to which all the Moores from Atherington came, did not distract her from worrying about Johnny. When George moved with Hannah into their house in Barum and she realised that she would not be seeing him any more at the weekends, her spirits really flagged. She was used to doing his washing and baking him food for the week and now Hannah would be taking care of all his needs. He might not be as far away as Eliza and Johnny but Mary knew that she had now lost George as well.

'You've still got me, Ma,' Albert said one day when he discovered her moping in the kitchen.

'How long for? I don't s'pose 'twill be many years before you'm wed and leaving us!' she said for Albert was nearly seventeen now and a favourite with the local girls.

'Not me! I won't leave Father, even if Fred and Joey do.'

'Fred and Joey?' She looked at him, startled. 'They bain't leaving, be 'em?'

'They'm talking about it — thinking of setting up on their own in South Molton. Seems old man Vickery, the town carpenter, died a while back. There's no sons to carry on after'n, so there could be a good opening for somebody.'

Mary was dismayed. 'Have they told their father?'

'Not yet.' Albert grinned. 'I wouldn't like to be in their shoes when they do!'

But nothing was said. Mary watched Reuben anxiously for any sign that he had been told. He was in his sixties now, heavier in build and not as agile as before, depending on his sons for ladder work when they took on any roofing jobs. She knew he would miss Joey particularly, just as he had missed James who had been so good with figures.

When several weeks went by with no announcement, she began to hope that Albert had been wrong or that the boys had had a change of heart. Then Reuben came home unexpectedly one Monday morning when she was in the middle of the week's washing and one look at his face told her that he knew.

She took her hands out of the tub, sluiced off the soap suds before drying them and pulled down her sleeves. 'What's up?' she asked.

He slumped into his old chair and looked gloomily at her. 'Joey and Fred,' he said. 'Leaving me.'

She nodded. 'Setting up on their own?'

He glowered. 'You knew? Did 'em tell ee before me?'

'No. Albert said summat but I hoped 'twould blow over.'

Reuben sighed heavily. 'They think they can do better in South Molton. P'raps they can. There bain't really enough work here for four of us. I've seed it coming but I hoped one of 'em would stay, at least till Albert got on a bit.'

'Will ee be able to manage?'

'Oh, us'll manage. Albert's a good boy. Not so quick as your George but he'll do.' Reuben gave a wry laugh. 'Twill be just you and me and our son from now on, Mary. All the rest'll have flown the roost!'

'But they'll be back! None of yourn be far away. If they don't come to us, us'll just have to go to them!'

The months passed and when she had almost ceased to expect it, a letter arrived from Johnny. He was working at a ranch in northern California, driving cattle with the cowboys and learning the ropes, sleeping out on the range under the stars, he told her, or riding into the nearest small town to spend the dollars he earned in the saloons there. It was a boastful letter, full of how he intended to have a ranch of his own one day and make a fortune so that he could send Mary the diamond brooch he had promised her.

She sighed when she read it, afraid he might be wasting his money on gambling or drink. But at least she knew where he was now and could write to him and to Eliza with the news.

'You spend half your time writing letters!' Reuben grumbled when he found her at Jane's old desk that evening.

''Tis the only way I can keep in touch. I've a lot to tell Johnny, and Lizzie likes to know what's happening in the family.' She put down her pen, having seen from his expression that he needed her company. 'But I can finish this tomorrow.'

She was glad afterwards that she had spent some time with Reuben because Philip arrived home unexpectedly the next afternoon. He walked in as if he had never been away, astonishing Mary, who clasped him in her arms and held him tightly for a moment.

'Philip!' she said. 'Why didn't ee let us

know? Your dad and Albert are out on a job.'

'They won't be long,' he said and kissed her. He had come to say goodbye because his battalion was being sent to India to reinforce the garrison at Jhansi which had been much reduced by a cholera epidemic. He had a week's leave as he would be abroad for at least two years and he hoped to see as many of the family as he could before he went.

'They'm spread about now,' Mary said, 'since Fred and Joey set up in South Molton. But us'll send messages or p'raps your dad could let ee have his new horse for a few days to get around to see 'em. Old Cap'n's been put out to grass and this young un's a lot livelier so you'll need to watch'n.' She took a better look at Philip. He was handsome and fit in his army uniform, smart with its new white facings. His cap badge, showing Exeter castle, was polished and gleaming. 'You'm looking well,' she said. 'Seems army life suits ee.'

He laughed. ''Tis all the training — plenty of square bashing and route marching. I'll be glad to leave the barracks and see a bit of the world.' His expression changed as he read the doubt in Mary's eyes. 'How's Lizzie?' he asked quietly.

'Pretty well. Johnny went with 'em to America but he split up from 'em before they got to Oregon. Now he's a cowboy in California, aiming to make his fortune!' She clutched at Philip's arm anxiously. 'Be it safe in India? I don't like the thought of ee going where there's cholera.'

'The epidemic's pretty well burned itself out and there's talk of moving to another camp near Lahore. Don't worry! I'm fit enough.' He looked around him and sniffed the air appreciatively. ' 'Tis good to be back. I fancy I can smell some of your pasties cooking and I've been dreaming about them ever since I heard I had leave.'

'Then you shall have one straight out of the oven!'

Mary hastened to feed him, telling him about George's wedding and how Joey and Fred were doing well, wondering at the back of her mind how Reuben would react when he met Philip again. They had not parted on good terms and she knew how difficult Reuben found it to forgive.

When she heard the clatter of the wagon coming into the yard that evening she left what she was doing and hurried out to meet her husband. He stared at her obvious excitement. 'Summat up, Mary?'

'Philip's here,' she said, 'come to say goodbye 'cos he's off to India. Now you be gentle with'n and treat'n as a father should!'

Reuben tossed the reins to Albert. 'See to Blacky!' he said abruptly and clambered down from his seat, glowering at Mary. 'I don't need telling how to treat me own son!' he growled. 'Where be'n?'

'In the kitchen, half asleep by the fire. Just mind what I told ee, Reuben!'

She waited outside while Albert unhitched the horse from the wagon. Once Reuben and Philip had been given a few minutes on their own she returned to the kitchen, finding them sitting at either side of the fire, talking earnestly. They were so engrossed they hardly noticed her. Relieved, she busied herself with putting the tea on the table.

When Albert came in, the conversation livened over the meal for Philip had a lot to tell them. He was disappointed at being sent to India as he had hoped for South Africa. He had been following the events there and had a new hero in Cecil Rhodes who had made a fortune out of the diamond mines in Kimberley and was using his money and influence to expand the British protectorate well beyond the Transvaal. But the Boers in the Orange Free State, who had been given independence by Gladstone were suspicious and Kruger still had dreams of bringing South Africa back into Dutch control.

'So what we've got needs protecting,' Philip

told them, 'and if Rhodes pushes still farther north there'll be even more to look after. The British army'll be needed over there for years to come. I could get there yet.'

'But how dangerous is it?' Mary pressed him. 'Would ee have to fight?'

'Only if there's trouble and no more than I might meet up with in India. I can't see much happening either place for the next couple of years, barring the odd skirmish.' He grinned. 'If there is, I'll keep my head down!'

'Caw!' Albert said. 'I wish I could see India!'

'Now I want none of that!' Mary scolded him. ''Tis bad enough Lizzie and Johnny going off to foreign parts without you getting ideas! Your father needs ee here!'

Albert looked abashed and Philip clapped him on the shoulder. 'You stay put, young Albert! The army bain't a bed of roses!' He yawned. 'Would ee mind if I turn in early? I'm half asleep on my feet.'

'You do what you want, boy!' Reuben said. 'You shall have Blacky tomorrow to ride into Barum. Tell Sally and your brothers and their wives to get up here on Sunday. I'll send a message to Fred and Joey, and Albert can fetch Charlie from Westcott so they'm all here to see ee off.'

Philip smiled. 'Thanks, Dad. Can I ask

Em'ly and Sam to come as well?'

For a moment, Reuben stiffened. Then he said, 'Ay, if they will. Tell 'em to bring young Alfred! 'Tis a while since I seed'n.'

'But how shall I feed 'em all?' Mary cried.

'Same's you always have, m'dear,' Reuben said. 'You've never let us down yet.'

So that weekend there was an early Christmas gathering in the carpenter's house, a full month before the proper day. The long table was crowded twice over and somehow Mary kept filling it with the help of her mother and her sisters who provided home baked pies, scones and cakes and trifles. George and Hannah came because Philip said George was as much a brother to him as all the others and Mary was only saddened because Eliza and Johnny were not with them. She felt proud when Reuben made a speech, wishing Philip a safe return from his posting. But just for a moment, when she looked at his large family, she had a cold premonition that this might be the last time they would all be together.

That night, when he turned to her in bed, she knew that he needed comforting. 'Philip'll be all right,' she whispered as he slipped his hands under her nightgown. 'And I'm glad Em'ly came. You did well today, Reuben, with both of 'em.'

'With your help,' he muttered into her neck. 'What would I do without ee, Mary?'

Or I without you? she wondered and shuddered as an icy tremor ran down her back.

'Not cold, be ee?' he asked.

'No. 'Twas just your hands for a minute.' She held him close and gave herself to him gladly, thankful that he, at least, was still with her.

But it was from that moment that she began to feel events were passing out of her control. Reuben had always kept a firm hand on his family and she had tried to guide hers but now their children had taken charge of their own lives. Even Albert, the only one they shared, was beginning to range farther afield for his friends and becoming secretive about what he did in his spare time. She asked him once if he was courting but he only laughed and told her to wait as he was going to surprise her one day. When he did, she and Reuben were astonished to hear that he had been doing nothing more underhand than learning how to ring the bells at St Andrews church. Now he had been taken on as one of the team and would be ringing with them for the first time that Sunday.

'Be sure to listen out for us, Ma!' he told her. 'You won't hear a single bell out of time!'

So, although Mary usually went to the little wooden chapel on Sunday evenings, she accompanied Reuben to church that Sunday morning and listened with pride as she walked down the hill, knowing that her youngest son was helping to ring the summoning bells of St Andrews.

In the middle of '86, Eliza wrote that she was expecting another child in November. The news sent Mary into a turmoil of worry as to who was to care for her and whether there would be a proper midwife on hand. She could not begin to imagine the ranch in Oregon where Eliza lived with Simon or the vast expanse of land where the sheep were numbered in thousands rather than hundreds. It was all so different from the patchwork fields at Westcott and the little cottage in the valley she had lived in with John.

'I don't even know if there's any other women on this ranch,' she complained to Reuben. 'Lizzie's never said.'

''Tain't likely Simon Tucker's the only chap there with a wife,' Reuben scoffed. 'They'd need women to cook and such. Lizzie's a healthy maid. Her didn't have any trouble with the first one.'

This was little comfort to Mary. She wrote at once to Eliza, demanding to know more about her situation and telling her to take good care of herself. While she was still waiting for a reply, George and Hannah arrived unexpectedly in Yarnscombe one Sunday morning when she was cooking the dinner. They'd come by horse and trap especially to tell her that Hannah was also expecting a baby, due in January.

Mary was so overjoyed she kissed them both. This was one grandchild she could be sure would be staying near at hand. She would be able to help Hannah if she was needed and the girl's own family was not far away. There were doctors and proper midwives in Barum so she would not be abandoned, like Eliza, somewhere in the wilds of Oregon.

All the same, Mary thought that the girl looked pale. She seemed thinner than ever and hardly showed at all that she was in the family way. 'You must take better care of her, George!' she admonished her son. 'Make sure her gets plenty of nourishing food!'

He laughed at that. 'Then, if there's enough, us'll sit down to your good Sunday dinner for a start, Ma. My mouth's been watering ever since us came in!'

A letter arrived from Eliza some weeks later, assuring her mother that there were several capable women on the ranch who would help her through her labour. Not only that, Simon had started building a wooden house with a porch for her and his growing family. Mary began to relax then and to look forward to being a grandmother again, twice over. But she was still relieved when she heard in late November that Eliza had given birth to another son they had called Wilfred.

'I told ee you was worrying for nothing!' Reuben said. 'Lizzie's strong and built for child bearing. Not like George's skinny maid. Too narrow by half, her be!'

Mary was visiting George and Hannah whenever Reuben could take her into Barum. The girl was still very pale and seemed constantly tired as if her slender body could not bear the weight she was carrying. But she made no complaint and was always welcoming. When Mary offered to be with her at her confinement she thanked her but said that her own mother was coming from Dolton and that they would send word as soon as the baby was born.

The message came early in January that Hannah had given birth to a son. Mary straightway persuaded Reuben to take her into town and it was the girl's mother who opened the door of George's house and let her in. She whispered that Hannah's labour had been difficult and long. She had lost a lot of blood and the baby's cord had been twisted round his wrist, marking it. Apart from that, he was beautiful.

Mary's heart jerked. 'They'm both all right, though?'

'Picking up now,' Hannah's mother said. 'Hannah will have to lie abed for a time and the doctor said her mustn't think of another one for a long while yet. But come on in! George is here and they'm both waiting to see ee.'

Hannah was propped up on pillows in her bed, cradling the baby in her arms with George standing awkwardly beside her. He grimaced with relief when he saw his mother. 'I thought I was going to lose 'em both,' he said gruffly.

Hannah looked exhausted but she smiled up at him. 'You worry too much!' she said and held out her baby for Mary to take. 'We've called him John, after George's father.'

John! Mary took the baby and gazed down at him. Her first John had died young and her second had almost broken her heart with his wild ways. This third John seemed like a promise of better things to come and she loved him on sight. He was a quiet baby, lying very still and there was a look of Hannah in his fine features. She saw the dark, circular mark on his left wrist but his tiny fingers, long and slender like his grandfather's, clutched strongly at one of Mary's.

'I'm glad you've called'n John,' she told George. 'He looks as if he could be musical, like your father. I should've kept that penny whistle for'n.'

George shook his head. 'Johnny always made good use of it so I don't begrudge it to'n. Have ee heard from'n lately?'

'Not for nigh on six months. Last time he wrote he'd teamed up with some chap to run a herd of cattle of their own. I just hope he bain't mixing with the wrong company, knowing the trouble he got into before with hosses.'

'I can tell ee one thing, Ma!' George said. 'My John means too much to me to let'n go astray. I'll put'n to the trade soon's he's old enough and we'll be partners one day.'

Hannah's tired eyes lit up when he said that. 'George is foreman for Mr Luxton now,' she told Mary. 'and he gets put in charge of all the best funerals. You should see'n, dressed up in his black tailcoat and top hat!'

'Albert's stood in for Pa Dark a couple of times,' Mary said, 'now that Joey's gone. But he don't care much for funerals. He'd sooner toll the bell at the church!'

'He'll get used to it,' George said. 'Last time I saw Albert he told me he wanted to be a builder one day, like me. You'll be proud of us both then, Ma.'

'I'm proud of ee now,' Mary said. 'You'm both good boys and that's all that matters to me.' She handed the baby back to his mother. 'Take good care of this one, Hannah! Then he'll make you and George proud, too, in the years to come.'

She hoped she would be spared to see him grow up. He was part of the next generation, like Eliza's children and Reuben's growing number of grandchildren, perhaps the beginning of a long line of descendants they would never know.

She shared that thought with Reuben when he called to pick her up but he rolled his eyes. 'Descendants? It don't bear thinking about, Mary.' He had been visiting Henry and his family and had been told that Harriet was expecting again, that James was soon to marry his Jessie and that Joey was courting a maid in South Molton. 'When will it all end?' he asked.

She squeezed his arm as she sat next to him in the trap. 'I don't s'pose 'twill ever end — not while there's feelings to draw a man and a maid together.'

'And us knows all about that! Albert be living proof of it. When anything happens to me, Mary, I want'n to carry on the business so's he can look after ee proper.'

'But what about your other boys?'

'I've done me best for 'em and they've all gone their separate ways. Albert's the last and he's your son so what I've got'll all be his.'

'Don't talk like that! You'm still in your prime!'

'I was in my prime twenty years ago when I married ee and I proved that on our wedding night.' He chuckled. 'Bless me if you ain't blushing the way you did then!'

'Then behave yourself and stop provoking me!' But she spoke fondly, grateful that he was making provision for herself and Albert even while she hoped they would not need it for many years to come. 'So let's have no more talk of dying!' she scolded. 'There's plenty of life in you and me yet!'

21

As the eighties rolled on into the nineties, Mary was sure time was moving faster. It was a period of relative calm so the days telescoped into one another and the weeks and months disappeared without trace. Yet things happened. James married his Jessie and Joey his Martha, the sweetheart he had kept secret for so long. More grandchildren arrived for Reuben and when his sons visited, his house was filled with the sound of children's voices and laughter. Mary was happy for him then but she could not supress a twinge of envy that he had so many grandchildren nearby while she had to content herself with George's little John.

He was nearly three years old now and delighted Mary with his chatter when he was brought to Yarnscombe or she could get into Barum to visit him. There was no sign of Hannah having another child but Eliza gave birth to a third baby at the end of '89, a little girl she called after her mother. It grieved Mary that she would never be able to hold her namesake in her arms and she cherished a photograph Eliza sent of her two boys cuddling their baby sister between them. Mary had it framed and kept it by her bedside, trying to imagine them all in the wooden house Simon Tucker had built for them.

Johnny wrote so rarely and told her so little she could only cling to the last memory she had of him on horseback and try to picture him instead riding the range in California. But she could not contemplate the extent of it or hear in her head the thundering of the cattle as he and his fellow cowboys galloped into the sunset. She knew he would be dressed differently, rather like Simon when he came back to marry Eliza and he would be growing older. They were all doing that, just as Philip was, thousands of miles away.

Reuben heard from him every few months. His battalion had marched to Rawalpindi after Lahore and wintered in the hills, gathering their strength after the cholera epidemic. According to his last letter, they had now moved to Calcutta, prior to taking ship for Burma where there was more trouble.

Reuben was gloomy for days after he read this. 'He'll be getting hisself killed, you mark my words! There's jungle in Burma. If he don't get a bullet in his head, he'll get ate by a tiger!'

'Philip's too careful for that!' Mary said. 'And he must be due for leave soon, after being abroad for so long.'

But Philip was not given leave and he did not write again until the middle of 1890 when he was in Rangoon. The third Burma war was underway and they were expecting to be sent into the thick of it.

'We shall be fighting alongside the Ghurkas,' he wrote, 'a fine body of men, I am told. We are not looking forward to it but we are well prepared. I wish you could see Burma, Father. There are mountains and forests like nothing in England. I often think of you all, sitting around the big table in the kitchen and pray it will not be too long before I am with you once more.'

After that there was a long silence.

Mary knew that Reuben was worried. He took to watching for the post, just as she did. He had often teased her about that in the past but now he was usually the first to pick up their letters. Yet it was not he who received bad news in '91. It was Mary.

A letter arrived from Eliza in July and it was about Johnny. He had written to Simon asking for money because he was in trouble again. He and his partner were in jail, awaiting trial after being accused of cattle rustling. Johnny swore he had done nothing wrong and blamed his partner for getting involved with a pair of card sharpers who had cheated them. All he wanted was two hundred dollars to bail himself out of prison so that he could prove his innocence.

'Simon cannot afford two hundred dollars,' Eliza wrote, 'and I told him he was not to borrow on Johnny's behalf. It would not be fair to get himself into debt now that we are just breaking even. Johnny must learn to stand on his own two feet and take his punishment like a man. We have helped him enough already and have had no thanks for it. I hope you will not think badly of us because of this, Mother, and that you are keeping well. The boys and Mary are thriving and will soon have another brother or sister to play with as I am expecting again next January. Your ever loving daughter, Eliza.'

Mary felt the blood leave her face as she read the letter. Her Johnny in prison! She could not bear to think of if. The fact that Eliza was pregnant once more hardly registered against the fact of Johnny's disgrace.

'How much is two hundred dollars in English money?' she asked Reuben.

'More than us can afford, if that's what you'm thinking of, Mary! Let'n come to trial! If he bain't guilty, you've nort to worry about.

If he be, 'twon't hurt your Johnny to cool his heels for a bit.'

Mary appealed to George but he was as adamant as Reuben that there was nothing they could do. 'Seems to me, Johnny always learns the hard way,' he said. 'Might be all for the best, Ma, if he gets stopped before he goes too far.'

'But what sort of prison be'n in? 'Tain't likely 'twill be the same as in England.'

George shrugged. 'Could be some sort of lock-up in that township he's told ee about, where there's a sheriff. 'Twill be a rough sort of justice, I reckon, but it won't do Johnny any harm.'

All Mary could do then was write a letter to Johnny, begging him to get in touch and let her know what was happening. More importantly, he was to keep well away from the men who had let him down so badly. She enclosed this with her reply to Eliza, asking her to send it on if she had an address. It was only when she re-read her daughter's letter that she properly took in the fact that Eliza was pregnant again, so soon after the birth of her last baby. Mary could not imagine how she would cope on the ranch with four little ones.

Mrs Pugsley sniffed when she was told. 'Lizzie made her bed,' she said, 'and if 'tis proving to be a hard one, that be her look-out. As for your Johnny, you spoiled'n from the start. I told ee that years ago.'

Mary bit back a retort. Her mother was in her middle seventies now and looking her age. She had worried her daughters during the previous winter which had been cold and damp, giving her a hacking cough. She had never quite shaken it off and had a fit of it now.

'Be ee taking that medicine the doctor gave ee?' Mary asked.

'I chucked the last of it down the drain. 'Twadn't doing me a bit of good!'

'You shouldn't have done that, Mother! I'll send a message, asking'n to call on ee again.'

'No need for that! You've got plenty to worry about, without me!'

Mary consulted her sisters and sent for the doctor, anyway. To their annoyance, he prescribed the same medicine as before, agreed that Mrs Pugsley's chest was bad but said she could not expect to throw things off the way she might have done when she was younger. She was a good age, after all.

'More or less told me I was on me way out!' the old lady grumbled. 'I could jump over his head any time!'

Mary laughed. 'Us all knows that, Mother! Just make sure you wrap up warm when the weather starts getting colder.'

She distrusted the back end of the year, so many things had gone wrong for her then, starting with John's death. She chided herself for being superstitious but could not ward off a feeling, as the Autumn days grew shorter, that the clouds were beginning to gather again.

She kept her fears to herself, not wanting to worry Reuben, but she visited her mother more often and waited anxiously for letters from America.

It was several months before one arrived from Johnny. He was jubilant because he had raised his bail money by winning at cards with the deputy sheriff while he was in prison. Instead of waiting to be tried, he had jumped bail and ridden off into northern California where he intended beginning a new, better life.

'I did not wait to be sentenced for something I had not done, Mother,' he wrote, 'and I took heed of what you told me about getting away from bad company. I have left all that behind me now and I have teamed up with one of the biggest cattle men in the west. I am earning good money and if I play my cards right I will make you proud of me yet.'

Reuben snorted when Mary showed him the letter. 'I told ee you was worrying for nothing,' he said. 'But 'taint playing his cards right your Johnny needs to bother about, 'tis keeping his nose clean. They'll catch up with'n one day!'

But not yet! Mary thought. Perhaps not ever! Perhaps Johnny had learned his lesson at last and would turn into an honest citizen. With hope in her heart, she wrote to the ranch where he was now based and told him to work hard, save his money and not bring any more disgrace upon the family.

She breathed more easily after that. Mrs Pugsley seemed no worse and it was almost time to think towards Christmas. Mary always liked to make her puddings early and she was in the middle of mixing them one morning in October when the post arrived. There was nothing for her but one for Reuben with a foreign stamp, the address written in an unfamiliar hand. She looked at it with foreboding. Reuben and Albert were in the workshop, making a back door for a cottage in the village and they hated being disturbed. She hesitated. But something told her that this was important so she wiped her floury hands on her apron and took the letter across the yard to her husband.

She watched his face as he opened it, fumbled in his pocket for his spectacles and began to read. When he looked up at her and handed her the letter, she saw fear in his eyes.

The letter had been dictated by Philip to the chaplain at the makeshift army hospital in Rangoon. Philip had been wounded, she read, so he was unable to write himself but wanted his father to know that he was being well cared for and hoped for sick leave once he was well enough to travel. 'So do not worry,' the letter concluded. 'I could be in England soon after you receive this.'

'When was it posted?' Mary cried and snatched up the envelope. But she could make no sense of the foreign markings. She read the letter again. 'It don't say how he's been wounded. P'raps 'tis his arm and that's why he couldn't write.'

Reuben shook his head and leaned heavily against his work bench. 'I don't like the thought of'n, Mary, lying in some foreign hospital where there's disease and filth. I want'n home where us can look after'n proper.'

'He could be home soon. That's what it says.' But there was such despair in Reuben's eyes she went to him and took his arm. 'Why don't ee come into the house for a bit and I'll make a pot of tea. Us've both had a shock.'

'You go, Dad!' Albert said. 'I can manage here.'

'I knew summat would happen when Philip

joined up,' Reuben said as Mary led him from the workshop. 'Once he got into Burma, I was sure of it.'

'Bear up, Reuben! He could be home for Christmas.'

Reuben would not be comforted and as the days and weeks passed with no more news, Mary became as despondent as he. Then, at the beginning of December, an official letter arrived for Reuben from the barracks at Exeter, informing him that his son, Private P Dark, was now in England and recovering from his wounds. His commanding officer regretted that, after a period of excellent service, he had been deemed unfit to continue with the regiment and would be invalided out and given an honourable discharge. He would be arriving, with an escort, on the morning train to Barum on December eighth when it was hoped that a member of his family would be able to meet him.

Reuben stared at the letter in disbelief. 'Honourable discharge — arriving by train — ! What do they think he is, some sort of parcel? This be my son they'm chucking out, soon's he's no more use to 'em! My God, Mary! This makes me ashamed to be an Englishman!'

'Don't take on!' Mary begged him. 'At least

Philip's alive and coming home. That's what us wanted.'

'But what sort of state be'n in to need an escort? Unfit for service? What do 'em mean by that? Why don't Philip write and tell us?'

Perhaps he can't, Mary thought but did not say so. Hiding her own anxiety she busied herself in preparing a room for Philip and on December eighth she went to Barum in the trap with Reuben to meet the morning train. As they stood shivering, arm in arm, on the cold platform of the Junction Station, they left unspoken their private fears and watched anxiously as the train clattered in and steamed to a halt.

The carriage doors opened and people began to descend. There were several soldiers and one stayed for a moment to lend a hand to his companion. Mary felt Reuben stiffen beside her as Philip was helped down and his bag hauled out after him. He picked it up with his left hand and, as he began walking down the platform with his friend, Mary saw that the opposite sleeve of his jacket was empty and pinned across his chest.

He caught sight of her and Reuben and quickened his step, smiling a greeting. She ran then and flung her arms round him, reaching up to kiss him on the cheek, half crying and half laughing as she encountered an unfamiliar beard. Reuben seemed transfixed until Philip reached him and put down his bag. Then he clasped his son's remaining hand in both his own. ''Tis good to see ee, boy,' he said huskily. 'God be thanked you've been spared to come back to us.'

'Not quite the man I was, Father,' Philip said wryly.

'That's no odds! You'm here and won't be going away again.'

'I told ee he'd be home for Christmas!' Mary cried, with tears in her eyes. 'All the family'll be there to share it with ee, Philip.'

She wanted the young soldier with him to come back to Yarnscombe for a meal but he had orders to return to the barracks by the next train once he had seen Philip into safe hands. 'I'll miss ee, Phil!' he said as he clapped Philip on the back. 'Been through a few tight spots together, us have!' He turned to Mary. 'Look after'n, missus! He's one of the best.'

Mary already knew that and she had a renewed purpose now for her seasonal preparations. She set to them with a will during the next few weeks, determined to give Philip a Christmas to remember. He was trying to come to terms with his disability and was teaching himself to write with his left hand. He even offered to help Reuben with his books as he had done once before and said he hoped to return to his old job when he felt capable.

Just occasionally, Mary saw him wince if somebody brushed up against the stump of his right arm and she asked him once if it was still painful. He said it was well enough but there were days when his face looked white and drawn and shiny with sweat. He would not let her dress his wound, seeing to it somehow himself but he could not hide from her sharp eyes that his shirt sleeve and his bedding were often stained and odorous when she came to do his washing.

The doctor was still visiting her mother occasionally and he called during Christmas week. Without telling Reuben, she asked him if he would take a look at Philip while he was in the village. Taken by surprise, Philip submitted to being examined with bad grace. The doctor frowned at what he saw. The wound was not clean, he said. It had not been cauterised properly and would have to be done again.

Philip's face blanched at the suggestion. 'No!' he cried for he had been through it all before. 'Not that!'

'Either that or gangrene!' the doctor said bluntly. 'It needs to be done immediately so I'll call again tomorrow with my instruments.

Be sure you have a good fire blazing, Mrs Dark and a bottle of brandy for the young man. I'll give him a whiff of chloroform but he'll need something more when the effect wears off.'

Mary hid in the workshop with Albert the next morning when the doctor came for she could not bear to see or hear what was being done to Philip. Reuben, however, stayed with him, holding him steady on the kitchen table while the doctor cauterised the stump of his arm. All that night he sat at his son's bedside, watching and comforting him as the effects of the chloroform and then the brandy wore off and Philip tossed and turned in agony.

Lonely and cold in the double bed without her husband, Mary could not sleep either and several times took the candle to the door of Philip's room in case she could be of help. But Reuben waved her away and she realised that this was something he had to do himself, that it was his way of repairing the rift that has so recently divided him from his son.

Early the next morning she took tea up to them both but Philip had slipped into a more peaceful slumber by then. So they did not wake him but crept downstairs together. 'He could be over the worst,' Reuben said. 'My poor boy! I wouldn't wish a dog to suffer so.'

'Do ee think he'll be fit for Christmas?' Mary asked.

Reuben shook his head. 'Doctor said he should rest. But Philip always had plenty of spirit, like his mother and he's been looking forward to everybody coming. Us'll just have to wait and see.'

The doctor called again the next day with a fresh dressing. He expressed himself well satisfied, pocketed his fee and departed, wishing them all a happy Christmas. He was hardly out of the door before Philip had managed to pull on his shirt and was struggling into his trousers, determined to get downstairs again.

'You should rest awhile longer!' Mary pleaded with him. 'There's no need to get up yet.'

''Tis only my arm that's missing and 'tis Christmas Eve tomorrow. I don't want to be stuck up here, away from all the fun. My brothers and sisters are coming and I've a few trinkets in my bag for the children.'

'Trinkets? How did ee manage to buy trinkets when you was in hospital?'

''Tis things I collected before from the markets. I've something for you, too, and for Father. Nothing much — just something to remember me by.'

'Remember ee? Us won't have to do that now you'm here.'

Philip laughed but Mary thought there was still something feverish in the glitter of his eyes and the colour of his cheeks. She said no more to deter him but helped him with his socks and the rest of his clothes and made sure he had a comfortable chair to sit in when he came downstairs. Then she busied herself with her final preparations.

She was glad she had started early because the worry over Philip had held her back. Some of the family were arriving late on Christmas Eve, the others, who could walk home, in time for Christmas dinner the next day. George and Hannah would be there with little John as they had spent the previous Christmas in Dolton with Hannah's folks. The house would be full to bursting as all Philip's brothers and Sally wanted to see him and even Emily sent word that she and Sam and the children would come by pony and trap in time for tea.

Reuben's long table was filled twice over again, just as it had been before Philip went to India. He sat next to his father with Tommy on the other side of him and Mary was touched to see the unobtrusive way Tommy cut up his brother's meat as if they had never once quarrelled and come to blows over Eliza. An almost tangible aura of affection seemed to envelop Philip as he sat surrounded by his family and held them enthralled with tales of his exploits in India and Burma.

After the meal he produced the presents he had brought for the children who were wide eyed with amazement and seemed not to notice that he had only one arm. There were little brass bells or bamboo flutes for the boys and shiny necklaces or bracelets for the girls. George's John made everybody laugh by asking his father solemnly, 'Is'n Father Christmas?'

Philip had brought Mary a brooch carved out of ivory and an embossed leather tobacco pouch for his father. He apologised for not bringing anything for his brothers and their wives but produced from his bag a folded paper lantern decorated with coloured pictures of birds. He handed it to Tommy and asked him to hang it up where everybody could see it.

''Tis my contribution to Christmas,' he said and they all clapped and cheered when Tommy climbed on to a chair and hung the lantern from a beam next to the sprig of mistletoe.

Mary brushed the tears from her eyes as she watched them all and turned to her mother who had come as usual for the Christmas dinner. ''Tis good to see Philip back home again and so happy,' she said.

Mrs Pugsley pursed her lips. 'That boy won't last long, Mary. 'Tis written in his face. He'll be lucky to see the year out.'

'Don't say that, Mother! Doctor's well pleased with'n.'

'You don't want to pay heed to that old fool! He gived me up months ago and I'm still here.'

'Ay. And I wish you'd keep your opinions to yourself!'

Distressed, Mary left her mother and went to thank Philip for her brooch. 'I'll always cherish it,' she told him, 'it's so pretty.'

'Wear it then!' he said. 'That's what 'tis for.'

She pinned it to her blouse straightaway and made a point of wearing it regularly after that to please him.

The year ended and January came in bitterly cold. Mary began to notice a change in Philip. He became irritable easily and there were often beads of perspiration on his face as if he suffered. He did not complain but slept badly and had frightening dreams, often calling out in the night. Once, when she went to him, he was sitting up in bed staring straight ahead and looking so like her John, she was afraid.

'What is it, Philip?' she asked.

He started as if he had not realised she was there. ' 'Tis Lizzie. Lizzie's calling me.'

'No! Lizzie's a long way off. I showed you her last letter. Her baby's due about now.'

'The baby?' He furrowed his brow. 'The baby's dead.'

The shock made Mary's heart lurch. 'No! You've been dreaming, Philip. A nightmare — that's all. I'll turn your pillow and make ee more comfortable.'

She felt uneasy, especially when she saw in the light of her candle that his pillow was stained again and his nightshirt blotched under his wound. She poured him a cup of water from his jug and steadied his hand while he drank but when she bent over him the stench from his wound made her turn her head away. 'Try to sleep,' she whispered as he lay back with a sigh.

Back in her own room she shook Reuben's arm to wake him. 'You must get the doctor again for Philip,' she said. 'That stump needs seeing to. 'Tain't right.'

Reuben groaned. 'He couldn't stand having it burned back again and I couldn't bear to see it done! There must be another way.'

There was only one other way that Mary knew of and she prayed that if it came to that, it would be quick. Reuben rode to High Bickington the next morning to fetch the doctor but by the time he came back with him Philip was slipping in and out of consciousness. The doctor looked at him and shook his head. 'I'm sorry,' he said. 'There's nothing more I can do.'

'You mean you'll let'n go,' Reuben cried, 'after making'n suffer the way you did?'

'I did my best. I warned your son of gangrene. I was called too late, I fear, Mr Dark.'

He went without asking for a fee, leaving Mary and Reuben to watch and grieve over Philip. He did not open his eyes again but died peacefully the next morning just after the sun came up.

22

Philip's death left Reuben inconsolable. He retreated into himself, into some dark place Mary could not reach. Only the making of his son's coffin seemed to give him relief.

He chose the finest oak for it, lined it with soft embossed material and gave it solid brass handles and a brass breastplate engraved: 'Philip Dark, 1859 to 1892. Died of wounds on January 12th, after action with the Devonshire Regiment in Burma.'

Walter informed the barracks of his brother's death and the commanding officer offered to send two young privates to represent the Devons at his funeral. But Reuben would have none of it. The army had destroyed his son, he maintained, and was never to be mentioned again.

So the funeral at St Andrew's church was a quiet, family affair. Albert presided as undertaker so that his father could lead the mourners with Walter, his eldest son, at his side. Mary walked behind with George and the womenfolk while Philip's six other brothers carried his coffin.

Yet it seemed as if all the village was there

for the church was full. Everybody had known and liked Philip and the vicar spoke movingly of the sacrifice he had made for his country. Mary heard Reuben mutter angrily under his breath when the vicar said that and after the burial, when they had seen Philip interred next to his mother's grave, he hardly spoke to the people who came up to offer their condolences. It was Mary who thanked them and later on welcomed the members of his family when they came back to the house for the usual meal.

It seemed a mocking travesty of their happy Christmas gathering and they were all subdued, especially as none of the children had been brought to such a sad occasion. Reuben was silent and remote and disappeared altogether when Mary and the girls began setting out the cold ham and pickles and the pies and cakes on the long kitchen table. She went looking for him at last and found him in Jane's little sitting room, slumped in her old armchair with his head in his hands.

'Reuben?' she murmured. 'What be doing in here, all on your own?'

He stared up at her, his eyes smouldering with grief and anger. 'Sacrifice!' he said harshly. 'You heard what the vicar said. But twad'n a sacrifice for his country! 'Twas for your maid, Lizzie, he gave his life!'

Mary shrank back as if he had hit her. 'That bain't fair, Reuben! 'Twas Philip's choice. Lizzie never wanted'n to go into the army!'

'Lizzie never wanted'n at all, and that be the truth of it! Her should be sorry now!'

'Lizzie'll be as sorry as any of us when her's told. She loved Philip. But 'twas as a brother, Reuben. That wouldn't have made a marriage!'

'What sort of marriage have her got now, stuck miles away from anywhere on a sheep ranch? Then there's your boy, Johnny, lying and cheating his way through life while my poor Philip, the one Jane loved best — ' His voice broke. 'I can't bear it, Mary. What have I done that the Lord should strike me so hard?'

Mary sank down on her knees before him. 'Oh, don't! Don't cry out against the Lord like that or be so bitter against me and mine! If I've been at fault, I'm sorry. I never wished Lizzie to go off to America and I would've kept her here for Philip if I could. But they go their own ways and there's no gainsaying 'em. Us both know that, Reuben.'

'Ay! More's the pity!' He pushed her roughly away and stood up. 'Oh, get back to the kitchen, woman, and feed them that's still left to us! I'm going out.'

'Where? 'Tis bitter cold and could snow.'

He ignored her and headed for the door with Mary running after him as he stumped through the kitchen, past his astonished family and out towards the porch. 'Take your heavy jacket,' she cried, 'and your cap and muffler!' She pulled them from the clothes hooks and tried to fling them on him. He snatched them from her without a word and left the house, slamming the door behind him.

Distraught, she stumbled back to the kitchen. Sally hurried towards her and took her arm. 'Where's Father gone?'

'The Lord knows. He's so angry, Sal! So hurt and angry! Somebody'd best go after'n.'

'I'll go,' James volunteered and Walter jumped up to join him. 'He won't go far. I think I know where he'll be.'

'He blames Lizzie for Philip,' Mary told Sally, 'and he blames me. Did I do wrong, then, when I married'n?'

'No!' Sally said firmly. 'You did right! You made a good life for Father and for all of us. You made him happy after Mother died and he'll come to remember that. Sit yourself down! You've had nothing to eat with serving the rest of us.'

Mary could only pick at her food while she

waited for Reuben to return. When his sons brought him home an hour later, Walter whispered to her that they had found him in the churchyard, on his knees between Jane's grave and Philip's. 'He often went there just after Mother died,' Walter murmured. 'It seemed to calm him. He'll be all right now.'

Reuben had made straight for his old chair beside the fire and was filling his pipe from the tobacco pouch Philip had given him. He sat quietly, detached from them all and as if by common consent they made no move to approach him. Yet Mary felt he was comforted by the presence of his family whereas she was still excluded. She wanted to run to him and clasp him in her arms but she knew, with despair, that this time it was going to be harder to break through his isolation.

As January slipped almost unnoticed into February there was still no change in Reuben's manner towards her. Albert noticed and wanted to speak to his father but Mary would not let him. She went about her household tasks hardly knowing what she did for something else was beginning to trouble her. She had not had a letter from Eliza with word of the new baby which should have been born weeks before. Letters took a long time to come but she felt she should have heard by now. She tried to tell herself that there could have been storms at sea, delaying the ships but could not banish from her mind the memory of Philip's face when he had said, 'The baby's dead.' Could he have had some strange premonition when he was so close to death himself?

She began sleeping badly and could not turn to Reuben for comfort. He lay stiff and unapproachable beside her and, rather than disturb him, she sometimes slipped from their bed and spent the rest of the night in the room Sally used when she came home. He made no comment when he found her missing the next morning, which only made her feel that they were drifting farther and farther apart.

A letter arrived at last at the end of February. When she saw that the address had not been written by Eliza she dared not open it but sat staring at it, her heart thumping. Reuben and Albert were working out of the village and would not be home until the late afternoon. The thought of hours of waiting, alone in the house, made her snatch up her shawl and run all the way to her sister Anne's cottage where she thrust the letter into her hands and blurted out, 'Open it! I can't.'

She sank into a chair and watched as Anne opened the letter and began to read. When her sister's face changed, Mary covered her own with her hands and cried out, 'Which is it, the baby or Lizzie?'

Anne came over to her and put an arm round her shoulders. ''Tis both, Mary,' she said gently. ''Twas a breech birth and took so long the baby came dead. Lizzie lost a lot of blood and was left weak but Simon said they hoped to save her. She lived for several days but never recovered and died, he thinks, partly of grief. He says her last thoughts were of you — ' Anne's voice broke. 'Here — read the rest yourself! I — can't — '

Anne was weeping as Mary took the letter. She read it slowly and carefully, trying to make sense of it. Then she stood up and said, 'Thankee, Anne. I'd best get home now.'

'No! You must stay a while.'

Mary shook her head. 'I have to get back. There's things to do before Reuben and Albert come home. Will ee — will ee tell Mother and Lou about Lizzie?'

'Don't go, Mary! I'll fetch 'em here. You've had a shock and you don't look well.'

'I'm well enough. I just — need to be by meself.'

She left her sister's cottage and walked steadily back up the hill to the carpenter's house. She felt very cold when she got inside and sat close to the fire, shuddering. Her hands were shaking so much she could hardly unfold the letter and had to smooth it on her knee to read it again. The words were the same but this time she could sense Simon's sorrow behind them as he told of his own loss and how he would strive to be a good father to the three little ones Lizzie had left behind. 'She often spoke of you before she died,' the letter ended, 'so I will send you news of the children from time to time. I hope you will write to them as you did to Lizzie. She was a good wife and mother and I will never forget her.'

Mary folded the letter carefully and put it in the pocket of her skirt. She was filled with a kind of numbness and sat for a long while, her mind a blank. When her mother and Lou came red-eyed she stared at them as if she could not remember who they were.

Lou kissed her and her mother clasped her to her bosom, something she had not done for years. 'Lizzie never should've gone off with that Simon Tucker!' she said bitterly. 'I told ee 'twould come to no good! Her couldn't have had proper care in that wild place!'

'Hush, Mother!' Lou admonished her. ''Tis no use going back over what's done! You'm only upsetting Mary.'

But Mary was deaf to what they were saying, she had so sunk into herself. She drank some of the tea Lou made, holding the mug in her cold hands to warm them. Then she stirred herself and stood up, saying that she should be tidying the house and preparing a meal for Reuben and Albert when they came home. Her mother protested that she should come back to her cottage and not be left alone to grieve but Mary was stubborn. 'I must be here for Reuben,' she said.

Because she would not be persuaded, Lou sent her mother home and stayed to help her sister with the housework, watching her anxiously for signs that she might break down. But Mary went about her tasks steadily, following her familiar pattern without rest or conscious thought. It was only when she heard the sound of the horse and wagon pulling into the yard that she flinched and became still.

Noticing that, Lou hurried out to forewarn Reuben. When he came in he stared at his wife in disbelief.

'Mary?' he asked. 'Be it true?'

For answer she took Simon's letter from her pocket and handed it to him, watching as he fumbled for his spectacles and began to read. When he looked up she ignored the dawning sympathy in his eyes and said, in a hard voice, 'So you won't need to blame

Lizzie now for Philip! The Lord has taken care of that and sent a terrible punishment on me and mine. But, oh, 'tis bitter hard to bear!'

She saw the shock in his face. 'You mustn't think that! The Lord never acts without a purpose. P'raps He took Lizzie so's her could be with Philip in Heaven. Can't us find some comfort in that, Mary, that they'm together now in a blessed place?'

'Oh, Reuben! 'Tis but cold comfort if us can't grieve together for what us have lost!' In despair, she held out her arms to him. 'So hold me! Help me now! Philip lies nearby and you know where he is. I could'n say goodbye to Lizzie and I won't even be able take flowers to her grave.'

She began to sob and when he reached her and cradled her in his arms she was able to give way at last. He wept with her as they clung and rocked together, mourning the son and daughter they had lost.

Lou crept away then and left them to their grief, knowing that only their combined tears could wash away the hurt that had festered between them.

But although they came to a new understanding that day Mary and Reuben never got over their double loss. Their marriage was changed by it for they were more careful with one another and watchful for signs of trouble. Reuben aged visibly and found it necessary to employ a young apprentice to help Albert with the work. He was a pleasant, biddable lad called Stanley Norman who fitted in well and almost became one of the family.

The rest of them came and went, providing comfort in their own way and Mary was pleased to get a letter from Johnny, expressing his sorrow at losing his only sister. 'I hope one day to take the trail to Oregon and visit Simon and the children,' he wrote. 'Then I can send you news of them. You will be happy to hear that I am courting the daughter of the local sheriff. She is a handsome young woman and we plan to be married in the fall. Her father is going to swear me in as his deputy so you can see how straight I am keeping myself now, Mother. I promise I will make you proud of me one day.'

Reuben grunted when Mary showed him the letter. 'They say it takes a thief to catch a thief,' he said, 'so your Johnny be the living proof of that!'

'At least he's trying to make something of himself,' Mary protested and she gave the letter to George to read the next time she was in Barum.

He laughed. 'Johnny a deputy and marrying the sheriff's daughter? Trust him to find a way of covering his back the next time he's in trouble!'

'You shouldn't say that, George!' Mary reproached him. 'I'm pleased he's found a good maid who'll help'n settle down. I'd like to feel all my boys are happily wed before anything happens to me. I've only Albert to think of now.'

Albert, however, showed no signs of finding a wife and he came in for some teasing as all Reuben's other sons were either married or courting. He took it all in good part and found his pleasure in bell ringing with the St Andrew's team, often in other churches in nearby villages for special occasions.

It was when he was ringing in St Michael's church in Torrington that he found a girl to suit him. Her name was Ethel, he told Mary, and she was the daughter of one of the Torrington team.

'So us got on fine,' Albert said, 'with ringing being in her family. 'Course, Ethel's young yet — only sixteen, so her mother wants us to wait a while before us gets wed. But can I bring her over one Sunday to meet you and Dad?'

''Course you can!' Mary was delighted. So a fortnight later, Albert borrowed the horse and trap and brought Ethel to Yarnscombe to meet his parents and those of his step brothers who happened to be at home that day.

Mary was reminded of when George first brought Hannah to the carpenter's house and of how shy the girl had been. At first, Ethel was shy, too. She was slightly built and pretty with a few stray curls that escaped from her piled up hair framing her face. She clung on to Albert's arm and had little to say for herself until she was helping Mary to clear away and wash the dishes after the Sunday dinner. Then she began to chatter about her young brothers and sisters and her parents who ran a hardware shop in the town and how she served behind the counter during the week.

'You must know nearly everybody in Torrington, then,' Mary said.

'Most of 'em. I often see Mr Dark's son, Will, when he comes in for screws and nails or some such. And I remember when your daughter got married at St Michael's. Father was ringing that day so Mother took me along to see the bride and groom come out. She looked lovely! I was only six then but I remember it 'cos people said they were going off to America.'

Mary's hands became still in the bowl of water.

'Oh!' Ethel put a hand to her mouth. 'I'm sorry, Mrs Dark! Albert did tell me about his sister but I forgot for a minute.' Her eyes were wide with sympathy. 'You must miss her terribly.'

'She was my only daughter,' Mary said painfully. 'But I have a good daughter-in-law in George's Hannah and perhaps — ' she tried to smile at Ethel, ' — perhaps I'll have another one in you one day.'

'Oh, I hope so! I do hope so 'cos I've never met a boy I like better than Albert.' Ethel giggled. 'D'you know what he said to me when we were driving up this morning? He said his father'd had nine sons and he hoped he'd have enough sons one day for a bell-ringing team of his own! Did you ever hear of such a thing — with us not even engaged yet?'

Mary smiled properly then. 'Albert's got more of his father in him than I thought! But such things can never be planned, Ethel. If you'm meant to have sons, they'll come. If not, they won't, so don't worry your pretty head about that!'

When she told Reuben what Albert had said, he laughed. 'I never thought the boy had it in him! Seems to me he'd better wed that little maid 'fore 'tis too late!'

But Albert was in no hurry. He would buy

Ethel a ring, but wait until she was eighteen and marry her in the summer of '97. This was going to be a year of national rejoicing because the old queen, if she lived that long, would have been on the throne for sixty years. A grand diamond jubilee celebration was being planned so the flags and bunting would be flying in all the towns and villages. Albert thought this would make his wedding to Ethel even more special.

She was already collecting for her bottom drawer and during '96 they began thinking about where they might live. Reuben could see no problem. They must live in his house in Yarnscombe so that when anything happened to him, Albert could carry on the business and look after his mother.

Mary tried to dissuade him. 'The young ones like to start out on their own,' she said, 'even if 'tis only in a little cottage in the village.'

'Why should 'em pay out for rent when there's room enough here and the workshop's handy in the yard? Ethel'll be company for ee, Mary, when I'm out working with the boys.'

Albert did not bother to argue with his father but set to work doing up two of the upstairs rooms in the carpenter's house, one for a bedroom and the other for a little sitting room where he and Ethel could be on their own when they wanted. She made fresh curtains and a patchwork quilt for their bed and they bought a few pieces of new furniture to make the rooms look more like theirs. Everything was ready by Christmas of that year and was duly admired by the rest of the family when they came for the usual festivities.

Then, as the year turned, the village was hit by an epidemic of influenza. One of the first to succumb was old Mrs Pugsley whose chest had been weak for some time. She could not withstand this new attack and died in January. Reuben made her coffin and presided at her funeral, leaving Mary and her sisters consumed with grief and guilt that they had not done more to look after their mother.

A few weeks later, Reuben himself fell ill. According to village whispers that was because he had buried so many and been too often close to infection. But he had always been strong and Mary was sure he would pull through. It was only when she lay next to him in their double bed on the third night and felt him burning beside her and heard him rambling incoherently that she was reminded of John and panicked. She called the doctor again but by the time he arrived, Reuben was barely conscious.

After examining him, the doctor shook his head and said that pneumonia had set in.

'No!' Mary cried. 'Not that! His son's getting married in June!'

'I'm sorry,' the doctor said. 'I've done what I could.'

'Like you did for my John and poor Philip?'

'I can't work miracles, Mrs Dark. And you shouldn't give up hope. Your husband could rally again. We must pray that he does.'

'Do ee think I bain't doing that already?' Mary knelt beside the bed and grasped Reuben's hand. 'He can't go! I won't let'n go! He's not ready!'

'He's in God's hands now, Mrs Dark. I think you should inform his family.'

Somehow, messages were sent, Mary never knew how. Her brother-in-law, Bert took charge, sending Albert off with the horse and trap to Barum and riding himself to Torrington and South Molton so that all Reuben's remaining sons and his two daughters could be at his bedside before he died. He rallied once before the end and raised himself up and stared at them. Then he smiled. 'I see you've brought Philip with ee,' he said and stretched out a hand. Mary grasped it as he fell back, his breath rasping in his throat. She stayed there, holding his hand and weeping until Sally gently led her away.

Albert was too upset to make his father's coffin so Fred and Joey stayed to help him with it while preparations were made for the funeral. It was held, like Jane's and Philip's, at St Andrew's church. Walter presided as Albert only wanted to toll the bell and Reuben's six other sons carried his coffin. He was buried in the plot already reserved for him next to his first wife, Jane.

Mary had George to support her and she was glad of his strong arm when they stood together in the churchyard. She was no longer the carpenter's wife, a fact brought cruelly home to her by Reuben's choice of final resting place. Later on, when all the family came back to his house, she was suddenly unable to face them. She knew that they would discuss her husband's will and would learn that everything had been left to Albert. There might be animosity from Reuben's other sons and she could not bear that. So she mumbled an excuse to Sally and escaped, running without thinking, to the little wooden chapel where she and John had been married.

It was looking shabby now but its plain, painted walls and lack of ornament were all she wanted. She stood just inside the doors, staring at the wooden cross above the communion table and whispered, 'Why? What was it all for?' When there was no answer, she let her tears flow free.

She had moved to John's grave when George and Albert came looking for her. 'This is where you must lay me,' she said, 'when my time comes. This is were I belong.'

'You belong with us, Mother,' Albert said. 'Us be all waiting for ee to come back home.'

Mary shook her head. 'I won't be wanted there now 'cos everything's going — all the folks I ever cared about.' She repeated the question she had asked in the chapel. 'What was it all for?'

'For them that's left,' George said, 'and for them that's yet to come.' He took her arm. 'I'm here and so's Albert. Hannah's back at the house with Ethel and my John's safe at home. There's plenty left for ee, Mother, and you won't want for ort 'cos Albert'll take care of ee, now he's been left the business.' There was a glint of envy in George's eyes as he pointed towards the little chapel. 'I see there's a job waiting here for ee already, Albert. That wants propping up before it falls down!'

'I won't just prop'n up. I'll build another one for Mother!' Albert boasted.

George glowered. 'Then when I'm set up on me own I'll build a row of fine houses in

Barum and Mother can choose any one of 'em she'd like!'

'Now don't start trying to best one another!' Mary pleaded. 'You'm both good boys. I'm just sorry your father didn't live to see ee married, Albert.' She sighed as she took his arm. 'How've 'em all taken it about the business?'

'Pretty well. Walter said he expected it and Sally told me to fetch ee home 'cos the place wad'n the same without ee.'

Mary began to feel better then. 'I s'pose I'd best get back. They'll all be wanting their tea and I can't leave everything for the maids to do.'

They moved off together, Mary between her sons. She was no longer the carpenter's wife but she was the mother of two craftsmen who would carry on his trade after him and might even become builders in their own right one day. Perhaps that was what it had all been for.

'Dew on roses.' The words in Jane's poetry book came back to her so clearly it was as if Jane herself had spoken them. Mary started and looked up. Thinking she saw her good friend smiling down at her, she smiled back and nodded.

'Mother?' George sounded concerned.

'I'm all right,' she said, for it was as if a

burden she had not known she was carrying had been lifted from her. It was Jane's turn to look after Reuben again, leaving her free to rebuild her life with those that were left, just as she had done once before.

THE END

We do hope that you have enjoyed reading this large print book.

Did you know that all of our titles are available for purchase?

We publish a wide range of high quality large print books including:
**Romances, Mysteries, Classics
General Fiction
Non Fiction and Westerns**

Special interest titles available in large print are:
**The Little Oxford Dictionary
Music Book
Song Book
Hymn Book
Service Book**

Also available from us courtesy of Oxford University Press:
**Young Readers' Dictionary
(large print edition)
Young Readers' Thesaurus
(large print edition)**

For further information or a free brochure, please contact us at:
**Ulverscroft Large Print Books Ltd.,
The Green, Bradgate Road, Anstey,
Leicester, LE7 7FU, England.
Tel:** (00 44) 0116 236 4325
Fax: (00 44) 0116 234 0205

Other titles in the
Ulverscroft Large Print Series:

STRANGER IN THE PLACE

Anne Doughty

Elizabeth Stewart, a Belfast student and only daughter of hardline Protestant parents, sets out on a study visit to the remote west coast of Ireland. Delighted as she is by the beauty of her new surroundings and the small community which welcomes her, she soon discovers she has more to learn than the details of the old country way of life. She comes to reappraise so much that is slighted and dismissed by her family — not least in regard to herself. But it is her relationship with a much older, Catholic man, Patrick Delargy, which compels her to decide what kind of life she really wants.